PHILLIP MARGOLIN

SUPREME JUSTICE

D0100926

HARPER

An Imprint of HarperCollins*Publishers*

This novel is a work of fiction. Any references to real people, events, establishments, organizations, or locales are intended only to give the fiction a sense of reality and authenticity, and are used fictitiously. All other names, characters, and places, and all dialogue and incidents portrayed in this book are the product of the author's imagination.

HARPER

An Imprint of HarperCollins*Publishers*
10 East 53rd Street
New York, New York 10022-5299

Copyright © 2010 by Phillip M. Margolin
ISBN 978-0-06-192652-5

First Harper digest printing: February 2011
First Harper premium printing: February 2011
First Harper hardcover printing: June 2010

Raves for *New York Times* bestselling author

PHILLIP MARGOLIN

"Margolin has mastered all the elements of a successful suspense mystery."
Pittsburgh Post-Gazette

"It takes a really crafty storyteller to put people on the edge of their seats and keep them there. Phillip Margolin does just that."
Chicago Tribune

"A master of plot and pacing—and one of those rare authors who can create a genuinely surprising ending."
Lisa Scottoline

"Margolin has turned the thriller on its ear."
Oregon Statesman Journal

"In the hands of bestselling writer Phillip Margolin, nothing is ever simple and no one is really safe."
Associated Press

"A master of plots that twist."
Palm Beach Post

"Margolin makes chills race down readers' spines."
Publishers Weekly

By Phillip Margolin

LOST LAKE
SLEEPING BEAUTY
THE ASSOCIATE
THE UNDERTAKER'S WIDOW
THE BURNING MAN
AFTER DARK
GONE, BUT NOT FORGOTTEN
THE LAST INNOCENT MAN
HEARTSTONE
EXECUTIVE PRIVILEGE
SUPREME JUSTICE

Amanda Jaffe Novels
WILD JUSTICE
TIES THAT BIND
PROOF POSITIVE
FUGITIVE

*This book is dedicated to the newest member
of the Margolin family,
Charles Joseph Messina Margolin,
who arrived in Portland, Oregon,
on September 29, 2009.
Welcome to the world, Joey.*

SUPREME JUSTICE

Part One

Ghost Ship

October 2006

Chapter One

John Finley's eyes snapped open. His heart was beating rapidly. Something had jerked him out of a deep sleep, but he didn't know if it was a dream sound or a real one.

Captain Finley sat up. The *China Sea* was moored at an isolated dock on the Columbia River in Shelby, Oregon, roughly halfway between Portland and the coast. No machinery was running, so every night sound was audible. As he waited for his eyes to adjust to the darkness, he slid his hand under his pillow and gripped his .38. He was never without a weapon on a trip like this, especially with the cargo they were carrying and a crew he didn't trust completely. The ship swayed gently against the pilings of the dock. Finley's breathing eased. He'd just convinced himself that he'd been dreaming when a groan slipped through the stateroom speaking tube.

The *China Sea* was an old supply vessel, originally built to take crews to and from oil rigs. She had been extensively refitted for her midocean rendezvous with the freighter from Karachi. There were intercoms throughout, but Finley had kept the old-fashioned speaking tubes on a whim. There was one on the bridge above his stateroom and one in the engine room.

The seven-man crew had acted professionally during the mission, but everyone had been hired by Belson, the man who had hired Finley. He didn't know Belson. He wasn't even certain that Belson was the man's real name. "Orrin Hadley," the name that appeared on Finley's passport and other identification, sure wasn't his.

Finley crossed the room quietly and pressed his ear to the door. A minute later, he unlocked it and eased it open. Bulbs trapped in wire cages lit the companionway outside his room. Shadows daubed the metal walls between each cage. The floor was carpeted, and the doors to the crew's staterooms were dark wood like Finley's. The trip was long, and he'd made sure that each stateroom was as comfortable as the cabins on a cruise ship.

Greg Nordland had the stateroom across from Finley. He was a professional painter who had touched up the scars left on the hull after docking at sea with the Pakistanis. Nordland's door was slightly ajar. Finley rapped on it gently. When there was no response, he nudged it open. There was no light in the cabin and it took a moment for the scene inside to register. Nordland's right arm hung off the bed, his knuckles and the back of his fingers touching the floor. The blood pooling on his sheets had seeped out of a deep knife wound in his throat.

Finley was no stranger to death, but the unexpected tableau still shocked him. He backed out of the room and was startled by an explosion that echoed off the walls in the narrow corridor. Then he crumpled to the floor, knocked down by the bullet that had been fired from the other end of the companionway. Steve Talbot walked toward him, adjusting his aim for the kill shot. The radioman's concentration on his projected point of impact saved Finley's life. Talbot was so intent on getting his next shot right that he didn't notice that Finley was armed. Finley squeezed off six shots. The sudden noise and the bullets that tore through him caused Talbot's shot to go wide, and he was dead by the time he hit the carpet.

Talbot's bullet had seared the captain's side. It hurt like hell but no other damage had been done. Finley gritted his teeth and struggled to his feet. His side burned, and he stumbled when he started down the corridor. There was another stateroom between him and the dead man. He knew what he'd find when he pushed the door inward. If the thunderous explosions of the past minute hadn't brought Ned Stuyvesant out of his room, Talbot had probably slit his throat. Finley took no satisfaction in being right.

It was four A.M. and Talbot was supposed to be on deck on guard duty. It made sense. The radioman had waited until everyone else was asleep before slaughtering the crew. Finley's habit of locking his door had probably saved his life. Talbot had been forced to use a knife because the captain would have heard a gunshot in any of the staterooms. Finley guessed that something had gone wrong with Talbot's plan when he went after the crewman who was in the engine room. When Talbot had been forced to use his gun, the ancient speaking tube had funneled the sound of the shot into the captain's stateroom.

Finley squeezed his eyes shut and breathed deeply to deal with a spasm of pain. Then he straightened as best he could and finished his journey down the hall to make sure that Talbot was dead. When he was certain that the radioman no longer posed a threat, he leaned against the wall and tried to think. Talbot had killed the crew and tried to kill him, but there was no way Talbot could move the cargo by himself, which meant that he was not acting alone.

Adrenaline coursed through Finley. He had to get off the ship *now*. He staggered back to his stateroom and reloaded his gun. Then he grabbed the duffel bag with the money and his fake passports and ID and threw in as much clothing as he could.

Finley felt light-headed but he forced himself to bury the pain and get to the deck. A cloud-covered sky obscured the moon. In his navy blue pea jacket and watch cap he wouldn't be easy to spot. It was cold outside. Finley turned up his collar for protection from the wind that blew off the river. Then he slid onto the deck on his stomach and scanned the shore. They were docked opposite a warehouse, and he'd parked his car next to it when they went to sea. To get to the car, he would have to go down the gangplank and cross a wide, open strip of asphalt. Anyone waiting for him would have a clear shot, but what choice did he have? If he stayed on board, the men who were working with Talbot would kill him for sure.

Finley sucked in a breath and staggered off the ship. Every step was agony, but he made it to his car without being shot or fainting. The captain's head was swimming. He thought he might throw up. When a wave of nausea passed, he started the car. Finley could think of only one place to go as he pulled onto the highway. He was so afraid of passing out that he riveted his attention on the road ahead. That's why he didn't see the headlights in his rear-view mirror.

Chapter Two

Tom Oswald got out of the police car just as a gust of raw wind whipped off the river. He ducked his head and bulled his 210 pounds through it toward the warehouse with his partner, Jerry Swanson, close behind. Below the warehouse, the current pushed the *China Sea* into and away from the dock.

The two Shelby cops found Dave Fletcher, the night watchman, inside the warehouse. He was wearing a rent-a-cop uniform and clutching a mug of hot coffee.

"You're Mike Kessler's uncle, right?" Oswald asked to put the jittery witness at ease.

"Bob's my brother."

"Me and Mike played ball together at Shelby High."

"I seen you," Fletcher said, but he didn't seem any more at ease. There was a tic near his right eye, and the broken capillaries in his nose told Oswald that Fletcher was a man who likely gave frequent testimonials at AA meetings.

"So, why are we out here, Dave?" Swanson asked. They'd been thirty-five minutes from the end of their shift when dispatch had sent them to the warehouse.

"Something terrible happened on the ship," Fletcher answered, his voice trembling.

"What do you mean, 'terrible'?" Oswald prodded. He was beat and had been thinking of crashing for the past hour and a half.

"I finished my rounds a little before four A.M. I go once around the perimeter every hour." Fletcher stopped to collect himself. Something had shaken him badly.

"I was getting ready to go in when I heard something. I did a hitch in the army. It sounded like shots. There was wind and the ship's hull is thick, so I wasn't sure."

Oswald nodded encouragement.

"Then a guy comes running off the ship, across the lot and around the back side of the warehouse. He was bent over and he was holding his side and he staggered like he was hurt. There's this car that's been parked around back for a few weeks. The boss said it was OK. Someone from the ship got permission to use the space when they rented the dock. That's where the guy went. By the time I got around the back side, the car was driving away."

Fletcher paused. His grip on the coffee mug was so tight that Oswald was afraid it would shatter.

"Right after the man from the ship drove off, an SUV passed by, but it could just have been driving down the highway."

"Do you know the make of either vehicle?" Swanson asked.

"I seen the one parked around back every day. It's a blue Honda. I don't know the plate. The SUV was black. It could have been a Ford. It was going fast and I didn't see the license."

"Dispatch said you reported a body," Oswald said.

Fletcher lost color. "There was one I seen in the companionway and one in a cabin. The one in the companionway, his face was shot off. I didn't stay long enough to get a good look at the guy in the cabin, but there was a lot of blood." Fletcher's voice was little more than a whisper. "That was enough for me. That's when I got out and made the call."

"How many victims are on the ship?" Swanson asked.

"All I saw was two, but there were a lot of shots."

"Do you think there's anyone alive on board?" Oswald asked.

"I didn't hear anything when I was inside."

"OK, Dave. Thanks. Now you stay here. Jerry and I are going to look around. You did great."

Oswald went to the police car and got the forensic kit out of the trunk. He ran up the gangplank and found Swanson waiting on the deck stamping his feet, blowing into his hands, and trying to stay warm.

"What do you think, Tom? Have we got ourselves an OJ?" Swanson asked excitedly. They didn't get a lot of big league crime in Shelby, Oregon. Judging by Swanson's tone, the young cop thought he was going to find the Yankees playing the Red Sox inside the *China Sea*.

"We'll soon find out," Oswald answered as he stepped through the hatch.

The policemen moved through the silent ship, guns drawn, and stopped when they found the bullet-riddled body in the companionway. A quick search of the staterooms turned up two more bodies.

"Let's split up," Oswald said. "I'll take the next deck and you check the one under that. As soon as we're done, I'll call the state police and the crime lab."

Oswald was halfway through his deck, when Swanson called up the stairwell.

"Get down here, Tom. I found two more bodies and something weird."

As he descended to the lower deck, Oswald wondered what could be weirder than what they'd already seen. Swanson was waiting at the bottom of the stairs.

"There's a body in the engine room and another over here," he said as he led Oswald to a short corridor behind the crew's head. "He was lying on his stomach. I rolled him over to check for a pulse and found this."

Swanson pointed to an almost invisible seam in a section of industrial carpet that covered the narrow hallway.

"Did you pry it up?" Oswald asked.

"Yeah, but I put it right back when I saw what was under it. I wanted to wait for you. You've got the kit."

Oswald squatted, dug his fingers under the seam, and lifted up a three-foot-square piece of carpet. Under it was a metal hatch.

"Shine your light on this while I dust for prints," Oswald said. Swanson's flashlight illuminated the steel surface. Oswald lifted three latents and put them in cellophane envelopes, which he slipped into his jacket pocket.

"OK, get it up," he said.

Swanson grabbed a metal handle that was affixed to the hatch and used his bulging muscles to wrench it open. Oswald shone his light into the pitch black interior of the hold. The space looked like a water tank, and he guessed it went down two decks. Someone had drained it. The beam of Oswald's light fell on several stacks of burlap-wrapped packages. He stared at them for a moment, then worked his way down the rungs of an iron ladder that was secured to the wall. When his head was even with the top of the nearest stack, he took out a knife and cut into one of the burlap packages. He stared at the substance and swore.

"I can't be certain until it's tested," Oswald said, "but I think this is hashish."

Oswald climbed out of the tank and shook his head. "What a clusterfuck. We have enough hashish to keep the city of Shelby happy until the next century and our own version of *The Texas Chainsaw Massacre*."

Oswald closed the hatch, and the policemen headed topside, discussing their possible courses of action. Just as they stepped onto the deck, three cars raced past the warehouse and screeched to a halt next to the dock. Car doors flew open before the engines were at rest, and men carrying automatic weapons poured out. Several men stationed themselves on the dock. The rest followed a tall blond man in a windbreaker up the gangplank. Oswald moved to the top of the gangplank to intercept them. The blond man displayed identification and kept walking.

"Arn Belson, Homeland Security," he said. "Who are you?"

"Thomas Oswald, Shelby PD, and you're trespassing on a crime scene."

Belson flashed a patronizing smile. "Actually, Officer Oswald, it is you who are trespassing." Oswald detected a faint Scandinavian accent. "You have stumbled into a federal investigation that has been ongoing for some time. I must ask you and your partner to leave the *China Sea*."

Oswald's mouth gaped open in disbelief. "You're kidding."

"I assure you I am not. There are national security implications in this operation, so I'm afraid I can't be more forthcoming, but your cooperation will be appreciated at the highest levels. I'm afraid that's all I can tell you."

Oswald fought to keep his temper in check. "I don't know what kind of yokel you think I am, but you're mistaken if you think you can waltz in here and take over the investigation of a mass murder by showing me a plastic ID that I can duplicate in a hobby shop."

Belson pointed to the men who were arrayed behind him. Their guns were aimed menacingly at the two officers.

"You do not want to question my authority, Officer Oswald. That foolhardy course of action will lead to your arrest and detention. Now, please leave this ship and the immediate area at once or my men will take you into custody."

Oswald was about to say something when Swanson put his hand on his partner's forearm. "We're outnumbered, Tom. Let's just get out of here and figure out what to do later."

Oswald glared at Belson, but he didn't need a fortune-teller to see who would come out on top if he resisted. He started to walk down the gangplank when Belson pointed at the forensic kit.

"Please turn over your kit," the agent said.

Oswald feigned reluctance as he handed over the kit.

"One question," he said. "How did you know this crime scene existed, and how did you get these men here so fast?"

"That's two questions, and I can't answer either of them. I wish I could, but it would compromise national security. Things have been very different since 9/11, as I'm sure you can appreciate."

The only thing that Oswald could appreciate was that he and Swanson were being fucked over, but he kept that thought to himself. Then he headed to his car with the fingerprints from the *China Sea* tucked away in his pocket.

When they'd driven out of sight, Oswald pulled to the side of the road and called Shelby chief of police Roger Miles. He could tell from the chief's tone that he'd been sleeping soundly.

"Sorry to wake you, Roger, but some really weird shit has just happened.

"What are you talking about?"

"We answered a 911 call from that dock near the warehouse. You know the one I mean?"

"Just tell me what happened, Tom," Miles said in a voice still thick from sleep.

"OK, well, there's a ship docked at the pier, and we found five dead men and a hold full of hashish on board."

"You what?" Miles said, fully awake now.

"There are five dead men on board. Some shot, some stabbed, and a hold full of drugs."

"Jesus. Call OSP. We're not equipped to handle something this big."

Oswald had expected Miles's reaction. The chief was a politician first and a law-enforcement officer second.

"I don't think the Oregon State Police will be welcome at the crime scene, Chief."

"What are you talking about?"

"About fifteen minutes after we boarded the ship, three carloads of armed men from Homeland Security showed up and ordered us to turn over our forensic kit and leave."

"They what? Can they do that? This is our jurisdiction."

"The leader, a guy named Belson, told me he'd arrest us if we didn't leave. I didn't want to press my luck. They were better armed than we were, and Jerry and I were outnumbered. So, what do you want us to do?"

"What a mess," Miles muttered.

Oswald could imagine the chief running his hand

through his hair. He waited quietly for Miles to develop a plan.

"OK," Miles said finally. "Your shift is almost over, isn't it?"

"Yeah."

"Head home. Forget about the ship. Let the feds handle it. We'd have to call in help anyway. Five dead men and a hold full of drugs. We'd be in way over our heads."

"Should I write a report?"

"Yeah, write it up, and be sure to mention how you were threatened. We need to cover our ass in case something goes wrong and someone tries to blame us."

"What should I do with the report when I'm done?"

"Just file the damn thing. If we're lucky, we'll never hear anything about this mess again."

Chapter Three

Tom Oswald parked the police car next to the warehouse. A full moon in a cloudless sky illuminated the dock. It was just after midnight the evening after the 911 call had directed him to the *China Sea*.

"It's gone," Jerry Swanson said as he and his partner peered through the windshield of the cruiser at the empty space where the ship had been moored.

Oswald didn't say anything. He was angry and he didn't know why. The mass murder and the drug smuggling had officially ceased to be any of his business as soon as Chief Miles told him to turn the matter over to Homeland Security. Still, the way the feds had barged in and thrown their weight around irritated the hell out of him.

"We've got company," Swanson said. Oswald snapped out of his reverie and glanced in the side mirror. A security guard was headed their way, flashlight in hand. He was at the rear of the car by the time Oswald could make him out clearly enough to see that he wasn't Dave Fletcher.

"Can I help you," the rent-a-cop said as he shone the light into the car's interior.

"Yeah. It'd be a big help if you'd get that light out of my eyes," Oswald snarled. Then he caught himself. It was late, he was tired and pissed off, but there was no reason to take that out on the guard.

"Sorry, rough day," Oswald apologized. "Where's Dave?"

"Who?" the night watchman asked.

"Dave Fletcher, the guy who's usually here."

"I got no idea. They just transferred me from the mall in Astoria." The guard shook his head. "I hope this ain't permanent. This place is too damned isolated for me. Know what I mean?"

"Yeah. Look, we're just taking a break. We'll be out of your hair in fifteen."

"OK, then," the guard said and he walked off.

"The fuckers disappeared the whole damn ship," Oswald said as soon as the night watchman was out of earshot.

"I saw David Copperfield make the Statue of Liberty disappear on TV once," Swanson said. "This is just like that, only Copperfield brought the statue back."

Tom Oswald lived by himself in a one-bedroom house that had been too small for Tom and his ex-wife and still seemed too small even with Linda out of his life. The house was dark and melancholy and held few good memories. Oswald had been depressed when he was discharged from the army, and his hasty marriage to a woman with a bipolar disorder and a drinking problem had not been the smartest of moves. The house was haunted by heated words and angry silences, and Oswald stayed away from it whenever he could.

Instead of going home when his shift ended, Oswald drove to the trailer park where Dave Fletcher lived. He stopped his car in front of Fletcher's trailer and knocked on the door.

"If you're looking for Dave, he's gone."

Oswald turned toward the voice. A heavyset woman in a housecoat was standing in the door of the next trailer. Her hair was in rollers and a lit cigarette dangled from the fingers of her left hand. Oswald crossed the yard between the mobile homes.

"I'm Tom Oswald. I'm with Shelby PD, Mrs. . . ."

"Dora Frankel."

"Where did Dave go, Mrs. Frankel?"

The woman took a drag of her cigarette and shrugged. "I got no idea."

"Can you remember when you saw him last?"

Frankel stared into space. "I saw him head out the day before, but his car ain't been parked by the trailer since then. Has something happened to him?"

"Not that I know. I just needed to talk to him about a case."

"He hasn't done anything wrong, has he?"

"He's a witness. He's not in any trouble."

"That's a relief. Dave's always been a good neighbor."

Oswald handed the woman his card. "If Dave comes back, ask him to call me."

"Sure thing," Frankel said. "I got to go in now. My program's starting."

When he got back in his car, Oswald made a mental note to talk to Fletcher's employers, but he didn't think they would be able to tell him what happened to Dave. His gut told him that the night watchman had disappeared along with the ship, the dead men, and the hashish. He hoped he was wrong about another victim being added to the body count, but nothing about the *China Sea* affair smelled right.

Oswald drove on automatic pilot while he thought about what the incident had taught him. He now knew that the inhabitants of Shelby, Oregon, were very little fish in a gigantic ocean where people, holds full of drugs, and entire ships could be made to disappear without any effort at all. He did not appreciate being pissed on by the big fish, but there wasn't a lot he could do about that, especially after Chief Miles had told him to forget everything he'd seen.

Oswald was halfway home when he conceived of a small act of defiance. He turned his car around and headed back to the station. He had the fingerprints he'd hidden from the goons from Homeland Security. It wasn't much, but he could scan those fingerprints into AFIS, the Automated Fingerprint Identification System, and see if he could get a match. He had no idea what he would do if he identified the person who'd left the latents. His satisfaction would come simply from doing something he'd been ordered not to do.

Part Two

The Court of Last Resort

2012

Chapter Four

When Brad Miller checked his tie in the mirror, he noticed that a few silver strands had insinuated themselves in his curly black hair. This was not surprising, given what had happened last year. But that was last year, this was now, and Brad smiled as he adjusted the knot.

Brad had several reasons to be happy, the biggest being Ginny Striker, his fiancée, who was standing next to him applying her makeup. Ginny was a few years older than Brad—a tall, slender Midwestern blonde with large blue eyes, whom he'd thought of as a commercial for Kansas when they'd met a year and a half ago as first-year associates at a law firm in Portland, Oregon. Ginny had moved to Washington, D.C., with Brad seven months ago when retired United States Supreme Court justice Roy Kineer helped her get an associate's position at Rankin Lusk Carstairs and White, one of the capital's most prestigious law firms. Her six-figure salary was the reason they could afford their apartment on Capitol Hill. Brad certainly couldn't have made their rent on the salary he was being paid to clerk for United

States Supreme Court justice Felicia Moss, a job Kineer had secured for Brad as a reward for helping expose the greatest scandal in American political history.

The clerkship was another reason to smile. It might not pay much, and Brad's workday might last ten to twelve hours, but a clerkship on the Supreme Court was every lawyer's dream job, one that opened the door to any position in the legal universe. The fact that he was clerking for someone as brilliant and as nice as Justice Moss was a bonus.

And there was one final reason to smile. Brad's life had been blessedly uneventful since he'd arrived in Washington. Uneventful was very, very good if the exciting incidents that had made your previous year event-filled consisted of being attacked by gun-wielding assassins, digging up a jar filled with severed pinkies that had been buried by a serial killer, and, last but definitely not least, bringing down the president of the United States.

"Guess what I did?" Brad said when he'd finished fixing his tie.

"What?" Ginny asked as she put the final touches on her makeup.

"I made a reservation at Bistro Bis for eight tonight."

"What's the occasion?"

"The six-month anniversary of no one trying to kill me and no reporter trying to interview me."

"Has it been that long?"

"Yup. I guess I've finally become a nonentity again."

"Oh, Brad," Ginny cooed. "You'll never be a nonentity to me."

Brad laughed. "I guess I can handle one person who still thinks of me as a god."

"I wouldn't go that far."

Brad kissed Ginny on the cheek. "Let's get going. You might have nothing better to do in the morning than look in the mirror, but I'm a busy man."

Visitors to the United States Supreme Court cross a raised plaza paved in gray and white marble, climb fifty-three broad steps that lead to the fluted Corinthian columns supporting the west portico, and enter the high court through a pair of magnificent bronze doors decorated with eight panels depicting *The Evolution of Justice*. When Brad Miller and the other law clerks came to work, they crossed a different marble plaza at the rear of the building and entered through the employees' entrance on Second Street. After punching in his code, Brad passed a small desk manned by a security guard. The guard didn't ask for identification because the Court security guards had memorized every clerk's face.

From day one, Brad had the sense that everything about the Supreme Court was *very* serious. Everywhere he looked he saw thick marble, dark wood, and no sign of architectural frivolity. Even the air in the building felt heavy. And the law clerks . . . There were thirty-six of them, and most had been the kind of students who had to be talked in off a ledge if they got an A-minus. Not that any of them had ever suffered a tragedy of that magnitude.

Many of the clerks regarded Brad as they might an exotic exhibit in a carnival side show. He had not

been Phi Beta Kappa, nor had he gone to a prestigious college or law school or clerked for a federal
appellate court judge. On the other hand, none of
the other clerks had brought down a president of the
United States. Brad felt self-conscious around these
legal geniuses even though he had been an editor
of his school's law review, and he was still nervous
about giving a legal opinion to Justice Moss, afraid
that he might have missed something that one of
the Harvard grads would have spotted with ease.
But Moss seemed pleased with his work, and he was
gaining confidence. Last week, she'd even compli
mented him on a memo he'd written. The judge was
stingy with praise, and her verbal pat on the back
had lifted him six inches off the ground.

Brad's day was taken up drafting opinions and
dissents, writing bench memos that helped Justice Moss prepare for cases the Court was about to
hear, crafting memorandums that commented on
the opinions from other chambers, recommending
whether to grant or deny petitions asking the Court
to review decisions from lower Courts, and advising
the justice on emergency applications, which were
often last-minute requests for stays of execution.

The work at the Court never slowed down, and
juggling these assignments seven days a week was
exhausting. Brad was thankful that the building
housed a gym, a cafeteria, a barbershop, and other
amenities that allowed him to groom himself, eat,
and exercise, activities normal humans did in loca-
tions other than their place of work. But Brad had
no complaints. He might work like a dog, but know-

ing that he had input into decisions that shaped American history was energizing.

Justice Moss had four law clerks, and Brad shared an office adjoining her chambers with Harriet Lezak. Harriet was perpetually frazzled. She had curly black hair that seemed never to have known a comb, and a tall, wiry figure, the result of running long distances and not eating. Brad was always fighting an urge to pin Harriet to the floor and force-feed her milk shakes. He often wondered if she ever left the Court except to take one of her long runs. The clerks had no prescribed hours of work, but Brad felt compelled to come in early. No matter when he arrived, Harriet was always at her desk, and she rarely left work before he did. Brad thought of her as a new species of vampire, who lived on legal research instead of human blood.

Brad and Harriet's office was one of several clerks' offices that lined a corridor on the first floor. The office was small and cluttered, with barely enough room for two desks. Its saving graces were a floor-to-ceiling window that let in light and the courtyard across the hall with its flowers and fountain that could be seen when the door was open.

"Good morning, Harriet," Brad said. Harriet's eyes were glued to her computer monitor and she flicked a hand at him rather than reply.

"Is the boss in yet?"

"She's waiting on this memo," Harriet answered distractedly as she maneuvered the cursor across the monitor screen and clicked the mouse. The printer whirred and Harriet stood over it, impatiently tapping her fingers on her thigh. When the machine stopped making noise, Harriet snatched the papers it had produced and raced next door.

Chapter Five

Every associate justice is assigned an oak-paneled three-room suite consisting of a private chamber for the justice and two rooms for staff. Carrie Harris, a forty-year-old African American who had been Justice Moss's secretary since the judge was appointed to the Second Circuit Court of Appeals, guarded the door to the justice's chambers.

"Is she ready for me?" Harriet asked.

"She's waiting on that memo," Harris said, nodding toward the sheaf of papers in the law clerk's hand.

Harriet rapped her knuckles on the doorjamb. Justice Moss was sitting behind a grand mahogany desk reading a file. She looked up and waved Harriet in.

The judge's private chambers had a fireplace and a private bathroom. The *United States Reports,* which contain the Court's opinions, took up a good deal of the wall space. On the rest of the walls were an oil painting of former Justice Thurgood Marshall, photographs from Justice Moss's days with the Reverend Martin Luther King Jr., framed copies of her briefs in the landmark Supreme Court cases she had argued, and a quote in a pink quilted frame that provided an example of the judge's sense of humor. The quote was from Justice Bradley's concurring opinion in the 1872 case of *Bradwell v. Illinois,* in which the United States Supreme Court held that Myra Bradwell could be denied the right to practice law because she was a woman.

> *[T]he civil law, as well as nature herself, has always recognized a wide difference in the respective spheres and destinies of man and woman. The natural timidity and delicacy which belongs to the female sex evidently unfits it for many of the occupations of civil life. The . . . domestic sphere . . . properly belongs to the domain and functions of womanhood.*
>
> *The paramount destiny and mission of woman are to fulfill the noble and benign offices of wife and mother.*

Felicia Moss was a sturdy, gray-haired, black woman who seemed more like a wise grandmother than one of the most powerful judges in the United States. The justice's real age was a closely held secret, and her response to those who asked was "None of your business," a line that got a lot of laughs at her confirmation hearing.

Anyone who didn't know Justice Moss's history would be surprised to know that she'd run with a teenage gang on the mean streets of New York before figuring out that her life expectancy would improve if she got out of the ghetto.

Moss had no idea who had fathered her. Her

teenage mother had given birth to her at home, and her grandmother raised her after her mother died of a drug overdose. The first person in her family to graduate from college, she'd paid her tuition at CCNY by working menial jobs that left her little time to study. Even so, her grades had earned a scholarship to Columbia University Law School, where she'd finished fifth in her class. Unfortunately, the legal profession of the midsixties had no place for a woman, especially one of color. Her anger at having to work secretarial jobs while the men in her class collected fat checks on Wall Street drove her to the Deep South, where she used her legal skills to help Reverend King. Moss had been a beauty in her youth, and there were rumors—never confirmed—that she and King had been lovers.

King's assassination drove Felicia Moss into a deep depression, away from the civil rights movement and to Wall Street, where she became the token African-American woman at a white-shoe firm trying to clean up its image. She lasted four years, during which she slowly became involved with the women's rights movement. Two pro bono victories for the ACLU in the United States Supreme Court established her reputation in legal and academic circles. After leaving Wall Street, Moss taught at her alma mater until President Jimmy Carter appointed her to the federal district court. President Clinton elevated her to the United States Court of Appeals for the Second Circuit, and President Nolan put the finishing touches on her judicial odyssey by nominating her to the high Court.

"Here's my memo on *Woodruff v. Oregon*, Judge," Harriet said when she was seated opposite her boss. The judge skimmed Harriet's analysis of the case while her clerk waited patiently.

"So, you don't think we should grant cert?" Moss asked when she was done.

"No," Harriet answered confidently. "Take the double-jeopardy claim. It doesn't stand up. Sure, Sarah Woodruff was tried twice for killing John Finley, but the first case was dismissed."

"After a jury was selected and she'd suffered the ignominy of having to go halfway through a trial because the government kept crucial facts from the defense."

"Which they had every right to do," Harriet responded. "Woodruff is arguing that her case is special, but she's just one person. Protecting all of our citizens outweighs the rights of a single citizen."

"You don't think the application of the state-secrets privilege should be scrutinized more closely when the defendant is facing the death penalty?" Moss asked.

"I don't. The type of charge has no bearing on the rationale that supports the privilege."

Moss talked about the *Woodruff* case with Harriet for a few minutes more, then ended the discussion when she saw that the time for her meeting with the other justices was drawing near.

"OK. I'll read your memo carefully. It looks like you did good work. Now scat. I've got to get ready for conference. And ask Carrie to bring me some coffee. I'm going to need a caffeine fix to get through the morning."

Harriet closed the door behind her, and Justice Moss frowned. Lezak was bright but she was mechanical. Her memo on *Woodruff*, like her other work, was exceptional, but she always concluded that the law is the law. It didn't hurt to inject some humanity into the law from time to time. After working with Lezak for half a year, the judge had concluded that she lacked soul.

Moss thought about Brad Miller and smiled. There was an advantage to having four clerks. They each brought something different to the table. Brad was as good on the law as the Ivy Leaguers even if he hadn't yet convinced himself that he was, and he came at the cases differently from the kids from the top-tier law schools. The plight of the people involved in the cases concerned him. There were times when his emotions got in the way of his logic, but the judge could sort that out. It was nice to work with a bright young man who possessed a healthy dose of empathy.

Moss glanced at the clock again and sighed. She had no more time for daydreaming. The issues in *Woodruff* were complex, and she still had no idea how she was going to come down on them. She hoped that she would do what was morally and legally right, but there were times when morality and the law dictated different results. As the final arbiter of the law in this great country, she had a duty to follow its statutes and cases even when her heart pulled her in a different direction.

Chapter Six

The only thing keeping many death-row inmates alive is a petition for a writ of certiorari, which, if granted, orders the last court to hear the petitioner's appeal to forward the record of the case to the Supreme Court for review. Twice each week, stacks of new petitions are circulated in the justices' chambers, where their law clerks write memorandums recommending that the petitions be granted or denied. The chief justice circulates a "discuss list" with cases deemed to have merit, and each associate justice may place additional cases on the list.

The decision to grant or deny the thousands of petitions that flood the Court each month is made in an oak-paneled conference room that adjoins the chambers of the chief justice. Only the justices attend the conference; no other Court personnel, including their clerks, are allowed to hear their deliberations. The conference room is illuminated by a chandelier and the light from several windows. The windows are flanked by bookshelves filled with reports of the Court's decisions. A somber portrait of John Marshall hangs above a black marble fireplace. From his position on high, the fourth chief justice of the United States watches his judicial descendants take assigned seats around a long mahogany conference table on which lie sharpened pencils and yellow legal pads.

Associate Justice Felicia Moss limped into the conference room aided by an ebony cane with a silver handle, a gift from her clerks to celebrate her return to the court after hip-replacement surgery three years earlier. Justice Moss eased herself onto one of the high-backed black leather chairs that surrounded the conference table, noticing that everyone but Ronald Chalmers was present. As soon as she sat down, Chief Justice Oliver Bates nodded. Warren Martinez, the most junior justice, closed the door and the chief justice began the meeting.

"Ron's not here," Moss interrupted.

"Sorry, Felicia," Bates said. "I told everyone before you came in. Ron's going to be delayed and he wants us to start without him."

Moss frowned. "Is something wrong? He hasn't missed a day since I started on the Court."

"He didn't tell me what was up. He just said to go on without him, so let's start. We have a lot to discuss."

Over the next hour, the justices debated the fate of several cert petitions before arriving at *Woodruff v. Oregon*. Millard Price—a barrel-chested, broad-shouldered man who had once been president of the American Bar Association, solicitor general of the United States, and senior partner in Rankin Lusk Carstairs and White—was sitting across from Moss.

Price was easygoing and could usually be counted on to defuse tension with a joke, but Moss thought he'd looked edgy all morning. As soon as the chief justice spoke the case name, Price leaned forward.

Warren Martinez had scribbled a request to speak about the case on the discuss list, and he outlined his reasons for believing that cert should be granted.

Chief Justice Bates and Kenneth Mazzorelli argued against granting the petition. Justice Moss was on the fence and decided to keep her views to herself. Millard was one of the last to speak.

"This is a waste of time," he said. "I don't see any thing certworthy in the case."

Moss was surprised to hear Price take a hard line in a capital case. The justice was a member of the conservative bloc on many issues, but he was a moderate on social issues, and he was usually fair and open-minded in death cases.

"The double-jeopardy argument is frivolous," Price went on. "The case was dismissed with prejudice the first time Woodruff was charged with Finley's murder. There was a completely different set of circumstances when she was charged the second time."

"But it was the government that was responsible for her being charged in the first case," Martinez said.

"And there's definitely a *Brady* issue," Justice Mary Ann David chimed in. "The government has an absolute duty to provide the defense with exculpatory evidence in its possession, and I don't think national-security concerns can trump that duty, especially when the defendant's life is at stake."

"That argument is based on guesswork and conspiracy theory, not fact," Price shot back. He seemed upset, and Moss found that strange. Millard's arguments were usually calm and well reasoned. This outburst was very uncharacteristic.

Before anyone could continue the discussion, the door opened and Ronald Chalmers entered the conference room. There were dark circles under his eyes and his broad shoulders were bowed.

"Glad you could join us, Ron," Chief Justice Bates joked.

"Out on the links?" Martinez asked with a smile. Chalmers was a serious golfer.

"I won't be staying," Chalmers said. Moss thought he sounded exhausted. "I just came from the White House. I'm resigning from the Court."

The justices looked stunned.

"I'm sorry to spring this on you, but I didn't know until yesterday afternoon. Vivian has Alzheimer's. It's in its earliest stage, so she . . ." Chalmers choked up and paused to collect himself. "We're going to Europe while she can still appreciate the trip. I've been putting it off and, well, I just can't anymore."

Justice Moss went to her friend and colleague and embraced him. The other justices gathered around.

"I am so sorry," Felicia said. "If there is anything I can do."

"There isn't," was Chalmers's weary answer. "I just want to spend as much time with Vivian as I can, and there's no way I can do that and carry on the work of the Court."

"When are you leaving for Europe?" Mary David asked.

"I've got our travel agent working out the details. It will be soon."

"Does Vivian want visitors?" Justice David asked.

Chalmers smiled. "I think she'd like that."

"I'll call, tonight."

The justices talked with their colleague a few moments longer. Then Chalmers excused himself.

"God, that has got to be so tough," Bates said.

"I can't imagine what he's going through," Martinez said.

The eight remaining members of the Court talked about their friend until Millard Price broke in. "I don't want to be insensitive, but we really should get back to work. It takes four votes to grant cert. With Ron stepping down, I don't think there are four votes in *Woodruff*, so maybe we can dispose of the case."

Several of the justices looked appalled at Price's lack of compassion. A few looked angry.

"The body's not cold yet, Millard," Martinez said. "I don't think this is the time to make a hasty decision about a case that some of us feel strongly about."

"Well, the votes aren't here," Price said. "We can take a poll, but I don't think a vote to grant cert will carry."

"I'm not going to be rushed into a vote, given these circumstances," Justice Moss said. "We have no idea how Ron's successor will vote, and I'm not certain how I'm coming down. I say we exercise the right under 28 USC, Section 1 to defer our vote."

A few of the other justices voiced agreement. Chief Justice Bates said, "I'd like a show of hands. How many of you are in favor of deferring *Woodruff*?"

Seven of the eight justices raised their hands, Price being the only dissenter.

"All right, then," Bates said. "Let's take a twenty-minute break to clear our heads."

Moss wanted to talk to Price about the way he'd acted, but he rushed out of the room.

"What was that about?" Justice Mazzorelli asked Felicia, his eyes on Price's retreating back. Mazzorelli, a staunch conservative, often clashed with Felicia on legal issues, but he was an amiable colleague.

"I have no idea. Millard doesn't usually get worked up about our cases."

"Maybe he didn't get enough sleep last night." Mazzorelli shook his head. "I bet Ron didn't get any at all. Poor bastard."

Moss let Mazzorelli steer the conversation away from Price and the *Woodruff* cert petition, but she couldn't stop thinking about the judge's overreaction.

Chapter Seven

Dennis Masterson worked a kink out of his neck as he carried his coffee mug to one of the floor-to-ceiling windows in his spacious corner office. Masterson's workplace was the largest of any partner at Rankin Lusk, which was fitting because he was the firm's biggest rainmaker. The oak-paneled walls of his domain were a testament to his power. They were decorated with pictures of Masterson posed with every important person who had worked inside the Beltway for the past thirty years.

Most of the partners in the major D.C. law firms labored in obscurity, known only to the members of their country club and the legislators and political appointees they lobbied, but Masterson was familiar to any American who watched the evening news or political talk shows. A quarterback at Dartmouth and a law-review editor at Yale, he had joined Rankin Lusk after two tours in Vietnam. Seven years ago, Masterson had taken a sabbatical to serve as the director of the CIA. Three years ago, there had been a very embarrassing incident in Afghanistan, and Masterson had rejoined Rankin Lusk when the president, in need of a scapegoat, had asked him to fall on his sword. Masterson had toyed with the idea of resisting the request, but there was a lot of money to be made in the private sector and it didn't hurt his business prospects to be owed a favor by the leader of the free world.

Masterson was six four with the patrician features of a man born to wealth. With his snow-white hair and steely blue eyes, he was the personification of wisdom and sincerity, and the perfect guest on any television talk show. During his CIA days, he had been the ideal person to bear witness before a congressional committee. Masterson's connections with the defense and intelligence industries made him indispensable to his firm.

Masterson's disposable and untraceable cell phone rang. Only one person had the number to this particular phone and that person only called with important news.

"The conference just ended," the voice on the other end of the line said, "and there's been a development. Justice Chalmers resigned. His wife has Alzheimer's and—"

"I've known that for two hours," Masterson interrupted. "What happened with the *Woodruff* petition?"

"It's still alive."

Masterson swore. "Millard couldn't kill it?"

"He tried but Moss stepped in and convinced the other judges to defer a vote."

"What's the count?"

"Justices David and Martinez want cert granted.

Moss won't take a position, but Price thinks she's leaning toward voting to grant."

"Thank God for Chalmers's wife. He would have been the fourth vote if Moss is in favor."

Masterson went quiet. The caller waited.

"I want Moss's chambers bugged," Masterson said. "We have to know which way she's leaning."

"I'm on it."

Masterson broke the connection and returned his attention to the world outside his office. In the streets below, people scurried back and forth with no idea of who was really running the world. From this height, they looked like ants, and Masterson viewed them with the same dispassion he viewed any other insect. Of the billions of people in the world, only a few counted, and he was one of them. But that could change if Sarah Woodruff's case didn't die in conference. As it stood now, *Woodruff* was just another criminal case from a Podunk state known for tree huggers, pretty mountains, and running shoes. Masterson could not risk the scrutiny it would receive if the Supreme Court took it up. *Woodruff* had to stay buried, and Dennis Masterson was willing to do anything to keep it six feet under.

Chapter Eight

The Supreme Court cafeteria is open to the public, but the clerks eat in a glassed-in section with a door that is always closed so they can discuss Court business freely without worrying about being overheard. Advance notice of, for instance, the way a business case is going to be decided can have all sorts of consequences, and the clerks were impressed from their first day with the need for secrecy. Brad never discussed his cases with anyone but his justice and his fellow clerks, and Ginny knew better than to ask about them.

Brad was grabbing an early lunch alone in the clerks' area of the cafeteria when a tall, fit-looking man with a military haircut carried his tray to the seat across from him.

"Mind if I join you?"

"No, sit," Brad answered. The man looked to be in his mid- to late thirties, which was old for a clerk, and Brad wondered if this was a visitor who had wandered into the clerks' eating area by mistake.

"Are you Brad Miller?" the man said as he set down his tray. Brad braced himself for questions about the Farrington case. "Your fiancée is Ginny Striker, right?"

"Do you know Ginny?" Brad asked, relieved that he wasn't going to have to fend off another nosy inquiry.

"I'm Kyle Peterson and I'm a senior associate at Rankin Lusk."

Peterson saw the panicky expression on Brad's face and laughed. "Don't worry. I'm temporarily clerking for Justice Price until he hires someone to replace Frank Sheppard."

Brad sobered immediately. "That was awful," he said. Brad had met Frank his first week at the court. All of the clerks were shocked when he was badly injured in a hit-and-run accident.

"I never met him, but I heard he's a very nice guy," Peterson said.

"He is. So how did you get to take his place?"

"I worked with Justice Price when I started at Rankin Lusk, and we stayed in touch after he went on the Court. He's comfortable with me, and he trusts my work. The firm thought it wouldn't hurt for me to work up here, so . . ." Peterson shrugged.

"Do you work with Ginny?" Brad asked.

"We worked on a project together. When Justice Price asked me to fill in, I mentioned it to her and she told me you were clerking. I knew your name and what you look like from the papers and TV."

"That is my curse."

Peterson laughed. "So, how do you like clerking?"

"I really enjoy it. Justice Moss is great to work for, and the work is so interesting and important. The load is overwhelming at times, but I'm really glad I got the position."

"It's a great place to work, and you'll be able to pick your job when you're through. You might think about Rankin Lusk, though I don't know what the firm policy is about hiring married couples."

"I worked for a big firm in Oregon, and I'm not interested in doing that again. I'm thinking about the Justice Department or maybe something in the Senate or House."

"That shouldn't be a problem. I bet Justice Moss has a ton of contacts. And speaking of your boss, do you have any idea what she did in conference that upset Millard?"

"No," Brad answered cautiously.

"It had something to do with the *Woodruff* petition."

"I didn't work on that one, and the judge never discusses what goes on during the cert conferences."

"Well, something set him off. He's usually pretty mellow. You don't happen to know how she's planning to vote on the petition, do you? That might have something to do with it."

"Like I said, it's not a case I worked on, and the justice hasn't said anything to me about it. I don't even know what type of case it is."

Peterson took a bite out of his sandwich and Brad did the same.

"So, you were working in Oregon," Peterson said when he was through chewing. "I've never been out there, but I hear it's nice."

* * *

Everything about the library on the top floor of the Supreme Court was majestic, appointed with rich oak paneling, plush red carpets illuminated by grand chandeliers, and long tables of polished wood on which to write and research. It wasn't unusual for Brad Miller to find his eyes drifting upward to the ornate ceiling or wandering to the figures representing law, science, and the arts that were carved on the seven huge arches on either side of the library.

By contrast, there was nothing beautiful about the gym located above the library. A set of narrow stairs led the way to a long, colorless room filled with weight machines, stationary bikes, and other standard workout equipment. Next to the gym was the aptly named Highest Court in the Land, a basketball court that was the scene of many spirited games played by brilliant attorneys who would all willingly trade their fancy degrees for a chance to play in the National Basketball Association.

This evening, Brad found himself in sole possession of the court. Using one of his patented moves, he faked Kobe Bryant out of his Nikes before firing a three-pointer over Shaquille O'Neal's outstretched hand. Unfortunately, the ball clanged off the rim, costing the Knicks the NBA championship. Brad swore and jogged dispiritedly to the wall to recover the ball.

"Nice form."

Brad turned his head and found a pretty brunette about his height, in shorts and a sports bra, watching him from the door that connected the basketball court to the gym. When he'd entered the gym, Brad had seen her hunched over one of the stationary bikes, her face tense, as if she were finishing a hotly contested leg of the Tour de France.

"Did you play college hoops?" she asked.

"High school, JV," he said, unable to lie, though he was tempted. "I was never good enough for a college team."

"Give it here," the woman said. Brad tossed her the ball. She glided across the hardwood before firing a shot from the spot where Brad had attempted his three. The ball swished through the net without touching the rim.

"Awesome," Brad said, reacting to the unexpected grace of the woman's moves. She laughed. Then she picked up the ball and walked over to Brad. As she drew closer, he realized that she was more than just pretty, and she was definitely sexy, with her flat bare midriff and long smooth legs.

"Did you play in college?" Brad asked.

"Point guard at MIT."

Of course, Brad thought, feeling more inadequate than usual. He'd been a decent tennis player in college and could usually console himself with the idea that he was a better athlete than his fellow clerks even if he wasn't as smart, but this clerk could not only play hoops better than he could, she had a degree from MIT.

The woman thrust out her hand. "Wilhelmina Horst. It's a horrible name. Everyone calls me Willie. You probably don't remember, but we met at Happy Hour," she said, referring to the courtyard get-togethers hosted in turn by each chamber, where the clerks could get to know each other over a beer and eats.

"Oh, yeah," Brad said, fighting to hide the discomfort he felt being this close to a very attractive, half-naked woman. The guilt the attraction elicited was due to his status as a man engaged to be married. "I didn't recognize you out of uniform."

Willie smiled. "I was probably wearing glasses along with my suit. I use contacts when I'm not trying to look lawyerly."

"Brad Miller."

"Yeah, I know; the president guy. You're famous."

Brad blushed. "I wish I wasn't. Being a celebrity isn't all it's cracked up to be, believe me. It's actually a big pain in the butt."

"Oh, come on. Bringing down a president has got to be a rush."

"Not really. Mostly, I was in a state of terror. So, whom do you clerk for?" Brad asked, desperate to change the topic. Willie wasn't the first clerk who had tried to pump him for inside dope about the Farrington scandal.

"Millard Price. You clerk for Justice Moss, right?"

Brad nodded.

"My boss is pissed at her."

"Oh?"

"Something she did at conference with the *Woodruff* cert petitions upset him."

Brad's mental alarm went off. Horst was the second of Price's clerks to talk to him about *Woodruff*.

"What did she do?" he asked.

"I don't know. He was just muttering about Justice Moss when he got back to chambers, and he looked concerned. Your boss didn't mention *Woodruff* when she got back from the conference?"

"Not to me. I didn't work on that one. I don't even know what it's about."

Willie looked directly into Brad's eyes, making him more nervous than he was already. Then she thrust the ball at him.

"Want to go one-on-one?"

Willie's voice sounded huskier than it had been moments before. Brad felt something stirring bellow his belt line and tried to control his panic. He looked over Willie's shoulder at the clock. It was almost eight.

"I should be going. My *fiancée* is probably waiting to have dinner with me."

"Maybe some other time?" Willie said, her voice full of promise. She was apparently unfazed by the revelation that Brad had a significant other.

"Not if I want to preserve my dignity," Brad answered with a nervous laugh. "You'd probably kick my ass."

Willie smiled. "It would be fun to try. Say, I've heard that Justice Moss's chamber is decorated with really interesting civil rights memorabilia."

"It is."

"Any chance you can give me a tour some evening, after work, when she's gone?"

"Uh, sure, maybe."

"Good."

"I really have to go. Ginny's probably starving."

"Right. Nice talking to you again."

Brad left the gym sweating more than he had when he was working out. The questions about *Woodruff* had raised a red flag. Something was up, and he decided he should tell his boss about his conversations with Millard Price's clerks as soon as he had a chance.

Brad took a quick shower, then headed down to his office to call Ginny.

"Are you up for dinner?" he asked when he got through to her.

"I would love to have dinner with you, but General Tso asked me first."

"Ditch the takeout. I can be at your office in fifteen minutes."

Ginny sighed. "I can't. One of the partners dumped a file on my desk at six and needs a memo first thing in the morning. You remember what that's like."

"Unfortunately, I do," Brad said as he flashed back to the bad old days at the law firm in Portland.

"I love you, and I'll see you at home."

"You'll probably be too tired for wild sex," Brad said, half joking and still aroused by his encounter with Willie Horst.

"Or any other kind."

Brad laughed. "Just kidding. I'm pretty beat myself. You're the best."

They traded kisses and Brad hung up. He smiled. Willie Horst might be sexy, but she was no Ginny Striker.

* * *

Ginny hung up the phone and sighed. In front of her was a sixty-page contract so boring that it would put a speed freak to sleep. To her right, a pair of chopsticks stuck out of a carton of greasy General Tso's Chicken. She would have given anything to be in her pajamas, snuggling on her couch with the man she loved while they watched a great old movie on the Turner Classics station. Unfortunately, she owed thousands of dollars in student loans and also found it necessary, for some strange reason, to eat and put a roof over her head. Ah to have been born a royal princess or heir to an industrialist's fortune. Life was definitely not fair.

Ginny plucked a piece of chicken out of the carton and washed it down with a swig of Coke. Then she slapped her cheeks to get her adrenaline going. She made it through the contract a little after nine and e-mailed her memo to the partner at 10:15. At this hour, Rankin Lusk Carstairs and White was a ghost town inhabited by the cleaning crews that moved silently through the plush offices of the partners and the Spartan broom-closet-size spaces occupied by oppressed associates who, like Ginny, had been saddled with last-minute assignments by their sadistic masters.

Ginny was almost to the elevator when she heard the *ding* that signaled the arrival of a car. A woman stepped out, followed by Dennis Masterson. Ginny was not surprised to see Masterson with a female. He had a well-deserved reputation as a womanizer. As new as she was to the firm, Ginny knew of two associates who'd had to fend off his advances. What did surprise Ginny was how ordinary the woman looked. She was dressed in a severe beige business suit and had thin, pinched features and mousy brown hair. Her eyes were her best feature, and they examined Ginny without emotion, the way a computer might if it could stare.

Masterson nodded at Ginny as he passed her on his way to his sprawling corner office. Ginny wondered if the woman was a client, then wondered why she would be meeting with Masterson in his office at this hour. She considered the possibility that the meeting was a tryst but discounted it. If Masterson was going to make love to the woman, they would be in a hotel room. Ginny was too tired to give any more thought to the pair, and they were forgotten by the time the elevator doors opened in the garage.

Chapter Nine

Inverness, a sleepy college town of roughly thirty thousand in northern Wisconsin, was founded by Scotch immigrants who migrated west from New York in the mid-1800s. The population of the town more than doubled each fall when the students at Inverness University and Robert M. La Follette School of Law started the fall semester, and it swelled again during hunting and fishing seasons. Hiking and camping were popular diversions for Inverness students, and the university orientation package contained maps highlighting the hiking trails that started at various points on the outskirts of the campus, and the location of the many lakes that could be found in the verdant forest that surrounded the town and the university.

Daphne Haggard was a redhead with green eyes and freckles but without the stereotypical fiery temper. She'd been one of five officers in Chicago's police department with an Ivy League degree when she arrived in the Windy City after her husband was accepted into the PhD program at the University of Chicago. She had moved to Inverness when her husband was hired to teach history at Inverness University. Her law-enforcement career had been on the ascendancy, and the decision to move had been difficult, but not as difficult as her husband's efforts to find a good job at a good college. Brett had been miserable working as an adjunct professor with no hope of tenure, who supplemented his income by teaching courses at a community college. Daphne loved her husband, and she'd been willing to make a sacrifice to see him happy.

Daphne's business card identified her as the chief homicide inspector of the Inverness Police Department, but she was usually working on crimes that had nothing to do with dead people, because there weren't many murders in Inverness, and it usually didn't take much sleuthing to solve them when they did occur. Inverness had never been the scene of a bizarre serial killing, and no one could recall finding a murder victim sealed in the locked room of an eerie mansion. Once or twice a year, someone who had too much to drink would hit his wife too hard and too often, or a bar fight would end in tragedy, and Daphne would make the arrest. There was usually a teary confession and a slew of witnesses, and the skills she'd developed in the Chicago PD were rarely needed.

Early one Saturday afternoon, however, the Inverness Police Department received a call from a terrified coed concerning a body part she'd stumbled over in the forest surrounding the campus. Daphne, an officer, and a forensic expert met Tammy Cole at the trailhead. The coed was dressed in running shorts and a sports bra. Her complexion was ashen and her arms were wrapped around her body despite the unseasonably warm weather.

Daphne showed the frightened girl her credentials. "Miss Cole, I'm Detective Haggard. This is Officer Pollard and Officer McCall. Can you tell us what happened?"

The girl swallowed. "I usually go for long runs around this time of day. I run different routes. There's a stream about five miles in on the trail I picked for today's run. I got thirsty. The underbrush is thick in spots and I tripped over a root. When I . . ."

Cole stopped and took a deep breath.

"Take your time," Daphne said.

"I threw out my hands to break the fall," Cole said when she was calm enough to continue. "It was soft, not like ground. There were insects, and it smelled rancid."

"What did?"

"I'll show you."

"It's human," Douglas McCall, the forensics expert, said after a brief examination.

The thigh presented Daphne with the only interesting case she'd had since she'd moved to Inverness—a chance to do some real detective work—but she suppressed her excitement for fear that McCall would think her ghoulish.

"Man or woman?" asked Daphne, who was squatting beside him.

"Tough to tell. Lots of men and women weigh in the neighborhood of 150 pounds, and their thighs would look similar after decomposition because the hair gets lost and the skin turns green, like it has here."

"Isn't there any way to tell who we've got? What about DNA?"

"You could send the thigh to NamUs, the National Missing and Unidentified Persons System. It's run by the Department of Justice, and they have a database they use to identify missing persons."

"How does that work?"

"We'd send a tissue sample to the University of North Texas, where they do the DNA testing. Their people can extract DNA from soft tissue, like the deep muscle in the thigh, and do nuclear testing on it."

"Make it radioactive?"

McCall laughed. "I thought you were the cop with the Ivy League degree."

"Spare me the wit. My degree's in English lit."

"Hey, that rhymes. I bet you aced poetry."

"Fuck you, Doug," Daphne answered with a grin.

"I didn't know you were so sensitive. Anyway, the term refers to the cell nucleus. That's where they get the DNA from. You can do that type of testing with blood, hair. When they extract the DNA, they put the sample in their database and try to get a match. But it takes a while."

"What's a while?"

"If this was a high-priority case you could get them to act pretty fast, but I'm guessing, realistically, we're talking three months at a minimum."

"Shit."

"Of course, the easiest way to do it is to find the rest of the body. Get me a hand, and we can print it; a pelvic bone, and I can give you the sex."

Daphne studied the grisly evidence. *Who are you?* she wondered. Then she stood up and looked around. Normally she would have found the *shush*-ing sound the stream made and the deep green of the forest restful. Today the woods had become a sinister place where the rest of the unknown victim might be hidden.

Daphne dialed headquarters on her cell phone. It was lucky that they were in a quiet time of the year, because she was going to need a lot of help search-ing the woods for the rest of Mr. or Ms. X. They'd have to mobilize the Explorer Scouts, get some ca-daver dogs from the state police. It would be a logis-tics nightmare.

Daphne briefed the chief and told him what she needed. It was only after she hung up that she re-membered the weather forecast. A storm was coming in, the first of the year. If they didn't find the rest of the body quickly, the parts might be buried under snow by tomorrow night.

Chapter Ten

Court had been in session, so Brad didn't get a chance to talk to Justice Moss until late in the day. When he walked into chambers, the judge was writing a draft of an opinion in longhand on a yellow legal pad. A computer stood on a worktable in a corner of the room, gathering cobwebs because Moss, who maintained that she was an old dog who could not learn new tricks, insisted on working with pencil and paper as she had during much of her legal career.

"What can I do for you, Mr. Miller?"

Brad sat in a high-backed, black leather chair across from his boss. "Something odd happened, and I thought you should know about it."

Moss laid down her pencil and gave Brad her full attention.

"Last night, I was working out in the gym, and Wilhelmina Horst, one of Justice Price's clerks, struck up a conversation. During it, she mentioned that Price was upset about something you did in conference that concerned the *Woodruff* petition for cert. Then she asked me what you were going to do in the case."

"What did you say?"

"I told her I didn't know anything about the case, which is true. I wouldn't have thought much about the conversation, except that earlier in the day, while I was eating lunch, Kyle Peterson, another of Price's clerks, did the same thing. I told him what I told Horst, and he dropped the subject, but I had the distinct impression that they were trying to pump me for information about your vote on the cert petition."

Justice Moss frowned and went quiet. After a bit, she looked across the desk.

"Justice Price and I had a disagreement during the conference, and the clerks probably overheard him venting. Thanks for telling me about the conversations, but I'm not concerned."

Brad started to leave. He was halfway to the door when Justice Moss spoke again.

"Don't mention this to anyone else, Brad. Millard shouldn't have talked about something that went on in conference, and I don't want anyone to know what goes on there."

"Don't worry. I've forgotten what happened already."

When Brad entered his office, it was empty. Harriet never left work this early, so he assumed that she had gone for a run. He continued to work on a memo outlining his views of the legal issues in a case he'd been assigned. After working steadily for three quarters of an hour, he took a break and printed out a section of the memo. Then he went on the Internet and Googled Millard Price's name. A long list of hits appeared, and he clicked on a biography on Wikipedia. The first thing that caught his eye was Price's long friendship with Dennis Masterson, a partner at Rankin Lusk, whom Brad had met at a party at the firm during Ginny's first week as an associate. With Masterson as Dartmouth's quarterback and Price at halfback, the Two Amigos, as they were nicknamed by the press, had won an Ivy League championship and had earned All-Ivy honors.

The friendship had continued at Yale, where they attended law school, and at Rankin Lusk, where Price ended up after law school and Masterson was hired after his service in Vietnam. Price had taken time off from his firm to serve as solicitor general of the United States, then returned to the firm until President Nolan appointed him to the Supreme Court.

"What are you doing?"

Brad turned quickly, startled by Harriet's silent return to the office. She was wearing a tight-fitting track suit, and her face was damp with perspiration.

"Don't sneak up on me like that," Brad complained.

"Sorry. Is that a biography of Millard Price?"

"Yeah."

"How come you're reading up on him?"

"I've been reading biographies of all the justices," Brad lied. "Aren't you curious about how everyone got where they are?"

"Studying the justices was part of my preparation when I *applied* for my clerkship."

"Did you apply to more than one chamber?" Brad asked, pretending that he hadn't noticed the subtle dig. Unlike every other clerk, with the possible exception of Kyle Peterson, Brad had been handed his job at the court.

"No, only Justice Price."

Brad was confused. "If you only applied to clerk for Justice Price, what are you doing here?"

"He hired too many clerks. There was some mistake. So he asked Justice Moss if she'd take me so he could keep Willie. Each justice is entitled to four clerks, and Justice Moss only had three after she hired you. She took me on as a favor to Justice Price because he didn't want to have to let me go after promising me the job."

"That would have been rough."

"What was rough was being shunted aside for that slut," Harriet said bitterly.

"Willie?"

"Is there any question why she was hired? Price has been divorced three times, and he always has one clerk with tits bigger than her IQ."

"Horst went to MIT."

"Is that what she told you?"

"She was on the basketball team."

"Her freshman year. Then she transferred to UMass. That's where she graduated."

Harriet stopped. "I shouldn't be talking like this. Sorry. I'm tired and it just slipped out. I'm going to shower."

"You coming back?"

"Yeah, I still have some stuff to do."

Harriet left, and Brad thought about what he'd learned about Willie. She'd never told him she was an MIT grad. All she'd said was that she was on the MIT basketball team, which was true. And she had to be pretty smart to get into MIT in the first place, plus she had been hired as a Supreme Court clerk, which was further proof that she wasn't a dummy, as Harriet had suggested.

Brad put all thoughts of Willie Horst out of his head and got back to his memo. He'd been working for fifteen minutes when someone tapped their knuckles on the doorjamb. Brad turned and found Willie Horst standing in the doorway. Her hair was down and she was wearing a tight-fitting black skirt and a white silk blouse, open at the neck, displaying the tanned and tantalizing curve of her breasts. Brad flushed, embarrassed by the sexual arousal Willie elicited. He also could not help entertaining the irrational idea that his visitor knew that he had been discussing her with Harriet.

"I came to take you up on your invitation to show me the memorabilia in Justice Moss's chambers," Willie said.

Brad didn't remember extending an invitation, but he wasn't certain he hadn't.

"Uh, OK. Let me log out."

Justice Moss had left the lights on in her chambers for the cleaning crew. Brad stepped back, and Willie walked in. Brad felt uncomfortable alone with Horst, and he wanted the tour of the office to go as quickly as possible. He started by pointing out the quote from Justice Bradley.

"So, you're seeing someone," she said, as she read the quote.

"We're engaged."

"Hmm. This is cute," Willie said when she finished. Then she wandered over to a photograph of a much younger Felicia Moss and Martin Luther King taken the day of King's assassination.

"I've heard they were lovers," Willie said.

"That's an unsubstantiated rumor."

"Have you ever asked her?"

"Of course not."

Willie laughed and walked over to the justice's desk. "You're not uptight about sex, are you?"

"No," Brad answered, too quickly. The truth was that he'd never been someone who took sex lightly. He was a one-woman man, and the women he'd slept with, with rare exceptions, were women with whom he'd had a serious relationship. His exhausting and painful relationship with one of those women, Bridgett Malloy, was the reason Brad had moved across the country from New York to Oregon after law school. When he'd arrived in Portland, Brad had wondered if he'd ever get over Bridgett, but Ginny had cured him of the symptoms of his tragic romance.

Willie ran her hand along the underside of the desk as if she were stroking a lover, while glancing at the papers stacked on top of the desk.

"I don't think you should be looking at the judge's work," Brad said. He crossed over to Willie to protect Justice Moss's privacy, even though he didn't want to get any closer to her than necessary.

"Sorry. Are those the covers of the cases Justice Moss argued in the Court?" she asked, crossing to the far side of the room.

Brad let Willie wander around the judge's chambers for a while longer. Then he told her that he had to meet Ginny for dinner. Horst took the hint and left. Brad noticed that she hadn't shown a lot of interest in the justice's memorabilia, and he wondered if the request for a tour had been a cover for something else.

Chapter Eleven

Dennis Masterson's driver powered down the tinted window of the limousine and identified his passenger to the guard at the east gate of the White House. The guard checked to see if Masterson was expected, then checked the attorney's identification before waving the car through. As the limo made its way along the horseshoe-shaped driveway, Masterson thought about the brief affair he'd had with President Gaylord when the then United States senator from Ohio was starting her second term. After Masterson had briefed the Senate Intelligence Committee in a closed-door session about a clandestine operation in sub-Saharan Africa, Gaylord had asked him to join her for drinks, ostensibly to pick his brain about what she would need to know to be more effective in her new assignment. Masterson suspected that Gaylord had more on her mind than self-improvement and was delighted when his suspicions were confirmed. The senator had been a Miss Ohio and had worked hard to keep her figure and looks. Masterson grinned as he remembered the few nights they'd spent together. Gaylord was unquestionably the only president who would have looked good as a *Playboy* centerfold.

The affair ended almost as soon as it began, and Masterson had no illusions about Gaylord's reason for beginning it. Every move she made was calculated to give her an edge. The president had grown up dirt-poor and had financed degrees in business and law with scholarships won in beauty pageants. She'd made a personal fortune and important contacts while serving as counsel to a major corporation, and her rapid rise in politics was well documented. The president was a shark with a dangerously high IQ, and Masterson knew he would have to be careful to gain what he wanted without being eaten.

The Rose Garden came into view, and the chauffer pulled up in front of a door that stood between the Oval Office and the State Dining Room. A Secret Service agent led Masterson upstairs to the private quarters and left him in a small study. After making Masterson wait for fifteen minutes, Maureen Gaylord walked in. The stately brunette was dressed in an understated outfit that the truly discerning would know was the product of a top fashion designer.

"Dennis," she said, flashing a warm smile that lit up her wonderful features. Masterson savored the moment. He knew the smile would disappear as soon as Gaylord learned the reason for his late-night visit.

"The presidency hasn't aged you a bit, Maureen," Masterson said after they'd cheek-kissed and were both seated.

"You were always great at flattery, but keep it up. I need to hear something nice after dealing with that asshole from North Korea all day."

"Then you should welcome my visit. I'm here to ease the burden of your office."

"Oh," Gaylord said. The president knew there was no such thing as a free lunch when the ex–CIA director was involved.

"Vivian Chalmers is a wonderful woman. It's got to be tough for Ron."

"He's devastated. I was one of the first people he told," the president said.

Masterson nodded sympathetically. "Ron is going to be tough to replace."

"I agree."

"But I believe I've found the perfect person for you to nominate." Masterson was relaxed. A calm smile illuminated his handsome features. "You know I had some terrific people working for me at the CIA. Well, the brightest person in the group is now a respected academic with a deep understanding of the world around us."

"And who would that be, Dennis?"

"Audrey Stewart."

"You're kidding?"

"You can use another woman on the Court."

"Audrey is to the right of Attila the Hun. There would be a donnybrook in the Senate, and the liberals would go insane."

Masterson stopped smiling and fixed Gaylord with a cold stare. "I guarantee that I can deliver the votes, Maureen."

"And how exactly will you do that?"

"The same way J. Edgar Hoover kept a string of presidents in line. The director of the CIA has access to secrets. I've kept proof of some very dark ones for a rainy day."

For the first time, Maureen Gaylord looked less sure of herself.

"Why Stewart? She's very smart, but so are any number of qualified candidates I could name."

"I regard Audrey very highly," Masterson answered evasively.

"Well, I don't, but I'll place her in my pool of possible nominees, and I'll see what my advisors think."

"I'd prefer something more substantial," Masterson said, his tone hardening.

"That's the best I can do, Dennis. You're not the only person advocating for a candidate. All I'll promise is that I will consider your suggestion seriously."

Masterson reached into his pocket and slid a DVD case across the coffee table that separated them. Under the DVD was a seemingly innocent photograph of Gaylord and a man who appeared to be of Middle Eastern origin sitting in a hotel lobby. Masterson watched the color drain from the president's face as he stood up.

"Thank you for seeing me on such short notice. I'd appreciate it if you'd consider Audrey as a possible nominee to the Court. Why don't you give me a call when you've made a decision?"

The president of the United States was still staring at the photograph when Masterson closed the door to the study behind him. Although he appeared supremely confident, the encounter had left him drained. As an attorney, he was well aware of the federal criminal statutes he'd violated by blackmailing the president, but the consequences of having cert granted in *Woodruff* were potentially far worse. Besides, he was certain that Gaylord would not want the conversation that had been recorded on the DVD he'd given her heard by anyone who didn't already know about it.

Masterson told his driver to take him home. Then he opened the bar in the back of the limousine and poured a glass of fifteen-year-old single-malt scotch. He took a sip and closed his eyes. When he was calmer, he considered his problem.

Masterson's mole in the Court had told him that if Moss was going to vote to bring *Woodruff* to the Court, the justices were just one vote shy of the four votes needed to grant cert. If Stewart was appointed, it wouldn't matter what Moss did, but Masterson didn't like leaving anything to chance. Moss was the wild card. She was the Court's brightest legal mind and she had a knack for bringing other justices over to her way of thinking. Gaylord was right when she said that the liberals would go berserk if Audrey was nominated. Masterson was pretty certain that he could leverage the votes he needed to get Stewart the appointment, but nothing was certain in politics. It always helped to have a contingency plan, and Masterson decided to put his into action.

Chapter Twelve

Daphne Haggard had grown up in New England. Then she'd moved to Chicago and Wisconsin. She should have been used to the cold, but she hated it. If the temperature had been in the eighties while she was standing in this land of majestic trees with its coat of sparkling white snow, she would have appreciated the forest's serene beauty. But each time she tried to lose herself in the picture-postcard landscape, a gust of wind would whip through the trees and lacerate her cheeks. If she had half a brain, she told herself, she'd be living in San Diego or Miami.

What was she doing out here supervising the search for more body parts? How likely was it that the search teams would find anything? Daphne hunched her shoulders, pulled her navy blue watch cap more firmly over her ears, and took a long sip of steaming hot coffee from the thermos she clutched in her gloved hands. She should be home in front of a fire instead of freezing her butt off on a fool's errand. Still, this might be their only chance. The storm that had prevented a search when the thigh had been discovered had lasted several days, but the weather had warmed and a lot of the snow had melted. It was getting cold again, but no more snow was predicted until the weekend, which meant they had a narrow window to blanket the area and pray for a miracle. Once the bad weather came in earnest, the search would have to be suspended for months. Of course, by the time they could resume, a match with a missing person would probably have been made from the DNA taken from the tissue sample that had been forwarded to NamUs and all of this suffering in the cold would have been for nothing.

Daphne was working herself into a deep depression when two Explorer Scouts crashed through the trees.

"We found a leg!" one of the boys shouted.

"It's on the other side of the stream," the second boy chimed in.

"Show me," Daphne said.

The two scouts raced to a place where the stream narrowed, and Daphne hurried to keep up. The water was high because of the runoff from the snow and moving fast. Daphne almost unbalanced on the slick stones that covered the streambed, but she caught herself before she fell into the freezing water. The bank on the other side was a gentle incline, and she made it to the top in time to see the scouts disappear into a copse of birch trees. The limbs were bare, and she kept her eye on the red ski parka one of the scouts was wearing. By the time Daphne entered the forest, the two boys had stopped.

"You're going to love this," said Patty Bradford, the county medical examiner, a tall, heavyset woman with dirty blonde hair and lively blue eyes, who was always upbeat despite the gruesome nature of her work. She and Daphne were standing over a stainless steel table on which lay a section of a decomposed leg.

"See this scar?" Bradford asked as she pointed to a strip of scar tissue that started beneath the kneecap and stopped about an inch above the stump. "Someone operated on this person. We X-rayed the leg as soon as we saw the scar, and this is what we found."

Bradford held up an X-ray for Daphne. She stared hard and noticed a straight dark line.

"That is an orthopedic appliance," Bradford said. "This person broke his or her leg, and this stainless steel rod was used to stabilize the fracture. When I take it out, we should find a maker's mark and a serial number. If we're lucky, the manufacturer will be able to tell you where this rod was shipped, and if we're luckier, the hospital that received it will be able to identify the patient."

"How long should the whole thing take?" Daphne asked, excited by the breakthrough but anxious about the speed with which the discovery of the victim's identity would occur.

"That I can't tell you. It will depend on how long ago the operation was performed and if all the records exist, but the rod will definitely give you something to work with."

Chapter Thirteen

Justice Moss was working on an opinion in a securities-fraud case in which Brad was not involved. Arnie Copeland, the clerk who had researched the case, had been in and out of the judge's chambers all day. Brad had finished a memo in a labor-law dispute out of the Deep South a little after five, and the judge had told him she wanted to see it as soon as he was done, but Brad knew better than to interrupt her. Justice Moss had tunnel vision when she was working and didn't appreciate distractions.

Harriet went for a run at six, leaving Brad alone. He kept watching the door to the judge's chambers, hoping to catch her before she left. At six thirty, Brad went to the restroom. When he came back to his office, he noticed the door to Moss's chambers was open. He peeked in and saw that she was gone.

"Where's Justice Moss?" Brad asked Carrie Harris, who was shutting down her computer.

"She just left."

"For home?"

Harris nodded. "If you hurry, you can catch her. She's headed for the garage."

Justice Moss had told Brad that she wanted the memo the minute he was finished, and he hated to disappoint her. He grabbed it and raced down the corridor to the elevator that went to the underground garage where the justices parked, his footsteps echoing off the walls of the nearly deserted building.

The elevator doors opened, and Brad found himself at the bottom of the ramp that led down to the garage from the street. A policeman sat in a booth at the top of the ramp to make sure that only authorized personnel got into the Court. Barriers blocked the entrance to the ramp until the policeman pressed a button and they retracted into the concrete to clear the way.

To Brad's right was another guard shack manned by another policeman. In front of him was the top of the ramp leading down to the first parking area. Justice Moss was limping down the ramp to her car. Brad was about to call out to her when a figure in black appeared from behind the concrete pillar at the bottom of the ramp. The intruder was wearing a ski mask and gloves and holding a gun with a silencer. Fear coursed through Brad as he flashed back to the only other time he'd encountered a man with a gun. His brain told him to flee but his legs moved on their own and he found himself racing down the ramp.

"He's got a gun!" Brad screamed.

The assassin turned toward Brad. Justice Moss didn't hesitate. She braced herself on the car beside her and whipped her cane across the killer's wrist.

The gun clattered to the concrete and skidded across it toward Moss. Brad launched himself and the assailant sidestepped gracefully before delivering a crushing blow to Brad's ribs. Brad crashed to the concrete floor chin first. He was dazed but he rolled onto his side so he could keep the assassin and Justice Moss in sight.

Moss was bent over, reaching for the gun. The killer started for her. Brad buried his pain and grabbed an ankle. The killer stumbled and Moss grabbed the gun. Brad struggled to his feet and the assassin ducked behind him, encircling his neck with a forearm.

Moss was unsteady on her feet without her cane. She grasped the gun with two hands and tried to aim. The killer dragged Brad up the ramp, using him as a shield, and the judge fired into the air to attract the attention of the policeman in the guard shack.

"Help!" Brad screamed as he clawed at the arm that encircled his throat. The stranglehold tightened, cutting off Brad's air. The policeman stepped out of his booth. The assassin dropped Brad and rushed at him. The policeman reached for his gun but a crushing kick buckled his leg. A knife strike to his throat, delivered with the killer's rigid fingers, dropped the officer to the concrete. Moss fired. The shot was wild and ricocheted off the guard shack. Brad covered his head and ducked. Moss fired again, just as the killer disappeared into the building. This shot hit the wall and was nowhere near its target.

"Stop!" Brad shouted. "You'll hit one of us."

Moss lowered the gun and fell against Justice David's tan Mercedes. Brad staggered toward his boss.

"Are you OK?" he asked.

"Better than you," Moss said. "That might need stitches."

Brad saw where she was looking and put his hand to his chin. It came away covered in blood.

Moss took a deep breath and shook her head. "I've never fired a gun before."

Given her lack of accuracy, Brad hoped that she never did again.

"Please get me my cane, Brad. Then see to the guard. I think his leg might be broken. And get the police down here."

Brad handed the cane to the judge and started up the ramp toward the policeman, who was holding his shin and writhing in pain. He was halfway to the officer when he noticed the pages of his memo scattered across the concrete. He picked them up on his way to help the policeman.

A security guard accompanied Brad and Justice Moss to her chambers. An EMT cleaned the cut on Brad's chin, decided that it didn't have to be stitched up, and applied a large Band-Aid. Then a member of the Supreme Court police force took their statements.

Brad was badly shaken. He and Dana Cutler, a private investigator from Washington, D.C., had been in a shoot-out in Oregon while investigating President Farrington's involvement in the murders of several young women, and it had been Brad's fervent wish to never be involved in another. His voice shook as he recounted what he remembered of the action in the garage, and his hand was trembling when he signed his statement. Before the police officer left, he assured them that a search of the building was under way, a guard was stationed outside Justice Moss's chambers, extra security was being provided for the judge, and the FBI had been notified.

Aside from asking for a glass of water, Justice Moss seemed unaffected by the mayhem in the garage. Unlike Brad, her voice had been steady when she recounted what she'd seen.

"How can you be so calm?" Brad asked as soon as they were alone.

"When I was a teenager, I ran with a pretty tough crowd. We didn't have the firepower that you can get so easily today, but I was in my share of knife fights, and there were chains and zip guns." She shook her head. "Of course, that was a long time ago. I haven't been in a fight since high school, and this took the wind right out of me."

"You sure reacted quickly. If you hadn't knocked the gun out of the killer's hand, we'd both be dead."

"Amen to that. I guess my old instincts aren't too far beneath the surface."

"Lucky for us."

"Lucky isn't the half of it. I was seconds away from being an obituary. But it's not the attack that's bothering me; it's the reason I was attacked that has me worried."

Chapter Fourteen

Keith Evans had gotten home a little before six and nuked a TV dinner. It was chicken something with a side of something else, but ten minutes after he'd tossed the tray into the trash, he couldn't remember what he'd eaten.

After dinner, Keith channel-surfed for ten minutes before turning off his set. One mystery Keith wished the FBI could solve was how, with two million cable channels, there was never anything on TV that could hold his interest. He dropped the remote on an end table and wandered over to the bookshelf that stood against the front wall of the small living room in his small apartment. Keith could have afforded something a little bigger, but he was home so rarely that he'd decided it wasn't worth the money to upgrade. He looked at the titles of a few books he'd picked up from a used-book bin at a local mystery bookstore, but nothing excited him.

Keith hated to admit it, but he was bored. He had started his professional life as a cop almost twenty years ago in Nebraska, where an intuitive leap had helped him track down a serial killer who had baffled the FBI for five years. The agent assigned to the case had been so impressed that he'd recruited Keith for the Bureau. Keith had never duplicated his uncanny series of deductions in any other case since joining the FBI. His successes were the result of dogged police work. At forty years of age, he had given up on any dreams he may have had of being the Bureau's Sherlock Holmes, but his involvement in the D.C. Ripper case, which had ended Christopher Farrington's presidency, had revived him. Now that the case was over, he missed the excitement of being at the center of the law-enforcement universe.

Keith was trying to decide what to do next when his cell phone rang. The display identified Maggie Sparks, his partner. It had to be important if she was calling so soon after he'd left the office.

Brad was in the middle of a conversation with the judge when Keith Evans and Maggie Sparks walked into Justice Moss's chambers. The two FBI agents represented a study in contrasts. Evans was six two with thinning blond hair, streaked with gray, and tired blue eyes. He was carrying extra weight around his middle, and his once broad shoulders were stooped. Sparks was slim and athletic with glossy black hair, high cheekbones, and a dark complexion. She looked young and vigorous, and the grim tasks that had weighed down her partner's psyche did not appear to have touched her yet.

"What are you doing here?" Brad asked Keith.

"Maggie and I have been assigned to investigate

the attempt on Justice Moss's life," Keith said. The agent pointed at Brad's chin. "What happened to you?"

"Mr. Miller was wounded in the line of duty," Moss said.

Brad turned to his boss. "You lucked out, judge. The FBI has put two of their best on this case. Keith was the head of the D.C. Ripper task force and his investigation was one of the threads that brought down President Farrington's presidency."

"I've seen Agent Evans on TV," Justice Moss said. "Pleased to meet you."

"This is Maggie Sparks, my partner. May we sit down?" Keith asked, indicating two armchairs positioned across from the couch on which Brad and Justice Moss were sitting.

"Please."

"I know you've already given a statement to the police," Keith said to the judge, "but would you mind telling us what happened?"

Justice Moss gave a detailed description of everything that occurred from the time the killer stepped from behind the pillar until her assailant fled into the Supreme Court Building.

"Has there been any luck finding this guy?" Brad asked when the judge was finished.

"The building is being searched, but it's pretty big. Hopefully, he'll be found, but he could have left the building before the search was organized."

"I'd be surprised if the person who tried to kill me is still here," Justice Moss said. "He seemed very professional."

"Why do you say that?" Maggie asked.

"I had the impression that he knew what he was doing, and I assume that includes working out an escape route. When you go to the garage, you'll see that he couldn't have planned on getting away by car. There are barricades at the top of the exit ramp that would have been up if the alarm was raised. So he must have worked out a way to get out of the Court once he was through with me."

"Why are you so certain your assailant was a professional?" Keith asked.

"It was the way he moved. He handled Brad and the guard easily, and his gun was equipped with a silencer. He definitely had some type of training."

"Can you think of any reason for this attempt on your life?" Keith asked.

"No, I can't. My assailant may just be a mental case or some right-wing fanatic."

"Are you considering a case this term that might set off someone like that?"

"No, we don't have any hot-button issues like abortion or gay rights before the Court this term."

"What about a case that affects an individual or a business?" Agent Sparks asked.

"That would be almost any case. They're all very important to the litigants, but I honestly can't think of a case that would get someone so upset they would try to kill me. And what would be the point? There are eight more justices. There have been instances where a justice has had to recuse himself or herself or has been unable to sit because of illness, and the Court has conducted business as usual."

"What about personal enemies? Can you think of a court employee who was fired or someone in your personal life with a grudge?"

Moss shook her head. "I'll give it some thought, but right now . . . No, I can't think of anyone who would want me dead."

Chapter Fifteen

Felicia Moss had lived alone for most of her life. There had been a brief marriage to a civil rights lawyer when she was in her late thirties, but that had only lasted two years, through no fault of her spouse. After the divorce, there'd been an occasional lover, but her work had been her real significant other. Felicia didn't regret the lack of companionship. She had decided long ago that she preferred to live alone, so the only tics and foibles she had to put up with were her own.

With the exception of her stint on Wall Street, the judge had never had an income comparable to those of men like Millard Price, but she had been a wise investor, and the returns from her portfolio allowed her to afford a pleasant apartment in an old and elegant high-rise in the Kalorama Triangle near Connecticut Avenue. Three policemen accompanied her home from the Court. One watched her door while the other two searched her apartment to make sure no one was waiting for her inside. When the search was complete, two of the officers left, leaving the third on guard in the hall outside her apartment.

Felicia could tell that Brad had been shaken by the attack in the garage, but she had always possessed the ability to shuck off the violent emotions that crippled others when they faced danger. She experienced no trembling of the hand or shortness of breath when the officers left her alone. However, she was overwhelmed by fatigue, and she dropped into an armchair and closed her eyes as soon as the door closed. She had always possessed an inordinate amount of energy, but she was in her midseventies, and age was catching up to her more rapidly than she would have wished.

After she'd been sitting for a while, Felicia became aware of a second sensation, hunger. With all the excitement, she had forgotten about eating. Her apartment building had been built in the early 1940s. An antique clock graced the mantel of the marble fireplace that was the centerpiece of the high-ceilinged living room. Felicia was shocked to see that it was after nine. She pushed herself to her feet and walked to the kitchen. Felicia was a talented chef, but she had only enough energy to slap together a sandwich made from odds and ends she found in her refrigerator. After pouring a glass of milk, she sat at the kitchen table. She barely tasted her sandwich because she was preoccupied by the events in the garage. She was too old to fear death, but she was as curious in her seventies as she'd been in her teens. What was the motive for the attack? The assassin could just be a fanatic, but she didn't think so. There was nothing going on in her personal life that could have engendered such hate. She examined a number of possible reasons for the assault and kept coming back to the same one. The only odd things that had happened recently were Millard Price's overreaction during the discussion of the *Woodruff* case and the attempts by two of Price's law clerks to pump Brad Miller for inside information on her vote, but Felicia couldn't believe that someone would kill her to prevent cert from being granted in a case.

On the other hand, she really didn't know much about Woodruff's case other than the fact that the petitioner was facing execution in Oregon and that the most interesting legal issue concerned the state-secrets privilege, something she knew little about. Was it possible that Millard Price had some connection to the case? Felicia shook her head. Even if he did, it was absurd to think that her friend and colleague would try to kill her because of it. But as absurd as her theory was, Felicia couldn't shake the idea that she might be on to something. What to do, though? There was no way she could conduct an investigation personally. A Supreme Court justice was not allowed to go outside the record in a case that was before the Court. Even if she was permitted to play private eye, she didn't have the time or energy. Felicia smiled as a thought occurred to her. She couldn't play at being Sam Spade, but she knew someone who knew a real-life private eye.

Chapter Sixteen

Brad called Ginny just before he left for home and gave her a bare bones sketch of what had happened. Ginny watched the evening news, and Brad was afraid she'd worry when she heard about the attempt on Justice Moss. The judge was concerned that her assailant might want revenge on Brad for foiling his plans, so she arranged for a policeman to drive him home and guard his apartment. When Brad opened the door, Ginny threw her arms around him, which balanced all the awful things that had happened but caused excruciating pain in his ribs where he'd been punched. Brad winced and Ginny backed off.

"What's wrong?"

"My ribs. They're a little sore."

A policeman followed Brad inside.

"This is Officer Gross of the Supreme Court police," Brad explained. "He's going to watch the apartment tonight. Officer Gross, this is my fiancée, Ginny Striker."

"Ma'am," Gross said.

"Why do we need a police guard?"

Brad decided to fudge the truth. "I don't think

we do, but Justice Moss insisted. I think she wanted to protect us if reporters came around. The Court frowns on clerks speaking to the press."

Officer Gross made a cursory inspection of the apartment before borrowing a kitchen chair to sit on in the hall.

"Are you really OK?" Ginny asked as soon as the door of their apartment closed. She had noticed the large Band-Aid on Brad's chin and remembered Brad's reaction to her hug.

"Honestly, the cut on my chin didn't need stitches, and my ribs aren't broken."

"I was so worried when I heard the news. It said a clerk had been injured but the reporter didn't name him. Then you didn't come home on time."

"I'm sorry you were worried." Brad pulled Ginny back to him and held her tight. "The person who attacked Justice Moss is probably a nut case."

"I just can't stand the idea of you being in danger."

"Well, I'm not." Brad pushed Ginny to arm's length. "Now enough of this mushy stuff. Is there anything I can eat? I'm starving."

While Ginny heated up some takeout Chinese, Brad told her about the incident in the garage.

"You idiot," Ginny blurted out when Brad told her how he'd rushed the killer. "What were you thinking?"

Brad looked down, unable to meet Ginny's eye. "I wasn't. I just did it," he answered meekly.

"God, I hate this. I thought we were through with guns and killers."

"We are, believe me. They'll find out this guy

is a member of some right-wing fringe group that hates African Americans or liberals. I was never the target."

The microwave dinged. Brad carried his food into the living room while Ginny brought him some tea. It was time for the late news, and Brad switched on the TV. A blonde anchorwoman was looking at the camera with her most serious expression.

"The Supreme Court dominated the news today as an assassin tried to kill a justice inside the historic building and President Maureen Gaylord nominated a woman to replace Associate Justice Ronald Chalmers."

A picture of Felicia Moss took over the screen.

"Never in our nation's history has an assassin struck at a sitting justice inside the walls of the Supreme Court Building," the anchorwoman said. "But that changed this evening when an assailant tried to shoot Associate Justice Felicia Moss in the Court's garage. Only quick thinking by one of her law clerks prevented the tragedy. The identity of the clerk has not been revealed, but Brad Miller, who figured prominently in the recent scandal involving former president Christopher Farrington, is employed as a clerk by the justice."

"Great," Brad said. "Prepare to be besieged by hordes of reporters again. Shit! I so wanted to be done with being a news story."

Ginny squeezed Brad's hand. "I'm not any happier than you are, but we weathered the storm once, and we'll do it again. Thank goodness, Justice Moss had the foresight to get you a person to guard the apartment. All I need is some reporter banging on our door in the middle of the night and—"

Ginny stopped talking suddenly. "I know her."

"Who?"

Ginny was pointing at the TV. "That woman."

On the screen, President Maureen Gaylord was introducing her nominee to fill the vacancy on the Court created by Justice Chalmers's resignation. The woman standing next to the president was a little over five feet tall, very skinny with pinched features and mousy brown hair. Her thin lips were drawn into a tight line and her eyes stared straight ahead. Brad thought that she looked completely humorless.

"Audrey Stewart is a graduate of Yale and its law school," President Gaylord was saying, "and has been a respected professor at Harvard and New York University law schools for several years. More important for these trying times, Miss Stewart spent several years in a high-ranking position at the Central Intelligence Agency. Her experience will give her a unique insight into many of the issues that will come before the Court."

"How do you know Stewart?" Brad asked.

"I don't really *know* her. Do you remember calling me a few nights ago and asking me to meet you for dinner and I couldn't go because I had to work late?"

"Yes."

"When I was leaving the office, Dennis Masterson came out of the elevator with Stewart. I thought it was an odd time to meet with a client, but Masterson must have been helping Stewart get the nomination. He was the head of the CIA, and I bet she served with him."

"That makes sense. Masterson is a major player in this town."

Audrey Stewart stepped to the podium and gave a saccharine thank-you speech.

"She looks a little scary," Brad said. "I wonder how she'll fit into the Court."

"If she worked at the CIA, I'm guessing she's going to beef up the conservatives."

"You can't always tell," Brad said. "Hugo Black was a member of the Ku Klux Klan, and he ended up being a big supporter of civil liberties, and everyone thought Harry Blackmun would be very conservative and he authored *Roe v. Wade*."

"If Dennis Masterson helped her get the nomination, Audrey Stewart is not a closet liberal. Trust me on that. I've learned enough about Masterson's politics during my short time at the firm to know he'd only help a dyed-in-the-wool right-winger get on the Court."

"Tomorrow, the bloggers and the newspapers will have plenty of articles analyzing her views."

The phone rang and Ginny and Brad stared at it.

"Let the answering machine take it," Brad said.

"Hi, this is Wendy Fellows from the *Washington Post*," the caller began.

Brad walked over to the wall and disconnected the phone just as Ginny's cell started to ring. They looked at each other and powered down their cell phones.

"Are you sorry you took up with me?" Brad asked Ginny.

"My life would certainly be more peaceful with almost anyone else as a fiancé. I just think of you as one of those trials God puts us through to test us."

Brad smiled. Then he took Ginny in his arms and kissed her. "We're not going to get any calls tonight, and there's nothing on TV. What do you want to do?"

"Are you sure your ribs can take it?" Ginny asked, only half joking.

"Why don't we see?"

Chapter Seventeen

Brad was so exhausted that he overslept, but the policeman who'd relieved Officer Gross drove him to work so he wasn't too late. Normally, the security guard at the employees' entrance nodded at Brad when he walked by, but this morning he said, "Good work, Mr. Miller."

Brad blushed and mumbled something inane before rushing off. The last thing he wanted was for everyone to think he was a hero when he didn't think of himself like that. He'd read interviews with men who had been awarded the Medal of Honor and citizens who'd rushed into burning buildings or leaped into turbulent rivers to save a life. Many of them were humble and embarrassed at being labeled a hero. Brad could see why. If he'd had time to think, he believed he would have run away from Justice Moss's assailant as fast as he could. But, like many other real-life heroes, he had acted on instinct, and it bothered him that he would be given credit for saving the judge's life when he was on automatic pilot when he did it.

"Thank you," Carrie Harris told Brad when he walked by the door to the judge's chambers on his way to his office.

"I really didn't do much, Carrie."

"Uh huh," she answered, her voice dripping with skepticism. "Well, whatever you didn't do kept the boss alive. So I'm still going to thank you. And speaking of Justice Moss, she wants to see you."

"I'll be there in a minute. I'm just going to dump my stuff."

As soon as Brad walked into his office, Harriet jumped to her feet.

"Are you OK?" she asked, examining his taped-up chin.

"Yeah, I'm fine."

"Did you really have a karate fight with the guy who attacked the boss?"

"Karate fight? I don't know any karate. Where did you hear that?"

"All of the clerks are talking. I think they heard it from the security guards, but I can't swear to that."

"There was karate, but there wasn't any fight. I was on the floor before I knew what hit me."

"Then how did you fight him off?"

"I didn't. Justice Moss knocked the gun out of the guy's hand with her cane while I distracted him by letting him beat the hell out of me. Then she fired the gun to keep him from killing me. She's the real hero."

"I think you're just being modest."

"I'm just being honest. Look, Harriet, the judge is waiting for me. Please don't tell anyone I'm the

Bruce Lee of the Supreme Court, because that is absolutely false."

"Hold my calls and shut the door," Justice Moss told Carrie Harris when she ushered Brad into chambers.

"How are you feeling?" the judge asked Brad as soon as they were alone.

"Not too bad. A little sore, that's all."

"Roy Kineer called me last night," Moss said when she was satisfied that he wasn't just being brave. "He heard about the attack on the news. He asked after you. I told him you saved my life."

"I hope you didn't exaggerate what I did."

Justice Moss threw her head back and laughed. "You charged a man with a gun armed only with a legal memo, young man. How do you exaggerate that?"

Brad smiled.

"Roy wasn't surprised by what you did. He had some very nice things to say about you, some of which I'd heard before when he recommended that I hire you. You should know that there aren't many people who impress Roy."

Brad blushed and looked at his lap. He didn't know what to say, so he said nothing. The former chief justice had acted as the independent counsel who investigated the charges against President Farrington, and they had met because Brad and Dana Cutler were the key witnesses in the case. Kineer was an icon in the legal community and one of

Brad's heroes. It was hard for him to believe that Justice Kineer thought about him at all, let alone was impressed by him.

Moss stopped smiling. "I have a problem, and you're the only person I can think of who can help me."

Brad sat up straight. "Anything I can do, just ask."

"Don't commit yourself until you hear what I want you to do. It's . . ." Moss paused. "Irregular. No, more than irregular. If someone discovers what we're up to, it could lead to some very unpleasant consequences for both of us. If you tell me you don't want to do it, I'll respect your decision, and I'll forget this conversation even took place."

"Now you're making me nervous," Brad said.

"When I told the FBI that there was no case I could think of that could have triggered last night's attack, I wasn't being completely honest. Millard Price's reaction in conference to *Woodruff v. Oregon* was very unusual. And you've told me that two of his clerks told you that I upset Millard by the way I acted in conference and tried to pump you for information on how I'm going to vote." Justice Moss paused. "Brad, I think there's a possibility that the attack on me and the *Woodruff* case are connected."

"You think Justice Price is trying to kill you?" Brad asked incredulously.

"No. But his reactions were so odd that . . ." Moss shook her head. "There's something about that case that's upsetting him, and I can't understand what it could be."

"Why didn't you tell Keith Evans about your suspicions?"

"What goes on in conference is sacrosanct. I would make an exception if I had evidence that the case was the reason I was attacked, but I don't have one scintilla of proof. I just have a feeling. That's why I need your help. I need to know if there's any hard evidence to support my suspicions."

"I still don't know what you want me to do," Brad said.

"We justices are prohibited from going outside the record in a case when we're deciding the legal issues it presents, but I can't help thinking that Millard may have some connection to the *Woodruff* case that he hasn't disclosed. I need an investigator to find out if such a connection exists and, if it does, what it is."

Brad frowned. "You want me to go to Oregon and play private eye?"

"No, of course not. You'd be missed instantly. Besides, I can't afford to be short a clerk. Last night, when I was talking to Roy, he reminded me that your friend, Dana Cutler, was working as a private detective when the Farrington affair broke."

Even though they were friends, the mention of Dana Cutler made Brad shiver. Brad liked Dana, but he'd led a sheltered life before getting involved in the Farrington affair, and he wasn't used to associating with people as potentially violent as he knew Dana could be. While working as an associate in an Oregon law firm, Brad had been assigned a hopeless pro bono appeal for a convicted serial killer and had stumbled onto evidence that linked President Farrington to the murder of several women. Simultaneously, in Washington, D.C., Dana had drawn similar conclusions when she discovered a link between the president and a murdered college student. When they'd finally hooked up in Portland, Dana had forced Brad into a situation that almost cost him his life.

"Is Miss Cutler still a private investigator?" Justice Moss asked.

"Yes."

"Do you think she would look into any possible connection between Millard and the *Woodruff* case?"

"I can ask."

"I'll take care of her fee and expenses, but she can't tell anyone who is employing her."

"That shouldn't be a problem." Brad paused. "Willie and Kyle told me that you did something specific that upset Justice Price. Do you feel that you can tell me what happened between you two? Dana is going to want to know."

"As you know, it takes four votes to grant cert. Oliver Bates, Kenneth Mazzorelli, and Millard spoke out against bringing *Woodruff* up here. Lucius Jackson usually votes with Ken, and Frank Alcott is more conservative than anyone on the Court. Mary David and Warren Martinez made it pretty clear that they want *Woodruff* heard. I'm leaning their way. Ron Chalmers was going to vote to grant cert. So there were only two sure votes for cert after Ron stepped down, and my vote wouldn't have been enough.

"As soon as Ron Chalmers left the room after

telling us he was going to resign, Millard tried to force a vote on *Woodruff*. I told him I wasn't sure how I was going to vote, and I precipitated a vote to defer. I'm responsible for cert still being a possibility in the case. Now it all depends on how Ron's replacement votes."

"You told Keith Evans that people don't kill justices of the Supreme Court to keep cases from being heard."

"I hope I'm right."

"And, from what you're telling me, even if cert was granted, the petitioner would probably lose five to four."

"That's true. And all this could be the work of an old woman's overactive imagination, but it's the only unusual thing that's happened in connection with a case, and it's got me worried."

"If Dana agrees to help, what do you want her to do?"

"I think she'll have to go to Oregon and find out as much as she can about what really happened there, and whether Millard had a connection to any of it."

"I'll see if Dana can meet with me tonight. Then we—"

A knock on the door startled them. Millard Price walked in. Brad had to struggle to keep his composure.

"Sorry to interrupt, Felicia, but I just heard that you were attacked last night. Are you OK?"

Brad watched Price closely. He seemed genuinely concerned.

"Thanks to Brad's quick thinking, I'm just fine."

"Thank God."

Brad stood up. "I should get hopping on that memo, Judge."

"Fine. Come in, Millard."

Brad took one final look at Justice Price before shutting the door. Then he went around the corner to his office. Harriet was working away at her computer, and Brad saw her cast a nervous glance at Keith Evans, who was sitting in Brad's chair. The FBI agent stood up as soon as Brad walked in.

"I just dropped by to see how you're doing," Evans asked.

"I'm fine, just a little sore, that's all."

"Good. Is there someplace we can talk? I want to go over what happened yesterday in more detail, now that you've had a rest, and I don't want to disturb Miss Lezak."

Brad led Evans through the halls until they reached the spacious, elegant, and architecturally identical East and West Conference Rooms, which faced each other across a corridor near the courtroom. Each space was bordered by a courtyard that provided natural light to the interior rooms. No meetings were being held in either place, so Brad led Keith into the East Conference Room. The carpets and drapery were rose colored, and the walls were paneled in American quartered white oak. Crystal chandeliers from Czechoslovakia hung from a ceiling glazed in two tones of gold. Portraits of the first eight chief justices graced the walls. Rows of beautifully carved, straight-backed wooden chairs had been set up for some special occasion that was to take place the next day. Brad took one chair and Evans sat next to him.

"This is some place," the agent remarked as he took in the stylish setting.

"Working here can be a bit overwhelming at times. Especially if you grew up in a ranch-style tract home on Long Island."

"I can see what you mean. So," Evans said, transferring his attention to his friend, "has anything occurred to you since we spoke last night?"

Brad knew he should tell Keith about Justice Moss's suspicions, but he would never violate her confidence.

"Not a thing, and believe me I've given what happened a lot of thought."

"I bet you have. What about the assailant?"

Brad shook his head. "He was covered from head to toe. I can tell you he was about my height and wiry, but that's it. I was on the floor most of the time or being dragged across the concrete with my back to the guy when he had me in that choke hold."

Evans sighed. "I was hoping you could give me something, because we're coming up empty. The perp vanished without a trace."

"What about security cameras?"

"They only tracked him so far. He knew areas of the building that weren't covered, and that's where we lost him."

"So he knows the layout of the Court pretty well?"

"That would be my guess," Evans answered.

"Do you think it's someone who works here?"

"That's a definite possibility."

"Well, I can't think of where to point you, but I'll get in touch if I get any ideas."

"So, are you enjoying yourself?" Keith asked.

"Yeah, this is the best job," Brad answered with a broad smile. "Except for the part where you get beat up by ninja assassins."

Keith laughed. "Hopefully, that was a one-off." He pushed himself to his feet.

"Make sure you've got Justice Moss covered, OK?" Brad said. "She's a great boss and a brilliant justice. The country needs her."

"We're beefing up her security. Do you think you need someone watching your back?"

"No. The killer was going after Justice Moss, not me. I wasn't even supposed to be in the garage. I shouldn't be in any danger."

Chapter Eighteen

Normally, Dana Cutler turned down matrimonial work. It was sordid and boring, and her clients were usually angry no matter what she reported. But Mark Shearer referred a lot of business her way, and he was genuinely worried about his client. Rachel Kelton, a sweet, plain-looking woman in her late thirties who had never been married, had inherited a fortune when her parents died in a plane crash. Eight months ago, she had met Erik Van Dyke, the president of a hedge fund, at a charity fund-raiser. Van Dyke was five years Rachel's junior. He had wooed her for five months before proposing. On the surface, he appeared to be an ideal prospect for matrimony, but something about her fiancé bothered Rachel, and out of an excess of caution, she had asked Mark to conduct a discreet investigation into his background.

That was why Dana found herself following Van Dyke in the inconspicuous brown Toyota she used for surveillance. She had begun detecting a sour smell shortly after looking into Van Dyke's business dealings. Although she couldn't prove it, she suspected him of running a Ponzi scheme, in which he gave initial investors excellent returns by paying them with money he received from newer investors. Rachel's fortune would be very attractive to a con man.

Dana also had a funny feeling about Van Dyke's social life. He didn't appear to have any. When he wasn't courting Rachel, he worked or stayed in his apartment. That would be normal if Van Dyke was the genuine article. But it would be abnormal if he was a predator. On a few occasions, Dana had followed Van Dyke into a seedy part of town known for street prostitution, but he had not made a move. This evening, he did.

The girl was young and had the reedy, waiflike build of a woman with a serious jones. She was pale and could have passed for twelve. There were dark circles under her eyes, which were constantly scanning the street, and her stringy blonde hair looked like it hadn't been washed in days.

Van Dyke usually drove a flashy sports car or an expensive sedan. Tonight, he'd chosen a low-end Chevy, which he pulled to the curb. The girl leaned into the car through the open passenger window. After a brief negotiation, she got in the front seat, and Dana followed them to a by-the-hour motel.

Dana was worried. The girl looked very vulnerable. Van Dyke could afford high-priced, sophisticated call girls. What was he doing with a junkie who could be loaded with a sexually transmitted disease? Dana suspected that missionary position sex was not on Van Dyke's mind.

The girl waited in the car while Van Dyke secured the keys to a room at the far end of the building. The parking-lot lights were out near the room, and Van Dyke parked in the shadows. The girl got out and he followed. Dana noticed the navy blue gym bag he carried in his right hand.

Dana was five ten, lean and muscular, and she was always on edge. She looked hard and dangerous in her leather jacket, tight jeans, and black T-shirt, but there was something about her that would make a man think twice even if she was wearing a cocktail dress.

There was a reason for the aura of violence that enveloped Dana. She had spent a year in a mental hospital dealing with post-traumatic stress after she had butchered three men who'd tortured her in the basement of a meth lab while she was working undercover with the D.C. police. Since her release from the hospital, she always went armed and had shown no reluctance to resort to extreme violence during her involvement in the affair that had brought down President Farrington.

Dana was carrying two guns and a hunting knife, but she rejected these weapons in favor of a tire iron she kept under the driver's seat. Dana didn't think Van Dyke would be much of a physical threat to someone with her training, and she decided that she could always escalate if she was wrong and things got out of hand.

There was a window at the front of Van Dyke's room and another at the side of the building. Dana took her camera out of the car and knelt by the side window. Unless someone parked in the lot across from the room she would not be detected. The shade was up enough for Dana to see into the bedroom. So far, Van Dyke was acting the part of the perfect gentleman. Dana couldn't hear what the couple was saying, but Van Dyke was smiling as he pulled out his wallet and handed some bills to the girl. As soon as she tucked the money in her purse, the girl started to disrobe. Van Dyke watched her but made no move to take off his clothes. As soon as the girl was naked, Van Dyke smiled broadly and hit her in her solar plexus. The girl flailed for air. He slapped a piece of duct tape across her mouth to keep her from screaming. She was already oxygen deprived, and her eyes bugged out when her mouth was sealed. Van Dyke had no trouble turning her face down and handcuffing her arms and legs to the bedpost with restraints he pulled from the gym bag.

Dana could have rushed in immediately, but she decided that the girl would be safer secured to the bed where she wouldn't be a distraction. Van Dyke took a whip from his bag. Dana slipped on a ski mask, walked to the front door, and pounded on it.

"Open up, police," she barked in the authoritative voice she'd used when she was with Vice and Narcotics.

Dana thought she heard the door to the bedroom slam shut, and she pounded and shouted "Police" again.

"One second," a voice called. Dana guessed Van Dyke had covered the girl with a blanket and bedspread and had ditched the whip, which she noticed he'd held in his right hand. As soon as he answered the door, Dana broke Van Dyke's right collarbone and kicked him in the crotch. He collapsed on the floor. Dana took out one of her guns and closed the door behind her. Then she grabbed Van Dyke by the hair and pulled him into the bedroom.

"Get all of your clothes off," she commanded.

"You broke my shoulder," he whined as he rolled on the floor in agony.

Dana pistol-whipped him hard enough to get his attention before repeating her order. She enjoyed seeing the pain Van Dyke suffered as he struggled to take off his clothes with his collarbone broken. She hoped his pain exceeded the pain he had intended to inflict on his helpless victim.

Dana walked over to the girl. "I'm here to help you. I'm taking off the tape. Don't scream. You'll end up with every penny this asshole has before I leave, and he won't be able to hurt you, so please do as I say."

The girl nodded and Dana removed the tape so she could breathe. Dana pulled off the blankets that covered the girl before returning her attention to Van Dyke.

"Pick up the whip in your right hand and stand by the bed as if you're going to beat her," Dana ordered, knowing that the girl was in no danger from the whip because of Van Dyke's broken collarbone. As soon as Van Dyke obeyed, Dana snapped off several shots of the naked man that made it look as if he was going to flay the helpless girl. When she had enough pictures, Dana removed the girl's handcuffs and used them to secure Van Dyke faceup on the bed.

"I'm going to leave in a minute," she told the girl. "This creep won't be able to hurt you. I'll leave his car keys on the dresser. If you want to, you can drive somewhere, ditch the car, and take the money to your dealer. Or I can take you somewhere safe and get you into rehab. I'm not going to tell you what to do. I'm not your mother. You're sick. The first step in getting better is to start making the right choices. Think it over while I finish with this pervert."

Dana turned to Van Dyke. "I want you to refund the money you stole from your clients. Then I want you to leave Washington. I'll give you one week to take care of business. If I find you haven't followed my orders, I will publish these pictures on the Internet after I send them to the police. If you're still here after I publish the pictures, I will hunt you down and kill you. Tell me you understand."

Van Dyke was crying from the pain in his shoulder. "I understand," he managed.

"Good," Dana said.

Dana had a brief flashback in which she was lying on the cold cement in the basement of the meth lab after she'd been gang-raped. Rage raced through her. She slapped duct tape across Van Dyke's mouth and broke his left kneecap.

"You make me sick," she told him when Van Dyke's muffled screams stopped. Then she went through the man's wallet and handed his money to the girl.

"Heroin or rehab?" she asked.

The girl's head was down. She was crying. "Get me out of here," she gulped in a voice so low Dana could barely hear her.

"Good choice," she said.

Dana turned her back on Van Dyke and put her arm around the girl's shoulders. She would send Mark Shearer the photos and a report. The report wouldn't mention what she'd done to Van Dyke. That was private. Dana smiled. Saving the girl and humiliating Van Dyke had made this one of the most enjoyable evenings she'd spent in a while.

Chapter Nineteen

Dana Cutler was writing the report for Mark Shearer in the basement office of the suburban ranch house she shared with Jake Teeny. When the words began swimming across the computer monitor, she decided it was time to take a break. Dana stretched and her T-shirt rode up, revealing pale scars on her flat stomach. There was a coffee pot perched on top of a low filing cabinet. She walked over and refilled her mug before returning to the computer.

Dana had moved in with Jake at the conclusion of the Farrington affair, and that was working out. The flashbacks and nightmares associated with her scars had been infrequent visitors since they'd started living together. Dana figured that she was as close to happy as she was ever going to be. Close to happy was a big step up from the hellish months she'd spent in the mental hospital.

Dana's reflections about the state of her life were cut short by the ringtone on her cell phone. Few people had that number, and she was pleased to see Brad Miller's name on the readout. She and Jake had gone out with Brad and Ginny soon after the couple moved to D.C., but all four were so busy with their jobs that they hadn't hooked up again.

"Long time no hear," Dana said.

"I'm sorry about that," Brad said, "but this job eats up my hours."

"No need to apologize. I haven't called you either. What's up?"

"Can we meet for coffee?"

"Sure. When?"

"I was thinking now."

Dana looked at her watch. It was almost nine. She knew she should finish her report, but Brad sounded worried.

"OK. Where?"

"You know the city way better than I do. It would be best if we weren't someplace where we'll bump into reporters or anyone who'll recognize us."

"Are you in some kind of trouble?"

"Absolutely not, but I'd feel more comfortable talking to you face-to-face."

Dana told Brad where to meet her. Then she shut down the computer. Jake Teeny was a photojournalist whose assignments took him all over the world. Currently he was in West Africa, so Dana was free to ride his Harley. After being cooped up in the basement writing reports, the idea of tearing through the night on Jake's machine was very appealing. She had a smile on her face when she slipped into her leather jacket and settled her helmet over her short auburn hair.

* * *

Dana had worked on the report through her normal dinner hour, and she didn't realize how hungry she was until Brad talked about meeting someplace where you could get coffee. That was usually a place where you could also get something to eat, and thoughts of a juicy burger topped with cheese and bacon had her mouth watering and her stomach growling. When she was working undercover, Dana had discovered Vinny's in one of the less reputable sections of the District of Columbia. Vinny's served great burgers and fries and had not yet been discovered by the people who wrote the dining-out reviews in the *Washington Post*.

Dana was chomping on her dinner when Brad walked in. He looked nervous. Dana guessed that was because of the run-down state of the neighborhood and the disreputable look of Vinny's patrons. Brad's expression turned to relief when Dana waved from the dingy booth near the back of the tavern. He slid across the tattered red vinyl that covered his side of the booth and stared at Dana's burger.

"Is that any good?" he asked apprehensively.

"Don't let the decor fool you," Dana said. "Order the bacon cheeseburger with fries. You're in for a treat."

Brad gave his order to their waitress and added a beer to wash it down.

"So," Dana asked. "Why the clandestine rendez-vous?"

"I want to know if you can handle a sensitive assignment."

Dana rolled her eyes. "Like investigating whether

the president of the United States is a serial killer?" she asked.

"This isn't a joking matter, Dana."

Dana could see how concerned Brad was, so she decided to get serious.

"Does this have something to do with the attack on Justice Moss?"

"I'm not sure. It might."

"Is Justice Moss the client?"

"As far as you're concerned, I'm your client."

"Right."

Brad leaned forward and lowered his voice. "Imag ine you're under oath, testifying before a Senate committee, and the chairman asks you if Supreme Court justice Felicia Moss hired you. How do you answer, under pain of perjury?"

"I get your point. So, Mr. Client, what's this all about?"

Brad had read the statement of facts in the Sarah Woodruff case, and he gave her an overview. Then he gave her the details of the attack on Justice Moss and his boss's suspicions about Justice Price.

"I've just wrapped up two cases, so I have time to devote to your problem, but I'll have to go to Oregon, and I'll need to read the record in the case before I go."

"It's packed up and ready for you. You'll have it tomorrow."

Dana smiled. "You were pretty sure I'd take this case, weren't you?"

"I was pretty sure you were a friend I could count on."

Dana didn't handle compliments well, so she went quiet. Brad took the opportunity to bite a chunk out of his burger. Suddenly, Dana smiled. Brad's mouth was full so he arched an eyebrow.

"I'll need a cover story if I'm going to keep you and 'she who must remain nameless' out of this, and I just thought of one that's perfect."

When they were finished discussing the assignment, Brad told Dana what life as a Supreme Court clerk was like and filled her in on Ginny's job. Dana told Brad about a few of her cases.

"Most of what I do is pretty boring," she confided. "It's nothing like my days as a cop or my time on the run during the Farrington business."

"Do you miss the action?" Brad asked.

"Not really. Maybe I'm just getting old, but the idea of not having to look over my shoulder twenty-four hours a day has a certain appeal."

"I hear you," Brad said. He looked down at the table, his smile gone. "The fight in the garage shook me up pretty badly. It took me months to get over what happened in Oregon, and I'm having the same reactions again. I act brave, and I haven't told Ginny because I don't want to worry her, but I've had nightmares."

"Welcome to the club," Dana answered somberly.

There was a clock over the entrance, and Brad noticed the time.

"I should be going," he said.

"It's been great seeing you again. Say hi to your better half."

Brad smiled. "I will. When Jake gets back, we should double."

"It's a date," Dana said.

Brad walked to his car and Dana waved. The temperature had dropped, and she was grateful for the warmth her motorcycle jacket provided. Despite what she'd told Brad, she did miss the action. Her boring work paid well, and there was an upside to not having people trying to kill you 24/7. But action made her blood move faster and made the colors brighter, as it had the other night at the motel when she'd saved that girl. Still, now that she had Jake and she had a choice, she'd opted for the quieter side of life.

Dana stopped being introspective long enough to start Jake's Harley and check for traffic. There were a few cars on the road, and she waited for an opening, then eased out. At this hour, she figured the trip home would take half an hour, which would give her time to think about what she wanted to accomplish in Oregon. The car that was following her stayed far enough behind Dana that she didn't notice it.

Chapter Twenty

Ginny was in a good mood when she arrived at Rankin Lusk the next morning. What had seemed so frightening last night seemed to be meaningless worry in the light of a new day. Justice Moss, not Brad, had been the object of the attack at the Court, and the assailant was most probably, as Brad had assured her, some nut case with an irrational agenda.

"You're to go straight to Conference Room E, Miss Striker," the receptionist said when Ginny entered the reception area.

Ginny frowned. She had a lot of work to do, and the few times she'd sat in on a client conference, there had been a lot of intentionally wasted time, all of which counted as billable hours.

Clients waiting in Rankin Lusk's reception area could see through glass walls into Conference Rooms A and B. Clients meeting in these rooms could gaze out through floor-to-ceiling windows at a magnificent view of the Capitol. Conference Rooms A and B were used to impress the clients who met in them and to give the impression to clients in reception that the attorneys at Rankin Lusk were always involved in *big* deals and didn't really need their business.

Conference Room E, which was a floor below reception, had no windows and was in the rear of the building away from prying eyes. As soon as Ginny walked into the room, she knew why the meeting was being held in a conference room where the conferees would not be on public display. Audrey Stewart and Dennis Masterson had their heads together at the far end of the table. Seated to Masterson's left was Greg McKenzie, a fourth-year associate who worked with Masterson and made Ginny uneasy. McKenzie was huge and had been an offensive lineman at Iowa before going to Stanford Law. McKenzie always seemed angry, and Ginny wondered if he used steroids to maintain his pro wrestler physique.

"Ah, Miss Striker, come in and close the door," Masterson said. Everyone stopped talking and looked her way. Masterson introduced Ginny. Then he smiled.

"Want to guess what we're doing?" Masterson asked her.

"Helping Ms. Stewart prepare for her confirmation hearing?" Ginny asked cautiously. She hoped she had guessed correctly. If that was her assignment it would be the most exciting one she'd received since starting at the firm.

"A-plus," Masterson answered with a smile. Then he addressed everyone in the room.

"I was delighted when President Gaylord nominated Audrey to the Court. We met when we worked together at the CIA, and we've kept in touch since we both left. The Court needs first-class minds, and Audrey was far and away the sharpest person I worked with at the Agency."

Masterson stopped smiling. "Sadly, the liberals are going to attempt to discredit her by focusing on practices that kept them safe after 9/11 but have now fallen into disfavor. I've already heard from several sources that Senators Cummings and Vasquez are sharpening their knives. These liberals cowered in their holes while Audrey was facing fire on the front lines. Now they're going to cast stones at the very people who protected them. So we have our work cut out for us. But," Masterson said, breaking once more into a smile, "I feel confident that we will prevail, because our cause is just and we have God on our side, not to mention a bunch of very smart lawyers."

Chapter Twenty-one

The offices of *Exposed*, Washington's most widely read supermarket tabloid, took up two floors of a renovated warehouse within sight of the Capitol dome in a section of D.C. that was equal parts gentrification and decay. Abandoned buildings and vacant lots peopled by junkies and the homeless could be found within blocks of trendy restaurants, chic boutiques, and rehabilitated row houses owned by urban professionals. *Exposed* was an unrepentant rag that had gained a measure of respectability when it broke the Farrington case, thanks to a deal between Dana Cutler and Patrick Gorman, the paper's owner and editor. But its bread and butter still consisted of Elvis sightings, accounts of UFO abductions, celebrity gossip, and guaranteed miracle diets.

Dana found Gorman eating an extra large pepperoni and cheese pizza in his second-floor office. A good deal of the wall space was given over to framed copies of the paper's most outrageous headlines. The fact that none of them made Gorman blush said a lot about his regard for journalistic integrity.

Dana stared at a section of one wall displaying the Pulitzer Prize the paper had won for its coverage of the Farrington scandal.

"That's a nice addition to your wall of shame," Dana said.

Gorman hated to be interrupted when he was working or eating, but he broke into a grin when he saw who was standing in the doorway.

"How's my favorite anonymous source?" he asked as he motioned Dana into a chair. Most gentlemen would have stood when a lady entered, but Gorman was grossly obese. Dana knew it took a real effort for him to heave himself to his feet, so she forgave him for his lack of chivalry.

"I'm well, thank you. And you? How are you handling being a legitimate journalist?"

Gorman waved his hand. "I got over that months ago. Though I do get the occasional flashback in which I'm standing on the podium with our Pulitzer and looking down at the sickly green complexions on the faces of those effete snobs at the *Times* and *Post*."

"I have noticed that you haven't stooped to including any more legitimate reporting in your rag," Dana said.

"I didn't know you were a reader."

"It's one of my guilty pleasures. I hide *Exposed* in between the pages of my dominatrix magazines."

Gorman laughed hard enough to make his jowls shake. Then he pointed at the remnants of his dinner. "Pizza?"

"No, thanks."

"If you didn't come here to eat with me, to what do I owe this visit? You don't happen to have another juicy exposé for me, do you?"

"No, I'm here to ask a favor."

"For you, anything within reason."

"I want press credentials for *Exposed*, and I want you to back me up if anyone calls to verify that I'm one of your reporters."

"I'm intrigued. Why do you need the cover?"

"I'll tell you but I need your promise that this will stay between us."

"Sure, with the proviso that *Exposed* gets exclusive rights to any juicy stories."

"If I can. I'd need permission from my client."

"Who is?"

Dana wagged a finger at the editor. "You know better than that."

Gorman shrugged. "You can't blame a guy for trying. What can you tell me?"

"I've been hired to look into a fascinating Oregon murder case. Sarah Woodruff is on death row for murdering her lover, twice."

Gorman's eyebrows went up. "That sounds ready-made for *Exposed*." He lifted his hand, and formed them into a frame for an imaginary headline. "I MURDERED MY DEAD LOVER. I like this story already. Tell me how it's possible to kill someone twice."

"It's not. Woodruff was arrested for killing a man named John Finley. The charges were dismissed in the middle of the trial. Several months later, Finley's body was found; she was tried again and sentenced to death. My client wants me to go to Oregon and look into the case."

"Why not tell whoever you talk to that you're a private investigator? Why do they need to think that you're a reporter?"

"What was the first thing you asked me when I told you what I was doing?"

"Ah, I see. They'll want to know the identity of your client."

"And they may not talk to me if I refuse to tell them. I won't run into that problem if I'm an employee of the Pulitzer Prize–winning editor of *Exposed*."

Dana waited while Gorman pondered her request for a minute, but only a minute.

"Deal. I'll let everyone know you're on the payroll, and you'll give me the scoop, if your client consents."

"You got it."

Brad had hand-delivered the transcript and briefs in *Woodruff* earlier in the day. When Dana returned home from *Exposed*, she fixed a cup of coffee and a sandwich and looked at the mass of paper piled on her dining room table. The transcript was over one thousand pages long, and she decided that it would help to get an overview of the case before she tackled it. So she grabbed the petition for cert and read the Statement of Facts, which provided a summary of the two trials in which Sarah Woodruff had been accused of killing her lover.

Part Three

Sarah Woodruff

June–December 2006

Chapter Twenty-two

Policewoman Sarah Woodruff sat in Max Dietz's windowless cubicle in the section of the Multnomah County District Attorney's office that prosecuted drug offenses and explained why the *Elcock* case should be reviewed. Her frustration built as she tried to ignore the smirk on the Weasel's face and the way his eyes wandered to her breasts and rested there brazenly.

Dietz had not been nicknamed the Weasel because he looked anything like that animal. The assistant district attorney was actually rather handsome in a smarmy sort of way, resembling those greasy imitation Englishmen in low comedies who con little old ladies out of their fortunes. His nickname referred to the underhanded way he practiced law.

Sarah had worked several cases Dietz had prosecuted, and he'd come on to her twice. When she didn't swoon, he'd become distant. Sarah wondered if his resentment at her rejection was fueling his attitude toward her request to reexamine the case against Harvey Elcock. Sarah also knew that she had to be diplomatic where Dietz was concerned, because the word was that a string of successful prosecutions had earned him a promotion to Homicide and the ear of Jack Stamm, the Multnomah County district attorney.

"I don't see it," Dietz told Sarah when she was through. "Let's say the speed in the undershirt drawer was this Loraine's. She didn't cop to the package we found in the back room, did she?"

"It's pretty obvious her boyfriend planted that."

"Obvious to you, maybe, but not to me."

Dietz had been leaning back in his chair. Now he sat up. "Don't go all bleeding heart on me, Sarah. This fucker is playing you. He pretends to be a retard, but the Marauders aren't going to let a retard deal for them. There's more to this guy than meets the eye."

"I don't think so, Max."

Dietz shrugged. "That's your problem, then. But seeing as this is my case, I call the shots. Come back and show me evidence that someone planted the shit in the back room, and I'll take another look at Elcock. Until then . . ."

Dietz shrugged again and Sarah realized any further discussion with him would be useless. And he did have a point. Feelings weren't evidence, and all she had was a bad feeling about the case and a statement from a witness she'd stupidly failed to Mirandize who had now recanted.

The *Elcock* case had started promisingly when an anonymous informant tipped off an officer in Vice and Narcotics that Harvey Elcock was going to receive a shipment of speed from the Marauders motorcycle gang that he would then sell. Shortly after receiving the tip, detectives conducting surveillance of Elcock's tiny Cape Cod observed two bikers in Marauders colors enter the house.

Sarah started having reservations about the bust from the moment Harvey Elcock answered the door. He was bald with pale cheeks that were covered with salt-and-pepper stubble, and Sarah guessed he was in his late forties. He was wearing wrinkled tan chinos, a white, stained crew-neck undershirt, and a gray cardigan sweater over his undershirt even though the temperature was in the high eighties. Elcock stared at the officers through a pair of black plastic glasses with thick lenses.

"Mr. Elcock?" Sarah asked.

Elcock nodded.

"May we come in?"

Elcock looked puzzled. "Why?" he asked.

"We have a warrant to search your house for drugs," Sarah said, holding up the document the judge had signed an hour earlier.

"Drugs?" he asked dully. Sarah was starting to think that they were dealing with an ineffectual man with a low IQ, not exactly the type bikers picked to deal and protect their product.

"Yes, sir," Sarah said.

"I don't have any drugs, except my prescriptions. I have some for high blood pressure, and my cholesterol isn't too good so my doctor gives me some for that."

"We have information that you have metham-phetamine on the premises."

"Is that like speed?"

"Yes, sir."

Elcock looked frightened. "I don't have that. There's none of that here."

"We've been told that you were given these drugs to sell by a biker gang."

"Oh no. Tony didn't give me nothing. He was just looking for Loraine. But she left. I think she's visiting her aunt. She might come back if her aunt won't let her stay."

"Is this Tony in a biker gang?"

"Yeah, Marauders. I don't like him."

"Mr. Elcock, we do have to come in, but we'll be out of your hair in no time if we don't find any speed."

Elcock let the search team in. The officer who searched Elcock's bedroom found meth under a stack of undershirts in Elcock's drawer. Sarah was disappointed. She had hoped they'd come up empty-handed. The stash looked like it was for personal use, and it wasn't anywhere near the amount the informant had sworn they'd find. Then another officer found a more substantial amount hidden in a back room.

Elcock swore he didn't know anything about the meth, and he cried when he was booked in at the jail. Logic told Sarah that the drugs had to be El-cock's, since he lived alone, but she had an odd feeling about the bust, and it wouldn't go away.

Two days after Elcock was arrested, Sarah re-membered something he'd said. As soon as her shift ended, she drove back to Elcock's house. A very pregnant woman answered the door.

"Are you Loraine?" Sarah asked.

"Yeah. Who are you?"

Sarah was in plainclothes, so she showed the woman her badge.

"Do you know that Mr. Elcock is in jail?" Sarah asked as soon as they were seated in the living room. The color drained from Loraine's face.

"What did he do?" she asked. Sarah thought Loraine looked very nervous, and she watched her face carefully for the reaction to her next statement.

"We received an anonymous tip that Mr. Elcock was selling methamphetamine for the Marauder motorcycle gang." Loraine looked sick. "Our informant told us that we'd find a big shipment here."

"That cocksucker," Loraine whispered.

"The first thing we found was a small amount of speed under some undershirts in the dresser in Mr. Elcock's bedroom. That was your stash, wasn't it?" Sarah asked softly.

Loraine buried her face in her palms. "I never thought . . ."

"Is Tony your boyfriend, the guy who got you pregnant?"

Loraine nodded. "Harvey is a sweetheart. Tony beat me up. He don't want the kid, and he got mad when I wouldn't get an abortion. I ran away, and Harvey's been letting me hide here. He even gave me his bedroom. I thought I was safe, but I got warned that Tony was on the way over, so I took off for my aunt. Only she wouldn't have me. I was so upset I forgot my stash. Then when I remembered, I seen Tony drive up, so I split."

"We found a lot more speed in another room."

"Harvey don't do drugs. Tony must have set him up to get back at him for helping me."

"You think Tony was the informant?"

"Oh, yeah, definitely. He's real mean. I wouldn't have had nothing to do with him, but he had the speed."

"Will you tell this to the DA?"

Suddenly, Loraine looked very scared. "I don't know. I got to think."

"Harvey could go to jail for a long time. The feds might even go after him."

Loraine put her hand on her stomach. "I can't have my kid born in prison."

Sarah had been afraid Loraine wouldn't talk to her if she gave her the Miranda warnings. Since Loraine hadn't been Mirandized, her statements couldn't be used.

"Maybe I can work a deal for you so you won't be prosecuted if you help Mr. Elcock. Would you talk to the DA if I can do that?"

"I got to think."

"OK. That's fair." Sarah paused. "Will Tony come looking for you? I can put you up someplace he won't find you while we sort this out. This place probably isn't safe."

Sarah had paid out of her pocket for a week stay at a hotel with room service, over the river in Vancouver, Washington. When she'd visited the next day, Loraine had lawyered up, and her mouthpiece told Sarah that Loraine wouldn't testify even with immunity because of what she knew the Marauders would do to her. An hour later, Sarah was sitting in Max Dietz's office foolishly asking him to show compassion while he undressed her mentally and did God-knows-what to her in his fantasies.

The more Sarah thought about the *Elcock* case, the more convinced she became that Loraine's boy friend had set Harvey up, but Loraine had to talk if Sarah was going to have any chance of proving her theory. But her lawyer had made it clear that Loraine would not testify. Suddenly, Sarah grinned. There might be a way for Loraine to clear Harvey Elcock without testifying.

Two days later, Jack Stamm summoned Max Dietz to his office. Dietz had no idea why he was being asked into his boss's inner sanctum, but he couldn't think of anything he'd done wrong, so he assumed it was to receive praise for something he'd done right. That thought disappeared when he saw Sarah Woodruff sitting on a couch against the far wall.

Dietz forced a cheerful smile. "You wanted to see me?" he asked.

"Thanks for coming, Max. You know Officer Woodruff?"

"Oh, sure. We've had a couple of cases together. She's an excellent investigator."

"She speaks highly of you, too, and it's her investigation in *State v. Elcock* I wanted to talk about. I spent an hour with a woman named Loraine Cargo this morning."

Dietz forced himself to keep a placid smile on his face.

"From what I understand, part of your case against Elcock rests on the discovery of speed in his chest of drawers."

"Yes, that's part of it."

"Miss Cargo says it's hers, and she passed a polygraph on that."

"We found a lot more speed, Jack. Elcock probably gave her the stuff in the drawer, so technically it would be hers, and she wouldn't be lying."

"She says she got the meth from her boyfriend, Tony Malone, who is a member of the Marauders motorcycle gang. We had Elcock's house under surveillance. One of the detectives positively identified Malone as a biker who visited Elcock on the day of the search. Mr. Elcock has no criminal record, and he's also passed a polygraph. I think we've made a mistake arresting him. An understandable mistake, but one we should correct as soon as possible, unless you have evidence that contradicts what Officer Woodruff has uncovered."

Jack Stamm had given Loraine Cargo immunity and a guarantee that no one would learn about their meeting, her statements, or the polygraph. He'd also guaranteed in writing that she would never have to testify against any member of the Marauder motorcycle gang. Her statements had led to the dismissal of all charges against Harvey Elcock.

Sarah knew that Max Dietz bore grudges forever, but she wasn't worried about him, and she'd left the courthouse with a smile on her face.

Chapter Twenty-three

A loud noise jerked Sarah Woodruff upright out of a deep sleep. When she was certain that someone was in her condo, she grabbed her Glock 9mm and slipped out of her bedroom. Something heavy crashed into a wall on the first floor with enough force to knock over the table in the entryway. A man cried out in pain. Sarah edged down the stairs, her gun leading the way. When she was halfway down, she saw a man in a peacoat and watch cap wrestling with a man in a black leather jacket.

Sarah yelled, "Freeze!" and extended her gun over the banister. The man in the watch cap turned his head.

"John?" Sarah said as she rushed down the rest of the stairs.

A gun butt smashed into the back of her skull. She dropped to her knees. A second blow landed and Sarah's finger squeezed the trigger.

Sarah sat up slowly. Her head was aching and her vision was blurred. She touched the back of her head.

Pain lanced through her skull and made her jerk her hand away. She squeezed her eyes shut. When she opened them, she saw that her fingers were covered with blood. She picked up her gun, gritted her teeth, and struggled to her feet. She was alone, and there was blood spatter on the wall. The entryway end table was on its side, and a newspaper, a magazine, a lamp, and some envelopes were strewn across the floor. The rug in the foyer was a small Persian, heavy with red tones, but a damp red liquid, tough to spot at first, had soaked in at several spots.

The pain grew dull enough for Sarah to think. She remembered John Finley fighting with a man in a black leather jacket. Then . . . she couldn't remember what happened next, but there must have been someone else in the house, because the pain in the back of her head was proof that someone had hit her from behind. The intruders must have taken John.

Sarah staggered upstairs and into jeans, running shoes, a sweatshirt, and a jacket. It was October, and a cold front had swept in, bringing an arctic chill to Portland. Sarah grabbed her car keys and rushed downstairs as fast as her aching head would let her, pausing midway down so she could bend forward while a wave of nausea swept through. Then she straightened, sucked in a mouthful of frigid air, and made her way to her pickup truck.

What was John Finley doing in my house in the middle of the night? Sarah asked herself as she cruised the streets in her neighborhood looking for any trace of him or the men she assumed had taken him. *What was he doing at my house at any time of day?* After what had happened the last time they were together, Sarah had been certain she'd never see Finley again.

Last summer, Sarah had vacationed in Peru so she could climb Nevado Pisco, a nineteen-thousand-foot-high peak in the Andes. Two days after her ascent, she'd met Finley in a bar in Huaraz. He was handsome and smart, and they'd hit it off. Finley was a pilot, and they'd flown to an island resort in his rickety two-seater. For the rest of her vacation, Sarah and Finley scuba dived, sunbathed, dined in elegance, and fucked like rabbits. Then Sarah flew back to Portland.

Two months ago, Finley had called to say he was in Portland for business, and Sarah invited him to stay at her condo. Everything had gone swimmingly until Sarah began to wonder about Finley's business. He'd told her it was import-export, but he was evasive every time she tried to get him to be specific. During a weak moment, Finley had mentioned the name of his company. Sarah had investigated and found that it existed only in a post office box in the Cayman Islands.

Cops cannot afford to associate with people who operate on the wrong side of the law, so she'd confronted Finley and saw a side of his personality she'd never seen before. There had been yelling and an attempt to hit Sarah. The brief scuffle ended when the combatants realized that they could both end up seriously injured. Sarah had held her gun on her guest while he packed his gear and then stormed out.

Fifteen minutes after Finley left, matters got worse. Two patrolmen showed up in response to a neighbor's complaint. The cops left quickly when they recognized Sarah and learned that no one had been harmed, but the confrontation had been embarrassing.

Now Finley had broken into her condo and had been attacked. What was going on?

A police car was parked at the curb when Sarah pulled her pickup into her driveway twenty-five minutes later. She got out of the cab, and a chiseled young officer with a buzz cut walked out of the house, aiming a gun at her.

"Don't move," he yelled. "Drop the weapon."

Sarah's gun was hanging limply from her hand. She was so tired and woozy from the blow to her head that she hadn't realized she was holding it until the officer shouted.

"I'm a Portland cop," Sarah said. "I'm putting the gun down."

Sarah bent her knees and placed the gun on the driveway.

"Move away from the truck and show your hands."

"A man was kidnapped from my house. I've been out looking for him," Sarah said as she backed away from the gun.

"What's your name?"

"Sarah Woodruff. I work out of Central Precinct. Bob Mcintyre is my sergeant."

A hefty African-American officer who looked to be in his forties walked out of the house just as the younger cop scooped up Sarah's gun. Sarah reached into her jacket pocket slowly and pulled out her badge. The black officer examined Sarah's ID while the younger officer examined her gun.

"I'm John Dickinson, Sarah," the older man said. "Why don't we go inside, but be careful. There's blood on the carpet and the techs haven't arrived yet."

"Are you hurt?" he asked as Sarah passed by and he saw the blood that matted her long black hair.

"I got hit." Sarah was exhausted. She closed her eyes. "Can I sit down? I don't feel so well."

"Yeah, go ahead."

Sarah collapsed on the couch. She was nauseous and would have given anything to be able to go to sleep. The younger cop whispered something in his partner's ear. The older man nodded.

"Call for an ambulance," Dickinson said. "Officer Woodruff might have a concussion. And get a forensic team over here."

"Tell me what happened," Dickinson said as soon as his partner was out of the room.

Sarah touched the back of her head gingerly and grimaced.

"Do you want some water?"

"There's no time for that. John Finley's been kidnapped."

"Who is Mr. Finley?"

"A . . . an acquaintance. I was sleeping. I heard noise downstairs. I saw John fighting with another man. When I ran downstairs, someone knocked me out. When I came to, they were gone. I've been driving around trying to find them."

"Did you call for backup?"

"I should have. My head. I'm not thinking too straight."

"Did you recognize the man fighting with Mr. Finley?"

"I never saw him before."

"Can you describe him?"

"Not really. Everything happened so fast, and it was dark. I think he was wearing gloves and a leather jacket but I never saw his face."

"Did you fire your weapon?"

Sarah tried to remember what had happened after she was hit. She had no recollection of firing her weapon, so she told Dickinson that she had not.

"Were you surprised to find Mr. Finley in your apartment?"

"I was. He owns an import-export business, and he travels frequently. I thought he was on a business trip. He hadn't called me, and he'd been gone a while."

"How did he get in?"

Sarah hesitated. "He has a key. He was living with me before he went on his trip."

"I don't want to embarrass you, but . . ."

"Yes, we were sleeping together."

Sarah leaned back and closed her eyes.

"Don't do that," Dickinson said. "It's not smart to sleep if you have a concussion. I hear the ambulance. Let the EMTs examine you, and they'll tell you what to do."

Sarah nodded and grimaced immediately. The wail of the siren grew louder, and within minutes two EMTs were in the living room. A few minutes later, Sarah was strapped on a gurney and they were wheeling her out of the house.

"What did she say about the gun?" the younger cop asked Dickinson.

"Said she didn't fire it."

"Someone did," the young cop said.

Chapter Twenty-four

The first thing John Finley noticed when he came to was the pain. His side was on fire where he'd been shot, and he felt like someone had slammed a hatchet into the back of his head. He squeezed his eyes shut and clenched his teeth. When the pain was bearable, he tried to figure out where he was.

That proved to be easy. He'd been placed in a confined space that admitted almost no light. Suddenly his body was lifted up and his head struck a hard surface. The pain was excruciating. After one more jolt, Finley figured out that he was in the trunk of a car that was driving on an unpaved road. He set himself to resist the next bump, but his hands were cuffed behind him and his ankles were bound together. His head smashed into the top of the trunk again. Then, mercifully, the car stopped.

Finley tried to remember what had led to his imprisonment. There was the ship. He'd killed Talbot on it, and he'd been shot. He remembered driving to Sarah's condo. His wound had been bleeding badly when he arrived. The duffel bag! He'd hidden it, and he was heading for the stairs that led up to Sarah's bedroom when two men burst in through the front door.

Finley remembered putting all of his strength behind a punch that caught the first man flush in the face, sending him stumbling across the foyer. Then he was grappling with the second man on the floor, weak from blood loss and barely able to put up a fight. A forearm had been jammed across his windpipe. He'd been struggling for breath when Sarah called his name. The last thing he remembered was a gunshot.

Car doors opened and slammed shut. Moments later the lid of the trunk popped up. Finley could see the silhouette of two men from their knees to their shoulders. One man bent down and reached in to drag him from the car. Finley resisted and was hit in the face.

"Don't make this hard on yourself. You're going to die no matter what you do," said the man who had hit him.

Finley wanted to fight but he didn't have the strength. The two men manhandled him out of the trunk and threw him on the ground. Pain lanced through his head and side, and he had to fight to keep from throwing up. The men watched him roll back and forth. When Finley stopped, he saw stars and the outline of tree limbs and leaves high above. The cold, unpolluted air and the absence of ambient light told him that he was somewhere in the country-side, probably in the mountains.

"On your knees, fucker," one of the men commanded. Finley squinted at the speaker. He was thick with curly black hair, but the darkness obscured most of his features. When Finley didn't move fast enough, his reward was a vicious kick to his ribs near his gunshot wound. The pain almost made him black out. Rough hands grabbed his hair and yanked him upright, and a gun barrel was jammed against the back of his head. The man who was standing in front of Finley smiled sadistically.

"No more pussy for you," he said. Then he laughed.

Chapter Twenty-five

"Talk to me, people. What have we got here?" Max Dietz said.

"The biggest problem is the body, the one we don't have," answered deputy district attorney Monte Pike.

Dietz thought Pike was an irreverent little twit, but Jack Stamm thought Pike was brilliant because he'd graduated from Harvard. Dietz thought that Pike's intelligence was overrated and that he'd probably gotten into Harvard because he had a knack for acing standardized tests. Dietz didn't test well, and he hadn't gone to Harvard, but he did kick ass and take names, which was, as far as he was concerned, all that counted in the real world. But Stamm had insisted that Pike be part of Dietz's team because anytime his office went after a cop, the case became high profile.

"Claire?" Dietz asked.

Claire Bonner had been assigned the task of researching the problem presented by the missing body. Dietz liked having Bonner on his team because she was a suck-up who would do anything to gain advancement in the office. Unfortunately, she wasn't attractive enough to merit any extracurricular attention, but unlike Pike, she didn't challenge everything Dietz said.

Bonner self-consciously pushed a strand of hair off her forehead. "OK, well, in American jurisprudence, the term *corpus delicti* refers to the principle that you have to prove a crime has been committed before you can convict someone. The corpus delicti in homicide is established when you show a human being died as a result of a criminal act."

"Yeah, yeah, we know all that," Dietz said impatiently. "What if you don't have a body?"

"It's OK. We can prosecute using circumstantial evidence. There are plenty of cases in Oregon and in other states where a conviction has stood up. For instance—"

"I get it. Put the rest in a memo. So," Dietz said, turning his attention to Arnold Lasswell, the lead detective on the case, "what's our evidence?"

"It's not that strong, Max," Lasswell answered hesitantly. He knew that Dietz didn't like independent thinkers. The prosecutor had decided that he wanted Sarah Woodruff's head on a pike, and Dietz was like a pit bull once he decided to go after someone. But Lasswell was a fifteen-year veteran of the Portland Police Bureau, four with Homicide, and he did not arrest citizens without good reason. The detective fully appreciated the consequences to a person's reputation once the cuffs were snapped on. And he was particularly sensitive to the impact of an arrest on a police officer's career, even if the officer was ultimately cleared.

"Let me decide whether we can get past a grand jury, Arnie. I'm the lawyer. Just run down the facts for me."

"We can place Finley at Woodruff's house. Woodruff said he was there, and Ann Paulus, the neighbor who called 911 to report the shot and the argument, saw Finley go in."

"How did she know the guy was Finley?" Dietz asked.

"She's met him. He lived with Woodruff off and on over the past year. About six months ago, some of Woodruff's mail was delivered to Paulus's place by mistake. When she brought it over, Woodruff was at work and Finley answered the door. They talked a little, and he told her his name."

"So we've got the victim in Woodruff's house on the evening of the crime, we've got the victim's blood in the entryway. What else have we got?"

"Point of order," interjected Pike, who was slouching in his seat, working a fingernail. The knot in Pike's tie wasn't pulled all the way up, leaving the top button on his white shirt exposed. Then there was Pike's unruly brown hair.

Dietz dressed like a magazine model and got a pedicure and manicure when he was at his hair stylist. He found Pike's lack of personal grooming repulsive.

"Yes, Monte?" Dietz asked, demonstrating the patience with subordinates—no matter how annoying they might be—that leadership required.

"We don't know its Finley's blood. In fact, other than the photograph of him that Woodruff snapped in South America, we don't know much about him at all."

"Well, Monte, we do know that the blood type doesn't match Woodruff's, so whose blood could it be?"

"The guys who snatched Finley."

"That's her story, Monte. The neighbor didn't see anyone other than Finley go in or out and there's no evidence to corroborate Woodruff's assertion that Finley was snatched, right, Arnie?"

"The neighbor wasn't watching the whole time, Max. She just happened to be looking out her window when Finley went in. She's a nurse, and she has to get up early to make her shift. She was checking the weather. When she was dressing, she wasn't watching Woodruff's house. Then she heard the shouting and the shot.

"Paulus got worried because she'd heard arguments between Finley and Woodruff before. She even reported one fight as a domestic disturbance. We have a report of that. But she was away from the window when she called 911. If Finley was kidnapped, he could have been taken out when she was on the phone."

"Did she hear three or four people shouting?" Dietz asked.

"She has no idea how many people were yelling. She just heard a commotion," Lasswell answered.

"If he was kidnapped, where's the ransom demand?" Dietz asked.

"We still haven't addressed the problem of identifying our so-called victim," Pike persisted. "We don't know his blood type because there's no record of the guy. Arnie, you ran prints taken from the scene, right? Did you match any of them to someone named John Finley?"

"No. We've drawn a blank. We do have prints other than Woodruff's but none that match anyone named Finley," the detective answered.

"And none that match our fictional kidnappers," Bonner said, hoping to score points with Dietz.

"Woodruff says the kidnapper she saw was wearing gloves," Pike said.

"How convenient," Dietz answered with a smirk.

"But there are the prints we can't match to anyone," Lasswell said.

"Which could be Finley's," Dietz argued. "And what does it matter? If we found Finley's prints in the house, it would just add to all the proof that he was there."

"It doesn't bother you that this guy doesn't come up in our database?" Pike asked.

"Not one bit. We have him in the house, he's missing, and she lied about shooting her gun," Dietz said. "We also have previous domestic violence calls. Then there's the fact that the neighbor heard the shot, we have gunshot residue on her hands, and there's a bullet missing from her service weapon. Lying about the shot shows consciousness of guilt."

"Until we find a body, it's still thin, Max," Lasswell cautioned. "What if Finley was kidnapped and he's still alive? That's a possibility. It will be embarrassing if you go after Woodruff for homicide and it turns out Finley isn't dead."

"It will be more embarrassing if we let a cop get away with murder. Jack's thinking of running for

Congress. How tough on crime will he look if we don't prosecute a killer cop?"

Monte Pike knew that Dietz wanted to use the Woodruff prosecution as a stepping stone to the DA's job if Stamm went to Washington, but he was smart enough to keep those thoughts to himself.

"I'd go slow here, Max," Lasswell said. "I just don't feel this."

"Hey, we're not on *Oprah*, Arnie. Leave the touchy-feely stuff to the shrinks. My gut says Woodruff is guilty. Let's see if a grand jury agrees."

Chapter Twenty-six

"I'm in a lot of trouble, Ms. Garrett," Sarah Woodruff said as soon as they were alone in Mary Garrett's corner office on the top floor of the priciest office building in downtown Portland. The large picture windows gave clients spectacular views of the river, three snow-capped mountains, and the West Hills. The decorations were ultramodern: sheet-glass desktops, gleaming aluminum tube armrests, and abstract art that confused Sarah.

Mary Garrett was just as disconcerting as her office furnishings. The attorney wore the kind of designer clothing and spectacular but understated jewelry that were found in the glossy pages of upscale fashion magazines, but her clothes and accessories didn't look right on the diminutive, birdlike woman with her overbite and dense, unfashionable glasses. None of this discordance mattered to her clients. No one hired Mary Garrett for her looks, and Mary assumed that Woodruff wanted her in her corner because Garrett had taken Woodruff apart during cross-examination in a trial that should have been a slam dunk for the prosecution but ended in an acquittal for one of the least likable drug dealers Mary had ever represented.

If Garrett looked more like a sideshow oddity than an attorney, Sarah Woodruff definitely looked nothing like the stereotypical damsel in distress. Garrett estimated Woodruff's height at five ten, and she had the build of a female boxer, with long legs, wide shoulders, and a torso that tapered down to a narrow waist. Long black hair framed intense blue eyes and full lips that tension had drawn into a straight line. At a cocktail party or a classy restaurant, when she was relaxed and smiling, men would find Woodruff attractive, if severe, and even sexy. Today, under strain, she was all business. Strong, tough, and self-sufficient were Garrett's first impressions of her new client. If she felt she needed someone to help her, Garrett bet her problem was very serious.

"What sort of trouble are you in?" Mary asked.

"I'm a Portland police officer. A few days ago, some people broke into my house around five in the morning and kidnapped a man named John Finley. I tried to stop them and was knocked out. A friend called me less than an hour ago and tipped me off that the district attorney is in a grand jury right now, looking to indict me for murdering John."

"Who's your friend?"

"I can't tell you that."

"Anything you confide in me is confidential and protected by the attorney-client relationship."

"I know that, but I promised to keep him out of this. He did me a big favor by tipping me off, and I'm not going to get him in trouble."

"Fair enough," Mary conceded as she studied Sarah. Her navy blue pants suit and white, man-tailored shirt looked good on her, but they weren't expensive, and Mary knew a cop's annual salary. Garrett decided to get the business aspects of their relationship out of the way.

"Defending a murder case is expensive. By the time the smoke clears, we'll be talking six figures for my retainer in addition to hefty expenses for experts and investigation. I'll need fifty thousand dollars to start. As soon as I have an idea of the complexity of your case, I'll tell you how much more I'll need."

"I'll have the money to you tomorrow," Woodruff replied evenly. "I can't afford to have a hack represent me."

"OK. Do you know why the DA thinks you murdered Mr. Finley?"

Sarah shook her head. "I have no idea. I mean, there was blood in my house, but that was from the fight. And as far as I know, John is missing, not dead. My friend told me that no one has found his body."

"You can use circumstantial evidence, like the blood in your house, to prosecute someone for murder even if there is no body."

"But I saw a man attacking John. He was kidnapped." Sarah pointed at the back of her head. "Do you think I did this to myself?"

"The police might think Mr. Finley did that while defending himself," Mary answered. "Maybe they think you killed Mr. Finley, disposed of the body, and made up the story about his being kidnapped."

Woodruff's fists clenched in frustration. "But

I didn't. Those men broke into my home. I didn't make that up."

"Tell me some more about what happened."

Mary made notes as Sarah told her about the incident at her place, her futile search for John and his abductors, her talk with the police, and her trip to the hospital.

"Had you ever seen the kidnappers before?" Mary asked when she was through.

"My memory is fuzzy. I blacked out after I was hit on the head, and everything happened very fast. I don't have a clear picture in my mind of the man who was fighting with John. Also, when I was halfway down the stairs, I saw John and focused on him. I'm pretty certain the man who was fighting with him was wearing a black leather coat. And gloves. He was wearing gloves." Woodruff shook her head. "I'm sorry I can't give you much more than that."

"If you just woke up and you were hit hard, I wouldn't expect you to have total recall. Tell me, did Mr. Finley ever mention any enemies?"

"He didn't talk about himself very much. Anytime I asked about his business or his past, he'd joke around or give vague answers. He rarely told me anything of substance." Sarah hesitated. "He did mention a few names, and I heard him on a call once."

"Can you give the names to me? I can have my investigator run them down. Maybe we'll learn a little more about Finley's background."

"The ones I remember are Larry Kres . . . no, Kester, Larry Kester. And Orrin Hadley." She shut her eyes and concentrated for a moment. Then she leaned forward. "Dennis Lang. Those are the three I remember."

Mary jotted down the names. "And you have no idea why Mr. Finley was kidnapped?" she asked when she was through.

"No, but John . . . he may be into something shady."

"Like what?"

"I have no idea."

"Have you known Mr. Finley long?"

"Not really. We met in Peru about a year and a half ago when I was on vacation," Sarah said. "Several months later, he turned up in Portland. We lived together for a while, but I became suspicious of his business and threw him out."

"What type of business is he in?" Mary asked.

"Export-import is what he said."

"You don't sound convinced."

Sarah hesitated. "John was always vague about what he was doing. I was concerned that he was involved with drugs or smuggling. He slipped once and told me his company was called TA Enterprises. I asked him what it meant and he joked that it was tits and ass, you know, porno, but I got the impression that he was sorry he'd let the name slip and this was his way of distracting me.

"Right around the time I learned the name of John's company, he told me he was going to Asia and wasn't sure when he'd be back. I did a background check on him and the company. It's a shell corporation registered in the Cayman Islands. I'm not even certain that the board of directors, or any officer, is real. And I couldn't find anything on John. I confronted him. I asked if he was a drug dealer or engaged in some other illegal activity. He was furious I'd run the background check. We had a screaming argument, and he left without answering any of my questions. Honestly, I never expected to see him again."

"Did anyone hear your argument?"

"It was loud and the neighbors are close on either side. The woman next door reported it. Two officers showed up soon after he left." Woodruff colored. "It was embarrassing."

Mary was quiet for a moment. Then she frowned. "Is there something you're not telling me? The evidence doesn't sound nearly enough for a murder indictment."

"Max Dietz is running the grand jury, and he has an ego the size of Mount Hood," Woodruff said, making no attempt to hide her anger. "He's come on to me a few times, and I turned him down."

"Dietz can be an asshole, but I can't believe he'd indict you for murder because you wouldn't go out with him."

"There is something else," Sarah said, and over the next quarter hour she filled Garrett in on the *Elcock* case. "When Loraine Cargo and Elcock passed their polygraph tests, Jack ordered Max to dismiss the case. He's never forgiven me for going over his head and embarrassing him in front of his boss."

Mary made careful notes about *Elcock*. Then she continued the interview for another half hour.

When she had enough background information, she placed her pen on top of her legal pad.

"I think that's enough for now. I want you to stay at a hotel in case the grand jury hands down an indictment. If you're home, they might arrest you. I'll make the reservation in my secretary's name. I'll call Max and let him know I'm your attorney. I'll try to talk him into letting you surrender so we can avoid an arrest if he gets an indictment. That will also give me time to set up a bail hearing and you time to put some bail money together. I'll need a list of witnesses who can vouch for your character, so I can convince the judge to grant bail. As you know, it's not automatic in a murder case."

"Do you think you can keep me out of jail?"

"From what you've told me, the case sounds thin. No body, no eyewitness. I think we've got a shot."

Chapter Twenty-seven

People assumed that Mary Garrett led a lonely life because she was homely, unmarried, and had no children. They were in error. Mary had a close circle of loyal friends and her share of lovers. Those lovers were always glad that they had gotten beyond the superficial aspect of Garrett's looks. There had even been proposals of marriage, but Garrett preferred to live alone and valued the freedom her choice provided. The lawyer thought of her clients as her children, and she poured the passion she would have given to a son or daughter into their defense. Each case was a cause, and she protected her charges with the ferocity that a lioness displays when her cubs are in danger.

Mary was concerned about her latest client, Sarah Woodruff. For the third time, she checked her stainless steel Franck Muller watch. Sarah was late. Outside, dark clouds were drifting over the high hills that towered over Portland, threatening rain. On the streets below, pedestrians clutched umbrellas and walked fast so they could reach their destinations quickly and gain shelter from the bitter wind.

Mary had rushed to the courthouse for an early appearance and had not had time to read the *Oregonian*. While she waited for her client to show up for their hastily scheduled meeting, she glanced through the paper. The Dow was down, the Seattle Seahawks had lost their starting tight end for the season with a torn ACL, the bodies of two men linked to a Mexican drug cartel had been found shot to death in a logging area in the Cascades, and another movie-star couple were breaking up even though they were "still good friends." Mary sighed. Today's paper was an echo of every paper she'd read this week.

Mary's receptionist knocked on her door, then ushered in Sarah Woodruff. She looked pale and drawn, like someone who was not sleeping well, but the primary emotion Woodruff displayed was anger.

"They searched my condo," she said. "They did it while I was at the station. There are clothes thrown around. They broke dishes. I bet that prick Dietz told them to trash my place."

"I wouldn't put it past him," Garrett answered, with an anger that almost matched her client's. "I'll straighten this out and make sure you're treated with respect, if I have to get a court order."

Woodruff dropped into a seat and ran a hand across her forehead. "I'm a fellow cop. If they'd asked, I would have let them search. I don't have anything to hide."

"That's what I want to find out," Mary said. She looked grim. Woodruff's head snapped up. "Remember I told you that you had to be completely honest with me?"

"I have been."

Mary pushed a copy of a police report across the desk. "This was written by Officer Dickinson after he interviewed you on the evening John Finley disappeared from your condo. Read it and tell me if you think Dickinson got anything wrong."

Mary watched Woodruff as she read the report looking for any reaction that would tip her to whether Woodruff had lied during their interview. If it turned out she had, Mary would be disappointed, but she had been conned by clients before. After all, many of the people she represented made a living by bending the truth without being obvious. But she'd slowly become convinced that Sarah Woodruff was innocent.

The judge who'd granted Sarah bail had concluded that the State's evidence didn't meet the criteria for denying a defendant release in a murder case. The inability of the State to produce a body was the tipping point for Judge Edmond and a strong component of Mary's argument for release. Max Dietz had been angry when he left the courtroom because he had lost, and Max hated to lose. But Mary sensed that Max had not laid down all of his cards during the bail hearing. A few sentences Mary had read in the stack of discovery her investigator had received from Dietz had reinforced that belief.

Woodruff looked confused when she finished reading the police report. "I don't understand, Mary. What was I supposed to see?"

"You were carrying a Glock 9mm when you returned to your condo."

"Yes. It's my service weapon."

"You told Officer Dickinson that you didn't fire it."

Woodruff's features shifted for a second. Her brow furrowed. "I remember him asking about that. I don't remember firing my weapon."

"You didn't say you didn't *remember* firing the weapon. You said that you did not. There's a big difference."

"Mary, I'd just witnessed an attack on someone I knew. I'd been knocked unconscious. I'd been chasing around the neighborhood. My head was killing me. The doctor at the hospital said I'd suffered a concussion. I think I can be forgiven for being a bit inaccurate."

"Let's hope the jury thinks so."

"Why are you so concerned?"

"For starters, there was a bullet missing from your gun. And do you remember a detective running a cotton swab over the web area between the thumb and forefinger of your hand to test for gunshot residue?"

"Vaguely. I wasn't thinking very straight. Are you saying they found residue on my hands?"

Mary nodded. "They can prove you fired your weapon."

Woodruff put her hands on her temples. She squeezed her eyes shut. When she opened them, she looked panicky.

"I don't remember firing the gun. Wouldn't I remember something like that if I'd done it?"

The grilling had been a test, and Mary thought her client had passed.

"Maybe not," she said. "After my investigator found out about the inconsistency, she talked to the doctor who treated you at the hospital. He's certain that you suffered a concussion, a traumatic injury to the brain as a result of a violent blow.

"A blow powerful enough to knock you out can cause your brain cells to become depolarized and fire all of their neurotransmitters at once. This floods the brain with chemicals and deadens the receptors in the brain that are associated with learning and memory. The upshot of all this is that a person who suffers a concussion can experience unconsciousness, blurred vision, and nausea and vomiting."

"I had all of that happen," Woodruff said.

Mary nodded. "Another consequence of a concussion is short-term memory loss. Memories of things that happen just before and after the impact are obliterated. Some people even have difficulty remembering certain phases of their life. The memory loss is usually not permanent, but it could account for your statement to Dickinson."

"It has to, because I've never lied about what happened at my place. I didn't kill John, and he was kidnapped."

"If Dietz tries to convince the jury that you lied about firing your gun, I'm going to present the testimony of the doctor who treated you, and I've got a call in to one of the top neurosurgeons in Oregon."

"Then you believe me?"

Mary wanted to tell Sarah that she couldn't

answer that question because she hadn't been in her house when the events that had led to her arrest occurred, but Woodruff looked awful and Mary knew she needed moral support.

"Yes, I believe you."

"Thank you, Mary. I need someone on my side."

"There's another thing I want to discuss, Sarah," Mary said. "Those names you gave me, Larry Kester, Orrin Hadley, and Dennis Lang they're all dead ends."

"What do you mean?"

"No criminal records, driving licenses, social security records. These men are phantoms. It's the same for John Finley. And my investigator can't find any more information about TA Enterprises than you did. It's registered in the Caymans, but we can't figure out what kind of business it conducts. Can you remember anything Finley may have said that can help us here?"

"I've told you everything I know."

"OK. That's all I wanted to go over today. I'm filing several motions tomorrow. You'll get copies when I finish them, and I'll call you if there are any more developments."

"Thanks, Mary. Having you on my side means a lot."

"Yeah, well, I haven't done anything yet."

Woodruff reached into her purse and pulled out a wad of cash. "Here's the fifteen thousand you wanted for expenses."

"Thanks," Mary said. "Unless you have any questions, you can head back to work."

Woodruff looked sick. "That's not going to happen anytime soon. I was officially suspended yesterday afternoon."

"I'm sorry."

"Well, you make one person who is," Woodruff said bitterly. "I haven't been getting a lot of support from my fellow officers. You'd think some of them would have the guts to wish me well."

Mary thought of several empty phrases she could throw at Sarah, but she knew none of them would help.

Chapter Twenty-eight

The Woodruff trial was a week away, and Max Dietz was worried. He'd convinced himself that he was prosecuting Sarah because she was a murderer and not because she'd refused to go out with him and had gone behind his back to Jack Stamm in the drug case. Now he was beginning to wonder if indicting Woodruff so quickly had been a mistake.

Dietz's first problem arose the moment Woodruff hired the Troll. That was Dietz's pet name for Mary Garrett, whom he hated. Garrett was abrasive and pushy and showed Dietz no respect. Worse still, the Troll had beaten him in court the last two times they'd faced off.

Then there was the evidence. A key to the state's case was Woodruff's denial that she'd fired her gun, but Mary Garrett's witness list included the physician who'd treated the defendant at the hospital and Dr. Peter Wu. Dietz had never heard of Dr. Wu, so he gave Claire Bonner the job of briefing him on the witness. It turned out that Wu was a world-renowned neurologist who had written and lectured extensively on memory loss due to trauma.

A knock on his door brought the deputy DA out of his depressing reverie. Monte Pike walked in without waiting for an invitation.

"Guess what?" Pike asked.

"I don't have time for guessing games," Dietz snapped.

Pike grinned. "I got a match to one of the unknown prints from Woodruff's condo."

"What? I thought I told you to forget about the prints."

"Oh," Pike said, his features an advertisement for innocence. "I guess I misunderstood you. Anyway, I ran the prints through AFIS again and got a hit for a case in Shelby."

"Shelby? That little town on the Columbia River?"

"Yeah."

"What the fuck does Shelby have to do with a murder in Portland?"

"I don't know. I haven't followed up yet."

"Well, don't. Is that a clear enough instruction?"

"But this is *Brady* material, Max. It's exculpatory evidence. The Supremes say we have to turn it over to Garrett."

"Bullshit! What's exculpatory about some prints connected to a case in Shelby, Oregon?"

"Woodruff claims there were people other than her and Finley in her house that night, the kidnappers. This is proof someone else was there."

"No it's not. You can't date prints. Everybody knows that. Who the fuck knows when they were placed in the house? They could be from a previous owner. Forget about those prints, Monte. I don't want to hear about them again."

* * *

Pike knew it would be useless to argue with Dietz, so he went back to his office. It was almost lunchtime. He rounded up his usual lunch crew and tried to lose himself in Trailblazer sports babble for an hour, but he couldn't forget about the fingerprint. Max Dietz was an ass, but he was also Pike's boss, and he'd ordered him to forget about the print. But Pike was more than a lowly deputy DA. All attorneys were officers of the court and bound by ethical rules. If the fingerprint was *Brady* material—evidence that could conceivably be used to clear a defendant—a district attorney had an absolute duty to disclose the exculpatory evidence to the defense. Dietz was ordering him to act illegally and unethically. As Pike saw it, he had a duty to his office but a higher duty to the court. The question was how to act in an ethical manner and still stay employed.

"Shelby Police Department?" a woman answered seconds after Pike dialed.

"I'm calling from the Multnomah County District Attorney's office about a case you're handling that may have a connection to one of ours."

"What is the title of our case?" the woman asked.

"I'm not certain, but we found prints at a Portland crime scene, ran them through the Automated Fingerprint Identification System, and got a hit referencing a Shelby case."

"Hold, please, and I'll try to find someone to help you."

Pike thought about hanging up before it was too late. No one had his name yet. But there was a click on the line before he could make up his mind.

"This is Tom Oswald. Who's this?"

"Monte Pike. I'm a deputy DA in Multnomah County. We found a bunch of prints at a crime scene we couldn't identify, so I ran them through AFIS and got a hit on one that referenced the Shelby PD."

There was dead air for a moment. Then Oswald asked, "Do you have our case name, Mr. Pike?"

"No."

"Do you know what type of case we're handling where this guy is involved?"

"Sorry."

"When was the print put into the system?" Oswald asked.

Pike gave him the date. There was silence for a moment while Oswald tried to remember when he'd scanned the print from the *China Sea* into AFIS.

"The only thing I can do is have you send me the print, and I'll try to figure out the case it belongs to. It might take a while. Give me your number, and I'll call you if I come up with something."

Pike gave him his extension.

"What's the name of your case?" Oswald asked.

"*State v. Sarah Woodruff.*"

"Isn't that the cop who's charged with murder? The one where there's no body?"

"Yeah."

"And this print came up in connection with it?"

"The print was found in her condo. It could be nothing. You can't date prints. I'm just trying to tie up some loose ends."

"Yeah, OK. Get the print to me. I'll give you a call if anything pops up."

* * *

Pike hung up, but Oswald held the phone for a few seconds, his mind on the problem the call presented. He'd been furious with the way the feds had treated the Shelby police force, and he'd put the latent fingerprint into AFIS in a fit of pique. When he'd calmed down, Oswald had thought about what he'd done. The chief had told him to back off, and so had the government of the United States of America. If he told Pike about the *China Sea*, there could be consequences for his career, but a fellow police officer was in trouble, and the information might help her. Should he sit on what he knew or call Pike? Oswald decided the best thing to do was to think. A day or so wouldn't make any difference.

Chapter Twenty-nine

Max Dietz was in his office reading the motions Mary Garrett had filed in *Woodruff* when his intercom buzzed.

"Mr. Dietz," the receptionist said, "there's a police officer who would like to talk to you."

Dietz didn't like to be interrupted when he was working, and he hadn't scheduled any meetings with police officers.

"Who is it?" he asked.

"Tom Oswald. He's from the Shelby Police Department."

The word *Shelby* created a sense of unease in the deputy district attorney, but he didn't know why.

"I don't have any cases involving Shelby. What did he say this was about?"

"A fingerprint. He asked for Mr. Pike first, but Mr. Pike is in trial. When he told me his business concerned the *Woodruff* case, I told him you were lead counsel, and he asked to speak to you."

Suddenly everything fell into place. That little cretin Pike had disobeyed his orders and had spoken to someone at Shelby PD about the fingerprint that had been raised in Sarah Woodruff's apartment.

"Show Oswald back," Dietz ordered. He'd find out what the policeman had to say. Then he'd take care of Pike.

A minute later, the receptionist stood back to let Tom Oswald into Max Dietz's office. Oswald looked uneasy as he waited for the receptionist to close the door behind him.

"How can I help you?" Dietz asked as soon as the policeman was seated.

"It's about the fingerprint."

"Yes, the fingerprint," Dietz answered noncommittally, hoping that his confident tone would convey an impression that he knew exactly what Oswald was talking about.

"I don't feel completely comfortable being here, but I've been worrying that the print might be important."

"What's bothering you?"

"I was told flat-out by Homeland Security to back off, and my chief told me to turn over the case."

Homeland Security! What the hell did they have to do with Sarah Woodruff?

"I see," Dietz said out loud, "but you felt it was important to tell us about the fingerprint."

"It's a murder case, and the defendant is a cop. I wanted to make sure that the right person is being prosecuted."

"Certainly. So, tell me about the print."

Over the next twenty minutes, Oswald told Max

Dietz about the dead men and the hashish on the *China Sea* and the cover-up that followed. Each new revelation tightened the knot in the DA's stomach. Mary Garrett would have a field day if she learned that a fingerprint in Woodruff's condo matched a fingerprint on a hatch covering a mountain of hashish that had been confiscated by a government intelligence agency.

"The chief told me to write a report about what happened," Oswald said when he finished telling his tale to Dietz. He held out a rolled set of papers that had been stapled at one corner. "I brought a copy if you want it."

"Yes, thank you," Dietz said as he took the report. "And you were certainly right to come to me. But I concur with Chief Miles. You should put this incident behind you. Let me deal with it from here on out. I've got plenty of contacts in the U.S. Attorney's office and the FBI. If something odd is going on, I'll get to the bottom of it. By the way, did you conduct any lab tests on this so-called hashish to verify your opinion?"

"No, the feds took all of it."

"OK. Well, my advice to you is that you carry on with your duties in Shelby. Rest assured I'll keep this between us. I have no intention of telling Chief Miles about our meeting. I don't want to put your job in danger. And I certainly don't want anyone at Homeland Security or the CIA investigating you."

"Will you need me to testify?" Oswald asked.

"I'll try to keep you out of this, but give me your

number so I can get in touch with you if I conclude that your evidence is important."

Oswald thanked Dietz. He looked relieved that the incident on the *China Sea* was now someone else's problem.

Dietz was not aware that his door had closed behind Oswald. He was too busy fantasizing scenarios in which a fully conscious Monte Pike was dismembered by chain saws and his body parts scattered over the Willamette River from the back of Dietz's boat. The fantasies were cathartic and helped him relax.

He had no intention whatsoever of following up on Oswald's story. In *Brady v. Maryland*, the United States Supreme Court had made up a terrible rule that forced district attorneys to turn over to the defense any evidence that might possibly clear a defendant. Dietz hated the case, and he was a master at rationalizing the withholding of evidence that was arguably discoverable under *Brady*.

By the time Dietz left for the day, he had arrived at several conclusions. First, *he* hadn't seen a fingerprint or its supposed match, and no one knew when these alleged prints had been left on the ship or in Woodruff's condo. How did he know the prints even matched? Errors were made in the comparison of fingerprints all the time. Why, close to home there was the Brandon Mayfield case, in which an Oregon attorney had been accused of being part of a terrorist group that had blown up those trains in Madrid because the FBI mistakenly identified a print of a known terrorist as Mayfield's.

And the hashish—was it really hashish? Oswald hadn't tested it. Who knew what was in the hold of that ship?

No, Dietz didn't see a *Brady* issue here, and he certainly wasn't going to go out of his way to help the defense create an absurd alternative theory of the crime involving drug dealers and intelligence agents. Let Garrett do her job. He wasn't paid to do the work of the defense.

That left Monte Pike. If Dietz called him on the carpet for disobeying orders, he would have to tell him about Oswald's visit. The traitorous little prick might go behind his back and leak the information about the ship to Garrett. Better to let sleeping dogs lie, even if it deprived Dietz of the opportunity to ream out the little punk. The way Pike was acting, Dietz was certain other opportunities would present themselves.

Chapter Thirty

Of all the cases Mary Garrett would handle, Sarah Woodruff's had the strangest ending. When she entered the courthouse on the third day of trial, Mary was unsure how the case was going. She wasn't crazy about the jury, and Judge Alan Nesbit was someone she rubbed the wrong way for reasons Mary could never determine.

The Multnomah County Courthouse was a blunt, functional concrete building that had been completed in 1914 and took up the entire block between Main and Salmon and Fourth and Fifth in downtown Portland. Most of the building's center was hollow, creating four marble corridors. When Mary and Sarah got out of the elevator on the fifth floor, a herd of reporters surged toward them. Mary looked insubstantial but her personality was Shaq-size, and she bulled through the reporters like a middle linebacker, repeating "No comment" until the courtroom door closed behind them.

Max Dietz was in a hushed conversation with Claire Bonner at the prosecution's counsel table. When they saw Mary and Sarah, they stopped talking. Mary opened the swinging gate in the low fence that separated the spectator section from the bar of the court and stood aside to let Sarah in. She had just arranged her papers and law books on the defense counsel table when the bailiff walked over.

"The judge wants the parties in chambers right away," the bailiff said.

"What's up?" Mary asked the DA.

Dietz shrugged. "You know as much as I do."

Mary followed Dietz, Bonner, and Woodruff into chambers. The first thing she noticed was the television and DVD player standing next to the judge's desk and the presence of a court reporter. The judge looked upset. As soon as everyone was seated, Nesbit sat up straight.

"I've just received some disturbing information that will require me to dismiss the government's case."

"What are you talking about?" Dietz blurted out. "Garrett hasn't given me any—"

Nesbit held up his hand.

"Please, Max. This has nothing to do with Ms. Garrett. When I came to work today, I found a DVD on my desk. I have no idea how it got there, but you need to see it."

Nesbit swiveled his chair and hit PLAY. Sarah's hand flew to her chest and she gasped. John Finley was staring at her, holding a copy of that day's *New York Times*.

"My name is John Finley, and I'm sorry for the confusion my disappearance has caused. Sarah, if you're in the room when they play this, I can't tell you how awful I feel about everything that's happened to you. Unfortunately, I could not reveal the fact that I am alive and well until today. I hope this proof that I am alive will end your ordeal."

The DVD ended. Mary looked at Sarah. All the color had drained from her face. Judge Nesbit addressed the DA.

"You introduced a photograph of Finley that was seized from Miss Woodruff's condo," the judge said. "The man on the DVD looks exactly like him."

"This is ridiculous," Dietz said as he envisioned the disappearance of his career and his public humiliation.

"Please, Max. I know how unsettling this is, but you can see that I have no choice here. The man is alive. He was never murdered."

Dietz couldn't think of anything to say. Mary had plenty of questions, but she wasn't going to do anything to jeopardize the dismissal of the charges against her client. She turned toward Sarah and saw that anger was replacing shock. She started to say something, but Mary gripped her wrist and shook her head.

"Shall I prepare a motion to dismiss with prejudice?" Mary asked.

"No, I'd think that would be the district attorney's job, given the circumstances," the judge said.

Dietz stood. "I'll have it here before lunch," he said, not even trying to hide his anger.

Mary couldn't blame Dietz for being upset. Everyone in the room was reeling.

"I'll dismiss the jury," Judge Nesbit said. "There's no need for you to wait."

Dietz stormed out with Claire Bonner in tow.

Mary went into the courtroom and gathered up her books and papers from counsel table before leading Sarah out of court.

"That son of a bitch," Woodruff said as soon as they'd fought their way through the reporters and were out of earshot of anyone. "I'm sorry I didn't kill him."

"Calm down," Mary said. "The important thing is that you're free and you're not facing a death sentence."

Woodruff stopped dead and glared at her attorney. "No, Mary, the important thing is that I'm broke from financing the defense of a case that should never have been filed, and my career and reputation have been ruined."

"Under the circumstances, I'll be refunding the greater part of your retainer, and the bureau should lift your suspension immediately."

"I appreciate your generosity, but any hope I ever had of making detective is gone. The bureau will stick me in a desk job. After all this publicity, I'll be a liability on the street."

"The furor will die down. People forget."

"But the bureaucracy doesn't. Take my word for it: My days as a cop are over."

It took most of the day to organize the files in the *Woodruff* case because everyone in the office wanted to know what had happened in court and everyone had a theory about John Finley's disappearance. Around four, Mary wandered down to the lunchroom and poured a cup of coffee. Back in her office, she told the receptionist to hold her calls and closed her door.

It was nice to have peace and quiet. Mary closed her eyes. She felt good about the outcome of the case, even if she had no idea what was really going on. The big thing was that death row was no longer a possibility for Sarah Woodruff. Or so she thought.

Part Four

Déjà Vu

June 2007

Chapter Thirty-one

The nature trails of Tryon Creek State Park run through a lush ravine inside the city limits of Portland. Homicide Detective Arnold Lasswell could appreciate the natural beauty of the place even with a team of forensic experts rooting around in the shrubbery and a dead man sprawled facedown on one of the trails.

"Hey, Arnie," Dick Frazier said when he spotted Lasswell.

"What have we got?" the detective asked the forensic expert.

"Male, Caucasian, I'm guessing in his mid- to late thirties. Shot in the head and chest, but killed somewhere else and transported here. We've got almost no blood around or under the vic."

"How long has he been out here?" the detective asked.

"I'm guessing a day or so. The ME will be able to give you a more accurate read."

Frazier pointed at a bloodstained duffel bag that lay a few feet from the corpse. "We haven't opened it yet, but there's one thing I picked up on."

Frazier led the detective over to the duffel. "See the bloodstains?"

Lasswell nodded.

"Notice anything about them?"

Lasswell studied the stains and was about to shake his head when he brightened.

"Some look darker than others."

Frazier clapped the detective on the back with a hand sheathed in latex.

"Bravo. We'll make a forensic expert out of you yet. There's no chemical test that can determine the relative age of blood, but fresh blood is redder in color than older blood. Then you get brown and finally old dried-up blood that's black. Now this isn't super scientific, but just eyeballing the stains, I'd guess that some of them were put on the duffel bag at different times."

Frazier signaled to a man with a video camera and the uniformed officer who had been assigned to collect evidence. When they were next to him, the lab tech squatted, unzipped the duffel bag, and pulled out some pants, underwear, socks, and shirts. The uniform put them in a large black plastic garbage bag.

"This is more interesting," Frazier said as he held up a handgun. He checked it to see if it was loaded before handing it to the uniform. Then he dipped his hand back into the duffel bag.

"What have we got here?" he asked as he pulled out four passports and laid them on a section of the duffel that was not stained with blood. He picked up the top one and opened it. Lasswell bent down and looked over Frazier's shoulder. The passport was in the name of John Finley. Lasswell stared at the picture and frowned.

Frazier thumbed through the passport, taking in the stamps from various nations in Europe, sub-Saharan Africa, the Middle East, and Asia.

"This guy was well traveled," Frazier said as he handed the passport to the uniform, who put it in a plastic bag.

"Whoa," Frazier said when he opened the next passport. It was identical to the first one except it was in the name of Orrin Hadley. The third and fourth passports were for Dennis Lang and Larry Kester but also had the same photograph.

"We've either got a spy or a drug dealer, but he's definitely not your average citizen," Frazier said as Lasswell wandered over to the corpse.

"Is there anything else?" the detective asked as he did a deep knee bend to get a better look at the dead man's face.

Frazier ran his hand over the interior of the bag and came out with several pieces of ID in different names but with the dead man's picture.

"Only this," he said, turning to talk to Lasswell, who had pulled out his cell phone. The forensic expert did not catch the name of the person on the other end but he distinctly heard Lasswell say, "You remember that DVD of John Finley from Sarah Woodruff's case? Yeah, it was about six months ago. Woodruff was indicted for murder, but the guy turned out to be alive. That's the one. I want the DVD on my desk ASAP."

Chapter Thirty-two

"It's definitely him," Arnie Lasswell told Max Dietz.

Dietz's eyes moved back and forth between a crime-scene photo of the dead man and a still from the DVD. When he was satisfied that he'd seen enough, his lips curled into a malevolent smile.

"The bitch killed him," Dietz said. He needed Sarah Woodruff to be guilty almost as much as he needed air. After the Woodruff fiasco, Jack Stamm had humiliated him by taking him out of Homicide and putting him back in the drug unit.

"Max, please don't jump to conclusions again," Lasswell warned. "I brought this to you because you were lead counsel on the first case. Don't make me sorry."

"She probably figures that we wouldn't charge her again after what happened in her first case," Dietz said, more to himself than Lasswell, "but she's not going to get away with this."

"We don't have any evidence pointing to Sarah Woodruff as our killer," Lasswell warned.

"Of course, we've got to do a thorough investigation," Dietz said to placate the detective, who would have been a pretty poor detective if he didn't see that Dietz's answer was completely lacking in sincerity. Before Lasswell could respond, his cell phone rang.

"Remember Ann Paulus, the neighbor who called 911 the first time Woodruff was arrested?" Lasswell said when the call ended.

"Yeah."

"She wants to talk to me about something she saw at Woodruff's condo about a week ago."

Ann Paulus, a trim blonde in her midthirties, worked as a nurse at Oregon Health & Science University, the large hospital that sprawled across the southwest hills just above downtown Portland. Paulus met Lasswell and Dietz in the lobby of OHSU's main medical building and led them to a sitting area near the counter where patients checked in.

"This is very strange, isn't it?" Paulus said.

"Strange how?" Lasswell asked.

"Well, it's déjà vu, like the first time all over again. There's a fight at Sarah Woodruff's house. I call. The police come. It's like time rewound. The first time Finley wasn't dead, but now he is."

"I see what you mean. How similar are we talking about?"

"Very. They were arguing . . ."

"You saw Mr. Finley and Ms. Woodruff arguing?" the detective asked.

"No, but I heard the argument."

"But you saw Finley go into Woodruff's place?"

"Yes. It was around eleven. I was getting ready to

go to bed and I went into my kitchen to get a glass of milk. The curtains were open. He was going inside."

"And you're certain it was Finley?"

"It was only a brief glimpse, but I'm pretty certain."

"OK, so what did you hear?"

"Yelling and a loud bang, maybe two bangs."

"Gunshots?"

"That I can't say. But it was a bang."

"Could it have been something slamming into a wall or something breaking?" Lasswell asked.

"It was more like a crack than something slamming into a wall, but I want to be fair. I don't want to guess."

"Which is good. But I have a question. The first time, when we were mistaken about Mr. Finley being murdered, you called the police right away. This time you waited several days. Why?"

"To tell you the truth, I felt very guilty after it turned out that Mr. Finley was alive. If I hadn't called, Miss Woodruff wouldn't have been in trouble. It must have been awful for her—the publicity, the trial, everyone thinking she was a murderer when she wasn't. And I felt responsible for all of it. So I decided to keep out of it this time."

"But you did call."

She nodded. "When I heard that he'd been murdered, I knew I had to."

"Mr. Finley's body was found on Wednesday morning," Lasswell said. "When did you hear the argument?"

"Well, that's the thing. Today is Tuesday, and I

didn't call until today because I didn't know that Mr. Finley was dead. I didn't read the paper that had the story. This morning, Joan Pang, another nurse, asked me what I thought about Finley being killed. She was off last week, and I didn't see her yesterday, so we didn't talk. So I didn't know about this until this morning. Then I tried to think back to when I heard the fight, and I think it was last Tuesday, but I'm not one hundred percent sure."

"But you did see Finley?"

Paulus nodded.

"What about Miss Woodruff?" Dietz asked. "Did you see her when Finley went inside?"

"No."

"So you can't say Finley was in the house with Woodruff?" Lasswell said.

"No, it could have been someone else in her house. But who would it be?"

Lasswell and Dietz talked to Paulus for twenty more minutes before thanking her for her help and walking back to their car.

"What do you think?" Lasswell asked the deputy DA.

"I think we've got enough for a search warrant, and this time I'm going to get her, Arnie. I can smell it."

Chapter Thirty-three

Jack Stamm was a bachelor whose passions were law and distance running. He had thinning wavy brown hair, kind blue eyes, and a ready smile that made voters forget that he was north of forty.

"Sit down," Stamm said, motioning Monte Pike, Max Dietz, and Arnie Lasswell toward three chairs that had been set up on the other side of his desk.

"Monte," the DA said, "we've had an interesting development in an old case. Fill him in, Arnie."

Lasswell turned toward Pike. "A hiker discovered a dead man on a trail in Tryon Creek State Park."

"I heard about that," Pike said.

"The man had been shot somewhere else and dumped in the park along with a duffel bag that contained clothing and a handgun. Also in the duffel were four passports and other ID. They were all for the dead man but in different names. One of the names was John Finley."

"John Finley, like the guy who rose from the grave?" Pike asked.

"The same," the detective said.

"Holy shit!" Pike's eyes were bright and a huge grin spread across his face.

"Yesterday, Ann Paulus, Sarah Woodruff's neighbor, told me that she saw Finley going into Woodruff's condo. She's not a hundred percent certain of the day, but she's pretty sure it was the evening he was killed. She also heard an argument and a loud bang—maybe two—from the apartment.

"This morning, Dick Frazier called me from the crime lab with some very interesting news. During Finley's autopsy, the medical examiner found two hollow-nose, Smith & Wesson 140-grain bullets. She sent them over to the crime lab. Dick made a digital image of the bullets by putting them on a microscope and rotating it. Then he scanned the images into a computer and ran them through IBIS, the Integrated Ballistics Identification System.

"Three years ago, we investigated a gang- and drug-related murder. The victim was killed by a hollow-nose Smith and Wesson 140-grain bullet fired from a .38 Special. According to IBIS, the bullets that killed Finley and the bullet that killed the victim in the gang slaying were fired from the same gun. When I went down to the evidence room to retrieve the gun it wasn't there."

"Where is it?" Pike asked.

"That is a mystery. It was introduced during the trial, but we don't know what happened after the conviction, although I now have a strong suspicion. According to the log sheet, the gun was returned to the evidence room after the trial, and there is no record of it being taken out after that. The verdict was appealed, so I thought the gun might still be in the court of appeals, but they don't have it. What's important here, though, is that Sarah Woodruff was one of the officers who worked on the gang slaying, and the log sheet showing that the gun was returned has her signature on it."

"You think Woodruff logged in the gun but stole it?" Pike said.

Lasswell nodded.

"Then killed her boyfriend, *again*?" Pike asked gleefully.

"Right now, she's our prime suspect," Lasswell said.

"I'm already working the case with Arnie," Dietz told Stamm. "I'd like to prosecute."

"I know you would," Jack Stamm said. "That's why I called you in here. I wanted you to hear this from me, not secondhand. I'm giving this case to Monte."

"But—" Dietz started.

Stamm held up his hand. "You want to redeem yourself. That's natural. But you're too emotional about Woodruff."

Dietz cast a quick glance at Arnie Lasswell. Had the detective complained about him to Stamm?

"I want someone with an open mind handling the case," Stamm continued. "Monte is going to be lead counsel, and you're not going to be involved. I know that's harsh, but I've given this a lot of thought, and that's how it's going to be."

Anger darkened Dietz's complexion. "If that's your decision . . . ?"

"It is," Stamm said.

"I was preparing for a trial," Dietz said. "If you don't need me anymore . . ."

"Sure, Max," Stamm said. "And don't think my decision affects my high opinion of your work as a whole. I just don't think you're the best person for this case."

Dietz was too furious to speak, so he just stood up and left the room.

Stamm turned his attention to Pike. "Tread carefully, Monte. This blew up in our faces the first time through. I do not want to find myself on national television apologizing to Sarah Woodruff again."

Max Dietz stomped back to his office with his shoulders hunched and his fists clenched. A pulse beat in his temple. When he'd shut the door and slumped onto his chair, he closed his eyes and took long, deep breaths to get his emotions under control. He knew he had to do something if he didn't want his career to unravel completely, and he couldn't think in his present state.

When he was relatively calm, Dietz took stock of his situation. He had been in Stamm's doghouse ever since the debacle that was the first Woodruff case. Convicting Sarah Woodruff of murder would save his career, but he wasn't going to get that chance. Max had once been the heir apparent to Stamm's throne. Now Pike was Stamm's new golden boy. What could he do about that?

A sudden thought jolted Dietz upright in his

chair. He knew something Pike and Arnie Lasswell didn't. He knew about the *China Sea*. He hadn't told anyone about Tom Oswald's information. If anyone had gotten the bright idea that it was *Brady* material, he would have been forced to tell Mary Garrett what he knew, and Garrett would have argued to the jurors that John Finley was killed by drug dealers or spies.

But what if Finley *had* been killed by drug dealers or spies? What if Monte Pike indicted Sarah Woodruff and took her to trial, and it turned out that drug dealers or government assassins had killed Finley? Monte Pike wouldn't look like such a hotshot then, would he? The little prick would suffer the same humiliation Dietz had suffered, and Max would be the smart one again.

Dietz pulled out a legal pad and started to jot down ideas. He needed information, and the only people who could provide information in a situation like this were insiders. Dietz wrote the names of contacts in the FBI, the U.S. Attorney's office, and . . . Dietz grinned.

Max had met Denise Blailock four years ago while they were working on a joint task force investigating Miguel Fuentes, the advance man for a Guatemalan cartel that was trying to make inroads into the local heroin trade. The DEA agent was pale and plain with washed-out brown hair, but she had a nice smile and a body that had attracted the DA's attention the minute she'd entered the conference room.

Dietz's second wife had walked out on him two

months before he met Denise, and he hadn't been laid since. When the task force meeting broke up, Blailock and Dietz had dined at a local steak house. During a dinner of T-bones and scotch, Dietz learned several important things about the federal agent. First, she was totally devoted to her career in the Drug Enforcement Administration. Second, as a result of a brief, savage, and regrettable teenage marriage, the only serious relationship she was interested in was the one she had with her job. Third, she was a strong proponent of recreational sex, in which the couple had engaged after dinner at a motel by the airport.

Dietz and Blailock had seen each other occasionally since their first tryst, the longest stretch being a week in Las Vegas the previous winter. Dietz dialed DEA headquarters and asked Blailock if she was doing anything after work. Over dinner, the DA filled in his friend on the downward path his career had taken since the Woodruff fiasco and his plan to restore his fortunes. Blailock told him that she'd never heard of the *China Sea* or the incident in Shelby, but she promised to poke around.

Chapter Thirty-four

Mary Garrett had been expecting a call from Sarah Woodruff ever since she'd read about John Finley's murder. The first words Sarah spoke were tinged with panic.

"Mary, Arnie Lasswell is here—at my house—with another detective. They have a search warrant, and they want to question me."

"Don't say a thing, and put Arnie on the line."

"Hey, Mary," Lasswell said. The two knew each other because the detective had investigated a number of cases Mary had defended.

"What's up, Arnie?" Mary asked.

"We have a warrant to search your client's house and car in connection with John Finley's murder. We'd also like to talk to her."

"Can you tell me anything else, like why she's a suspect?"

"Monte Pike is running the show. You'll have to ask him."

"What happened to Max?"

"I guess Jack wanted to try someone new this time around."

"OK. Look, I'm coming over. I don't want anyone talking to Sarah, understood?"

"Gotcha. I put her in the kitchen with a cup of coffee."

"OK, and be gentle during the search, OK? Make sure nothing is broken or torn. You guys screwed up the first time. If Sarah is innocent this time, too, you won't want to put the bureau and the DA's office in an even worse light."

"She's a fellow officer, Mary, and I *am* sorry for what she went through. I'll be gentle as a lamb."

It took Mary twenty-five minutes to get to Sarah's house. When the uniform at the front door let her in, she saw a team of police officers working their way through the living room and heard drawers and closet doors opening and closing on the floor above. Arnie Lasswell came down for a few minutes and laid out the ground rules, which included staying in the kitchen with her client and staying out of everybody's way.

Mary made small talk with Sarah for a few minutes, then called Monte Pike on her cell phone. She'd had two cases with Pike, which ended in pleas, so she had not had a chance to see the young DA in action, but Mary's impressions of the prosecutor were positive. Mary thought that Pike saw law as a game like chess and didn't take his work personally. He was definitely smart and honest; he worked hard, but he had a good sense of humor.

"Monte, it's Mary Garrett," she said when they were connected.

"Yeah, Arnie said you were coming over to make sure his boys don't steal the silverware."

"With the mayor cutting down on overtime, I hear the rank and file are getting desperate."

Monte laughed. "So, what can I do for you?"

"How about you tell me why you're sifting through Ms. Woodruff's lingerie."

"Why did I think that would be your first question? God, I hate being right all the time."

"And?"

"I'll tell you some stuff but not everything. A grand jury hasn't even been convened—and it may never be—so I'm going to keep some info close to the vest. I will tell you that Ann Paulus, the neighbor who called 911 in the first case, saw Finley go into your client's house. She's pretty certain it was the evening of the murder."

"Why only pretty certain?"

"That's for me to know and you to find out until I'm required to give you discovery. But I will tell you she heard arguing and what she thought might have been a shot or two. And that's it for now."

"OK. Will you give me the courtesy of telling me if you indict Ms. Woodruff?"

"Sure thing."

"Will you let her surrender herself?"

"I guess she's entitled to a little leeway in light of the mess we made last time."

"Are you certain you're not stepping in it again?"

"Unlike some people who shall remain nameless, I don't shoot first and ask questions later."

"What are you thinking about for a charge?"

"You want to know if I'm going for a lethal injection?"

"Yes."

"I don't know enough to answer that question right now."

"Fair enough."

"Honestly, Mary, I sincerely hope this search is an exercise in futility. I don't enjoy making life difficult for someone who's already had one awful experience with the justice system. But I'll go after Ms. Woodruff full-bore if I believe, beyond a reasonable doubt, that she murdered John Finley."

As soon as the last police car was out of sight, Mary got down to business.

"Monte Pike is in charge of your case, and he isn't a loose cannon like Max Dietz. This guy is very bright and very methodical. He didn't tell me much, but he did tell me that your neighbor, Ann Paulus, will testify that she saw Finley go into your condo around the time he was killed. Was he here?"

"Yes. The bastard broke in."

"Why would he do that?"

"He said he was on the run."

"From whom?"

"He wouldn't tell me. He said I would be in danger if I knew."

"If he was on the run, why did he go to your place?"

"He came back for his duffel bag. He said there were passports and ID in different names he could use. He'd hidden the bag in my house just before he was kidnapped."

"Pike told me the neighbor heard an argument and possibly shots."

"There was an argument, but I didn't shoot John, even though I was tempted. When I caught the bastard sneaking around my house, I thought he was a burglar. I fired a shot into the floor at his feet."

Mary had seen an officer digging something out of the floor in the hall. She made a note to ask if it was a bullet.

"When I saw who it was, I went ballistic. The son of a bitch ruined my life, Mary. I'm pushing papers, my chances of making detective are slim and none, I was humiliated and forced to stand trial. I let John know what I thought of him. That's when he explained what happened and why he couldn't help me right away. I calmed down a little after that and told him to take the duffel bag and get out. When he left, he was alive and well."

"What did Finley tell you?"

"He said he was a navy SEAL with contacts in the CIA. After he left the military, he freelanced for the Agency on occasion, and they took him off the books so anyone who checked on him wouldn't know about his background. TA Enterprises was created to purchase and refit the *China Sea* and to provide money to finance the operation that almost got John killed."

"Tell me about that."

"John told me that the *China Sea* was anchored in the Columbia River near Shelby. On the night he was kidnapped, she had just returned from a rendezvous at sea where she'd picked up a cargo of hashish from a freighter from Karachi, Pakistan. John guessed that the hashish was going to be sold to pay for covert operations that couldn't be financed from budgeted funds because they were illegal.

"John told me that a crew member named Talbot murdered the rest of the crew. John killed him in a gunfight, but he was wounded. My house was the only place he could think of, so he drove here. He still had a key. He'd just finished hiding the duffel bag when two men broke in and attacked him.

"John thought that Talbot didn't know that the CIA was behind the smuggling operation and thought John was just another drug dealer. He thought Talbot cut a deal with a Mexican named Hector Gomez to steal the hashish. John's kidnappers worked for Gomez. They took him to a deserted spot and were going to kill him, but a team of government agents rescued him. Everything that happened on the ship was kept quiet so the people who were going to buy the hashish wouldn't get alarmed and back out."

"Why didn't John come forward earlier?"

"He couldn't stop my prosecution without blowing the deal. After he sold the hashish, he insisted on helping me. That's when he made that video."

"If I can corroborate your story, I might be able to convince Pike to drop the case against you."

"God, Mary, I hope so. I can't go through another trial."

Woodruff had been fighting to keep her composure, but she suddenly burst into tears and buried her face in her hands. Mary felt helpless as she watched her shoulders shake with each wrenching sob.

"I didn't do anything. You have to believe me. If anyone killed John, it would be the drug dealers or the CIA. I just wanted John out of my life."

"Well, he's back in it. Hopefully, he won't be for long."

Chapter Thirty-five

A rap on her doorjamb brought Mary's eyes up from the memo she was writing. Mark Gilbert, her investigator, dropped into a chair.

"I thought you might be interested in this," he said as he handed Mary a rolled police report written by Tom Oswald of the Shelby, Oregon, police department.

"You told me Miss Woodruff said Finley's ship was the *China Sea* and it was docked in Shelby, so I decided to see if I could find out anything about it, and sure enough this cop wrote a report. It's pretty interesting. I think you should give him a call."

As soon as Mary finished Oswald's report, she swiveled toward her phone and dialed Shelby PD. Ten minutes later, she turned to face her investigator again.

"We're meeting after his shift tonight."

"Do you want me to come along?"

"No, I think he'll talk more freely if it's just me. You know, he said something interesting as soon as we were connected."

"What's that?"

"He said he'd been expecting my call."

"I wonder why."

"I didn't want to push him. I'll ask tonight."

"One more thing," Gilbert said. "I still have informants from my days as a cop. I've been trolling for information, and I came up with some interesting stuff. A few days after Finley was kidnapped, two men were found on a logging road. They'd been murdered. The men worked for a Mexican drug cartel. One of them was wearing a leather jacket."

"Like the kidnapper Sarah described."

"There's a rumor on the street that Finley had a quarter million dollars with him when he left the ship and that's why the kidnappers were following him."

"Finley told Sarah that he was rescued by government agents. They must have taken the money when they killed the drug dealers."

"Makes sense. Tell me what happens tonight," Gilbert said.

"Will do."

If Mary hadn't run a MapQuest search, she might have missed the bar, which stood on an empty lot away from a run-down gas station on an otherwise unpopulated stretch of highway. There were no streetlights on this part of the road. A quarter moon and the neon beer signs in the tavern window provided a little light. A pickup and a beat-up Chevy were parked in the gravel lot that fronted the tavern. The isolation made Mary uneasy, but her hand gripped the handle of a .38 Special she carried in the deep pocket of her belted Burberry trench coat.

When Mary opened the door to the bar, she was hit by the smell of stale beer and sweat. The inside of the tavern was almost as dark as the outside, and it took a moment before her eyes adjusted to the gloom. Two men were perched on stools, nursing drinks at opposite ends of a scarred, liquor-soaked bar. The bartender and the two men turned and stared when the door opened. Mary didn't waste any time on them. She scanned the tables and found the only other customer nursing a beer in a booth in the back.

"Officer Oswald?" Mary asked as she sat on the bench opposite the policeman. Oswald nodded, and he didn't stare. Garrett was well known to people in law enforcement. Mary pointed at his beer.

"Can I get you a refill?"

"Sure."

When Mary returned from the bar, she placed a cold beer in front of the officer and took a swig from her bottle.

"Thanks for meeting me. As I said on the phone, I'm representing Sarah Woodruff."

"The cop who's charged with murder."

"Right. A ship called the *China Sea* came up in our investigation, and my investigator found your report. I'd appreciate it if you can tell me what happened the night you answered the 911."

"The ship was docked near a warehouse, and the night watchman reported shots," Oswald said. "We found five dead men on the ship and a lot of hashish in the hold."

Mary nodded. "That's in the report. What I don't understand is why there aren't any other reports. I mean, there were five dead men. I assume that's not run-of-the-mill in Shelby."

"Yeah, well this whole deal wasn't run-of-the-mill. We don't usually get invaded by Homeland Security, either."

"And they told you to back off, that they were taking over?"

Oswald shrugged. "And my boss agreed. He was right. We would have ended up turning it over to the state police, so why not the feds?"

"And that's everything that happened?"

"Didn't the DA tell you the rest of it?"

"What DA?"

"I talked to two of them."

"Look, Tom, all this information about the *China Sea* is new to me. So why don't you tell me what isn't in the report."

Oswald took a swig from his bottle. Mary got the impression that he was making a decision. After he thought for a few moments, Oswald wiped some moisture from his mouth and started talking.

"Jerry and I couldn't let go, so we drove back to the dock. This was a day later. The ship was gone, and Dave Fletcher, the night watchman who'd called in the 911, wasn't there either. I drove out to his place. It was deserted. One of his neighbors told me she hadn't seen Fletcher or his car since the night I was called to the dock. I talked to Fletcher's boss at the company that provides the security guards. He told me Fletcher didn't work there anymore and they didn't know where he'd gone."

"Do you know what happened to him?" Mary asked.

"I have no idea. He has family in town, and they filed a missing-person report. I've followed up from time to time, but he vanished off the face of the earth.

"If I had to bet, I'd put my money on the men who disappeared the ship. You read about the CIA kidnapping terrorists all the time and taking them to secret prisons."

Oswald paused. He looked ill. "Dave was a good guy, a veteran. I hope to God he's still alive."

"Did Mr. Fletcher tell you anything you didn't write in the report?" Mary asked.

"Yeah, the chief told me to make the report bare bones, so I didn't put in a lot of stuff. For instance, Fletcher told me he'd seen a man run from the ship and drive away. The man was staggering, and Fletcher thought he might be wounded. He also thought another car followed the man when he drove off."

Mary started to get a funny feeling in her gut. "When I called you and told you I represented Sarah Woodruff, you said you'd been expecting my call. Why do you think what happened on the *China Sea* has something to do with Sarah Woodruff's case?"

"Shortly before your client's first case came to trial, a Multnomah County DA named Monte Pike called me. You know that several prints were found in your client's house that couldn't be identified when they were run through AFIS."

Mary nodded.

"Pike ran them again and came up with a match to a print I put into AFIS a few days after I lifted it."

"You didn't turn over all the evidence to the Homeland Security guys."

Oswald leaned forward. "I do not appreciate being treated like a hick, and I especially do not appreciate being treated like a hick by some asshole whose salary is paid by my taxes."

Mary smiled. "Where did the print come from?"

"The hatch covering the hashish."

Mary let out a low whistle. "Did Pike know about the hash and the wounded man who ran from the ship?"

"That I don't know, but I assume the other prosecutor told him."

"What other prosecutor?"

"The one I saw in Portland—Dietz. My chief told me to keep my mouth shut about the *China Sea*, and I didn't want Homeland Security pissed at me, so I told Pike I didn't know anything about the print, and I never got back to him. But I started to feel guilty. You know, Woodruff's a cop, and this stuff with the ship didn't feel right. My conscience was really bothering me, and I was in Portland on business. When I finished what I had to do, I went to the DA's office to talk to Pike, but he was in trial and they told me that Dietz was lead counsel. So I told him everything. Didn't he tell you about the ship?"

"No, Tom, he didn't, and I'm going to find out why. Will you get in trouble with your chief for talking to me?"

"If he brings it up, I'll handle it. Woodruff is a cop. If she killed the guy, I've got no sympathy for her. But I'm not going to sit on information that can prove she didn't do it. What kind of person would I be if I did that?"

Chapter Thirty-six

The next morning, Mary called Monte Pike as soon as she got to work. A half hour later, she and Pike were seated in a conference room in the Multnomah County District Attorney's office.

"So Mary, what's up?" Monte asked when they'd concluded their small talk.

"Does a freighter named the *China Sea* mean anything to you?"

"No."

"Max Dietz can tell you all about it."

Pike's brow furrowed. The young DA seemed genuinely puzzled.

"Why does Max know about this ship, and what does it have to do with the *Woodruff* case?"

"Remember the fingerprint you found in Sarah Woodruff's house that you ran through AFIS?"

"Yeah. It matched a print from a case in Shelby. I talked to a cop there, but he never got back to me."

"The cop's name is Tom Oswald. My investigator tracked down his report about the *China Sea*. Oswald found the print on the ship. He came to Portland looking for you after you called Shelby about the latent. You were in trial, so he met with Dietz instead." Mary handed Pike a copy of Oswald's police report. "I talked to Oswald last night. He verified everything he wrote and added a few items that aren't in the report. Max knew everything Oswald told me."

When Pike finished reading the report, Mary told him about the disappearance of the ship and the night watchman.

"And there's more. Shortly after Finley was kidnapped, two dead men were found on a logging road. They'd been shot to death, and they were working for a Mexican drug cartel. I think they were the men who kidnapped Finley from Sarah's condo."

"What do you want, Mary?"

"I want you to dismiss the indictment. This is a clear case of prosecutorial misconduct. Max had a duty to tell me about this exculpatory evidence."

"Max may have violated the ethics rules, but any effect his misconduct had on Woodruff's first case was cured by the dismissal."

"Would you have gotten this new indictment if the grand jury knew everything I've just told you?" Mary asked.

Pike considered the question, and Mary waited anxiously for his answer. When she got it, she had trouble hiding her disappointment.

"Yeah," Pike said. "I would still have presented the case even with this new information. Everything you've told me applies to the first case, not this one."

"How can you say that? If Finley was involved with black ops and drug cartels, it presents several alternatives to the theory that Sarah killed him."

"This stuff about drug dealers and CIA assassins is total speculation. Do we even know that there was hashish in the hold of the *China Sea*? Was the substance tested in a lab?"

"Homeland Security absconded with the ship and its cargo. There was no opportunity to test it."

"So the answer is no. And you're conveniently ignoring a few things. This stuff about spies and drug cartels is fascinating, but it doesn't explain away these facts: One, Finley had an argument with your client on the night he was killed; two, he was murdered with a gun that was stolen from the evidence room of the Portland Police Bureau; and three, your client is the last person to have contact with that gun. Spies or no spies, the evidence says that Sarah Woodruff murdered John Finley."

"Don't be naive, Monte. The CIA has people on its payroll who could steal a gun from the police evidence room if they wanted to frame Sarah. Remember the Finley DVD? Someone broke into Judge Nesbit's chambers and left it. You can't honestly tell me that nothing about this case raises a reasonable doubt in your mind about Sarah's guilt."

"If I had a reasonable doubt, I wouldn't pursue the case. I believe your client killed John Finley. Just because we made a mistake the first time around doesn't mean Woodruff gets a free pass this time. In fact, it is her audacity in thinking that she can get away with murder because we screwed up in her first case that motivates me."

"I guess we disagree on what this case is really about," Mary said as she pulled a stack of papers from her attaché and handed them to Pike. "I was hoping we could resolve this matter once you learned about Finley's connection to the *China Sea*. These are copies of my motions to dismiss for prosecutorial misconduct and discovery that I'm filing as soon as I leave our meeting. Sarah Woodruff didn't kill John Finley this time any more than she did the first time you made the mistake of charging her. He was killed by drug dealers or agents of the United States government who want to keep the public from learning about the *China Sea*. I'm going to make sure that everyone knows about the CIA's dirty little secret."

Chapter Thirty-seven

Max Dietz had no idea why Jack Stamm had summoned him to his office, but he began to feel uneasy when he found Monte Pike and the district attorney waiting for him, looking like mourners at a funeral.

"What's up, Jack?" Dietz asked as he took a seat.

"Monte has just given me some disturbing information."

"Oh?" Dietz said, turning his head toward his fellow prosecutor.

"What do you know about a ship named the *China Sea*?" Stamm asked.

"Oh, that," Dietz answered, smiling to mask the fear that washed over him like a red tide. Dietz didn't know what Pike and Stamm knew, so he held his tongue, hoping one of them would fill the void with information he could use to figure out a cover story.

"Did a police officer from Shelby visit you while Sarah Woodruff was awaiting trial under the first indictment?"

"Yes."

"What did he tell you, Max?" Stamm asked.

"I don't remember everything," Dietz hedged. "It was a few months ago."

"Why don't you tell us what you do remember."

Dietz felt sick. "What's this all about, Jack? Why the third degree?"

"Mary Garrett met with Monte earlier today and told him about a discussion she had with Tom Oswald, the policeman you met with about Sarah Woodruff's case. Mary was upset. She thought you'd breached your duty to tell her about exculpatory evidence that you had a duty to disclose under *Brady v. Maryland*."

"Over that ship? What did it have to do with *Woodruff*?"

"Well, there were the fingerprints," Stamm said. "Monte told you about them, didn't he?"

This was all Pike's doing, Dietz told himself. The little prick had gone running to Stamm to build up brownie points and to sabotage Dietz's career. Dietz was fuming inside, but he knew he was doomed if he showed any weakness.

Dietz smiled and shook his head. "Monte was all excited about some prints from Woodruff's condo. I remember that."

"Do you remember telling Monte to forget about the prints, that you didn't want him pursuing them?"

"Sure. They had nothing to do with our case. Pursuing them would be a waste of valuable time. Pike had no idea who made them or when they were made, and they matched some case in Shelby. Our case had nothing to do with Shelby."

"Until Officer Oswald visited you," Stamm said. "He's a police officer in Shelby. Didn't he tell you that the print he lifted came from a hatch on the ship covering a shipment of hashish?"

"Hold up, Jack. Oswald said he thought it was hashish, but there were never any tests done on the stuff in the hold. And we didn't know that the print was Finley's. No one could ID it on either end."

"The prints were compared to Finley's prints this afternoon and they match," Stamm said.

"I didn't know that then."

"But you did know that the night watchman saw a man run from a ship where five dead men were found and drive toward Portland, possibly followed by another car. And this was about when Finley would have had to leave the ship if he was going to arrive at Woodruff's house when he did."

"Jack, this is speculation. We had nothing then that would have proved the guy who fled from the ship was Finley. No one had a match for those prints."

"Sarah Woodruff contended that men broke into her house, fought with Finley, and kidnapped him. That fits the information Oswald gave you."

"Only if we knew it was Finley who ran from the ship, and I didn't. Look, Jack, Garrett would have had the jury running around in circles if she introduced evidence of drug dealers and terrorists and God knows what else, which is exactly what would have happened if I had told her about the ship."

Dietz could see the disappointment on Stamm's face. "You're better than this, Max. We all want to win, but prosecutors have a higher duty, and that is to seek justice. Justice is never served if an innocent person is convicted."

"I honestly believed Woodruff was guilty. I know I was wrong, now. But I believed it then. And giving Garrett this incendiary information . . ."

"Evidence of innocence is always incendiary, Max."

"I didn't see the evidence pointing toward innocence. I thought it was about an incident that had nothing to do with Sarah Woodruff. It was a judgment call."

"Then you showed poor judgment."

"Where is this going, Jack?"

"I'm not certain. I want to give this matter serious thought. Why don't you do the same, and I'll get back to you."

"OK, but I didn't do anything wrong here."

Dietz left with his head held high, but his shoulders sagged as soon as the door to Stamm's office closed behind him. He felt dizzy, sick. Everything had gone downhill for him since Woodruff's first case had been dismissed, and his career was going to come to a crashing halt if something good didn't happen fast.

It was almost four, and Dietz couldn't concentrate, so he left the courthouse. When he got home, he shed his jacket and tie and fixed himself a stiff drink. What had he done to deserve this kind of treatment? Nothing, he told himself. It was Pike. The suck-up had run to Stamm as soon as Garrett complained. Pike was trying to destroy him. Would Garrett file an ethics complaint with the bar? Would Stamm sack him? What if he was out in the street in disgrace? What would he do then? Dietz slumped forward and held his head in his hands. He'd talked to several people about the *China Sea*, and no one had gotten back to him. It looked like the ship was not only a dead end, but he might end up going down with it.

Chapter Thirty-eight

Denise Blailock pulled a nondescript brown Honda to the curb in front of the Multnomah County Courthouse and looked around nervously as Max Dietz jumped into the passenger seat. After twenty minutes of evasive driving, Blailock stopped the car in a deserted gravel lot under a freeway overpass near the Willamette. As soon as the car was parked, Blailock got out and turned up her collar to cut the wind coming off the river. Dietz was dressed in a suit because he had court in the afternoon, and he started to shiver as soon as he got out.

"What the fuck have you gotten me into?" Blailock asked in a tone of voice he'd never heard her use before. Dietz sensed anger, but he also heard fear.

"I told you everything I knew," he insisted. "That's why I asked you to poke around."

"Yeah, well, you didn't tell me I'd be jabbing a hornet's nest."

"What happened?"

"I made a few calls, went on the Internet, nothing that exciting. The next thing I know, I'm called on the carpet by my boss and told in no uncertain terms that the *China Sea* does not exist, and never has, and any further inquiries I make about this phantom will be from my new posting in Butt Fuck, North Dakota."

"Geez, I'm sorry. I had no idea your boss would come down on you."

"Well, he has, and I know how to take a hint."

"Did he tell you why he threatened you?"

"He was trying to help me. He's a good egg. He watches my back, and he didn't want me to get in trouble. After I talked to him, he got curious and made a few calls. He was also upset that DEA was kept out of the loop in a federal investigation involving drugs. The people he talked to at Homeland Security said no one from that agency was anywhere near Shelby, Oregon, on the night in question. Ditto every other agency he contacted. A few days later, he got a call from someone so high up the food chain he had to put on an oxygen mask to talk to him. This person told my boss in no uncertain terms that the *China Sea* never existed and he was never to inquire about the ship again."

Dietz was about to apologize again when it dawned on him that Denise didn't have to drive to a place where they would have complete privacy to tell him what she'd just disclosed.

"You found something, didn't you?" he asked.

"Yeah, and I'm going to tell you because I think Jack Stamm screwed you. But we're never going to discuss this subject again, ever."

"OK, I swear. So tell me what's going on with this ship."

"Bad things, amigo. The *China Sea* has the makings of an urban legend. From what I know, two Shelby cops responded to a 911 and found five dead men and a large shipment of hashish on board. Shortly after they arrived, three carloads of armed men claiming to be from Homeland Security pulled up and told them they would be arrested for interfering in a federal investigation if they didn't leave and turn over any forensic evidence they'd collected. Then the ship vanished, along with the night watchman who made the 911 call."

"I was told this already," Dietz said.

"Did anyone tell you about the other two dead men and the money?"

"What dead men, what money?"

"Sarah Woodruff told the cops that two men kidnapped John Finley from her house and the one she saw was wearing a leather jacket."

"Yeah."

"Shortly after Finley disappeared, two dead men were found on a deserted logging road. The police reports say they were shot. One of them was wearing a leather jacket, and they were both known drug dealers linked to Hector Gomez, who works for a Mexican drug cartel.

"Well, there's a rumor making the rounds about a missing quarter-million dollars that was supposed to have been in the possession of the skipper of the *China Sea*. That's what the drug dealers were after, in addition to the hashish, and it was the reason they kidnapped Finley."

"Where did you get that tidbit? I thought the federal agencies won't admit the ship exists."

"They won't. This rumor has been circulating among drug dealers and drug users. The same people who were questioned about the dead men on the logging road. If the hash on the ship was going to be used by some agency to fund an illegal operation, the agency would never admit to it. Drug dealers wouldn't have the same motivation to keep quiet. That's all I know, and this is the last time I'm ever going to talk about this subject."

Denise dropped Dietz at the courthouse and sped off. The prosecutor went through security and rode the elevator to his office. It would take someone with a lot of power to scare the head of a DEA field office. Max wondered how many people had the clout to cover up a quintuple homicide. The more he learned, the more convinced he was that John Finley had been killed by drug dealers or government assassins. He wondered if he was putting himself in harm's way by continuing to ask questions about the *China Sea*. Maybe the smart thing to do would be to back off. He was in Stamm's doghouse, and his plan to get out of it had involved showing up Monte Pike by proving that Sarah Woodruff had not murdered John Finley. To do that, he'd planned to use the information about the ship, but everyone knew about the ship now. It would be better if Dietz showed up Pike, but the little prick would still be humiliated if Garrett won an acquittal.

By the time the elevator arrived at his floor, Dietz was ready to forget about the *China Sea* and move on with his life. The doors opened, and just as he started to leave the car, Dietz remembered something Denise Blailock had said. He froze with one foot in the car and the other in the hall. The elevator door bumped him and the insistent buzzing of the safety system drove him out of the car. Dietz's body was standing in the hall but his mind was elsewhere.

Chapter Thirty-nine

Tom Oswald had not told Jerry Swanson that he had scanned the fingerprint he'd lifted from the *China Sea* into AFIS, and he had not told him about his conversations with Monte Pike and Max Dietz, but the day after his meeting with Mary Garrett, he decided to bring his partner up to speed. He didn't get the chance right away, because they were called to a traffic accident minutes after they got in their car. As soon as they were able to leave the accident scene, the dispatcher sent them to deal with a domestic beef. Swanson knew the husband and was able to talk him down before any real damage was done. After a whispered conference, the officers decided to leave the now weepy couple in each other's embrace rather than make an arrest. Soon after they drove off, Oswald confessed.

"Fuck, Tom, the chief told you to forget about that fucking ship," Swanson said.

"I said I'm sorry."

Swanson looked away. He was very upset. They drove in silence for a while.

"Do you think we'll have to testify?" Swanson asked.

"We might," Oswald answered.

"I wish you'd talked to me before you did anything. I'm involved, too."

"You're right. I was just pissed off by the way that asshole from Homeland Security treated us. I wasn't thinking clearly."

"Amen to that."

"If we do have to testify, we'll just tell what happened. The whole thing stinks, and I'd love to expose the bastards who pulled this off."

"Amen to that, too."

"Anyway, it's out of our hands now, and I'm sort of relieved that the ship is someone else's problem."

The next hour was quiet, and Oswald was starting to think that they were going to have it easy until their shift ended. Then dispatch sent them to an all-night convenience store/gas station on a deserted stretch of road near a group of rental cabins. The cabins were on a river that was heavily fished in summer, but there were few people around now that winter was creeping in.

Dispatch had told them to contact Jeff Costner, a store customer, who had called 911 to report that he'd been robbed at gunpoint in the parking lot of the store. He said he had not been injured, but the dispatcher said that Mr. Costner sounded very frightened. A cop working a small jurisdiction like Shelby knew every square inch of his beat and everyone in it. Oswald guessed that Costner must be a fisherman who was staying in one of the cabins, because he'd never heard of him.

The cabins and the convenience store were owned by Jed Truffant and his wife, Tiffany. The couple made their nut during tourist season and turned a small profit out of season. They were never going to get rich off the store, but they both loved to fish and seemed content with what they had. They were regular churchgoers and compassionate people, so Oswald assumed they would be comforting Mr. Costner in the warmth of the store. That's why he was surprised to see a man in a windbreaker sitting on the curb outside the store with his head resting in his hands.

Swanson parked a few spots from the man, and the officers got out.

"Mr. Costner?" Tom asked as he walked in front of the patrol vehicle. The man stood up and smiled. When the officers were a few steps away, he pulled a coal black Glock 37 handgun out of his jacket and shot Swanson between the eyes. Oswald froze. Two bullets spiraled into his chest before he could reach for his weapon. The killer's next bullet blew through his forehead, and he was dead when he hit the asphalt.

The door to the store opened, and the blond man who had identified himself as Arn Belson of Homeland Security at the *China Sea* walked out. He had hidden behind the counter next to the body of Tiffany Truffant when he saw the patrol car pull into the lot because he was worried that the officers would recognize him from the *China Sea*. Belson studied the officers.

"It's them," he told the shooter. "Good work. Let's adios before anyone else shows up."

They walked around the corner to where their black SUV was waiting in the shadows.

Later that night, Jed Truffant would find the bodies of the officers and his wife when he came from their cabin to spell Tiffany. By that time, the killers were almost in Seattle.

Chapter Forty

Jack Stamm stood up as soon as Monte Pike, the heads of units in the DA's office, Arnie Lasswell, and the three in-house investigators were seated around the conference table.

"We have a problem," he said. "Max Dietz has disappeared."

Everyone looked surprised. Then they looked at each other and began to ask questions. Stamm held up his hand and the room quieted.

"Max has been depressed ever since I took him out of the Homicide Unit after the *Woodruff* case fell apart. Another problem arose recently, and don't ask me what happened. I'm not going to discuss it. But it made Max's situation worse.

"The last time anyone in this office saw Max was Thursday afternoon. His secretary says that he seemed excited. He asked her for some subpoenas, and then he shut himself in his office. Around three, Max left the office, and no one has seen him since. No alarms went off on Friday. Then there was the weekend. He missed two court appearances Monday and another one Tuesday. His secretary called his house, but she got the answering machine both days. After the Tuesday call, she came to see me."

Stamm nodded toward one of the investigators. "Bob went to Max's house Tuesday afternoon. There was no car in the driveway, and he didn't answer the door. I authorized him to go inside in case there was a medical emergency. The house was neat, and there were no signs of a struggle, and no signs of Max. So, my first question is, does anyone know where he is?"

Dead silence.

"OK, I want each unit head to ask your people if they have any information that can help us find Max. Most of you know Arnie Lasswell." The detective held up his hand. "He's heading up the investigation. Contact him if you get anything. Any questions?"

A few people raised their hands. When Stamm finished answering them, he ended the meeting. Monte Pike held back until everyone else had filed out of the room.

"You don't think Max . . . ?"

The word *suicide* hung in the air between them.

"Monte, I have no clue about why Max disappeared or where he is."

"He was really upset when you wouldn't let him try the case, and this *Brady* thing only made it worse."

"I know. I've been worried about Max, but I never thought he'd do anything stupid."

"I sort of feel responsible. I'm the one who told you about my meeting with Garrett."

"You had to tell me," Stamm said. "Max sat on

Oswald's information because he wanted to win. That was wrong. It was his choice to break the rules, and you had nothing to do with it. Don't beat yourself up because you did the right thing in coming to see me."

"Intellectually I get what you just said, but I'll still feel like shit if something bad has happened to Max because of something I did."

Chapter Forty-one

Great generals shone on the battlefield, Olympic athletes excelled on their playing fields, and Mary Garrett knew she had few equals in a court of law. She was smarter and better prepared than almost every lawyer she'd gone up against, and she truly believed that her work ethic and mental agility were second to none. When she strode through the doors of the Honorable Herbert Brandenburg's court, Mary appeared to be a force of nature, but this time, unlike almost every other time she had gone into battle, she was radiating a confidence she did not feel.

Monte Pike had filed motions *in limine* to keep out all evidence concerning the *China Sea*. Two days ago, her investigator had come into her office shortly after eleven in the morning and told her that Tom Oswald and Jerry Swanson, the eyewitnesses to the events on the ship, were dead. Without Oswald and Swanson, she had little chance of defeating Pike's motions.

Mary hadn't told her client, but Judge Brandenburg's decision on Pike's motions *in limine* would have a huge impact on Mary's ability to win the case. In the motions, Pike was asking the judge for a pretrial decision limiting the evidence the defense would be allowed to introduce at trial concerning the murders on board the *China Sea*, the substance found in the hold, and John Finley's connection to the ship. With that evidence, Mary could present the jurors with an alternative explanation for Finley's murder. Without it, Sarah's chances of an acquittal were slim.

From the outset, Mary had had grave misgivings when she had learned that Sarah's case had been assigned to the elderly jurist. Brandenburg had a full head of snow white hair, a Roman nose, and piercing blue eyes that gave him the appearance of high intelligence, but everyone in the legal community knew that there was a dim bulb beneath the elegant hairdo. Brandenburg had a massive inferiority complex and was loath to admit his inability to understand legal issues. He frequently took the easy way out by ruling for the State in criminal cases, banking on the low reversal rates in appellate courts. He also disliked complicated trials, which Sarah's would become if Mary was allowed to introduce evidence of clandestine government operations or drug smuggling by international drug cartels.

Monte Pike sounded almost apologetic as he outlined to Judge Brandenburg the arguments that would destroy Sarah Woodruff's chance for an acquittal. The young DA's logic was impeccable and left no doubt that his positions were correct. Even Mary was momentarily hypnotized by Pike.

As soon as Pike finished his opening statement, Judge Brandenburg asked Mary for her rebuttal.

"I'd prefer to put on my evidence, Your Honor. The evidence will establish a clear connection between what happened on the *China Sea* and the murder of Mr. Finley," Mary said with more conviction than she really felt.

"Very well. I've read the memos concerning the DVD that led to the dismissal of Ms. Woodruff's first case, and I see Judge Nesbit is in court. Let's hear evidence relevant to Mr. Pike's motion to keep evidence of the DVD from the jury so Judge Nesbit can go about his business," Brandenburg said.

As soon as Nesbit took the oath, Mary asked him a series of questions that established his profession and his connection to Sarah's case.

"Judge Nesbit, please tell Judge Brandenburg what happened in your office prior to court beginning on the last day of Sarah Woodruff's trial," Garrett said.

"I arrived at work an hour or so before court was to begin in order to read over some materials that had been submitted by the parties and found a DVD that had been left for me with a note stating that the DVD contained conclusive proof that John Finley was alive."

Mary turned to the bailiff. "Can you give the judge defendant's Exhibit 1, please?"

The bailiff handed a clear plastic envelope containing the note to the witness.

"Can you identify this object for the record, Judge?"

"That's the note that accompanied the DVD."

"Does it appear to have been typed on a computer?"

"Yes."

"Please give the judge Exhibit 2," Mary told the bailiff.

"Can you identify Exhibit 2?" she asked Nesbit.

"It's the DVD I found in my office."

"Your Honor, I'd like to play the DVD for you," Garrett said.

"No objection," Pike said.

Judge Brandenburg watched intently as John Finley said, "My name is John Finley, and I'm sorry for the confusion my disappearance has caused. Sarah, if you're in the room when they play this, I can't tell you how awful I feel about everything that's happened to you. Unfortunately, I could not reveal the fact that I am alive and well until today. I hope this proof that I am alive will end your ordeal."

"Was the case dismissed with prejudice as a result of this evidence that Mr. Finley had not been murdered?" Mary asked.

"Yes," Judge Nesbit answered.

"I have no further questions of the judge," Mary said.

"Good morning, Judge Nesbit," Monte Pike said with a calm smile. "Is there any place on the DVD where Mr. Finley says that he works for any agency of the United States government?"

"No, he doesn't."

"And there's nothing on the DVD that explains why Mr. Finley didn't come forward sooner, is there?"

"No."

"He could have been on vacation or doing consulting work in some faraway place where communication was difficult?"

"I have no way of answering that question," Nesbit said.

Pike smiled at the witness. "Thank you. I have nothing further to ask of the witness," he said.

"No further witnesses, Your Honor," Mary said.

Pike started to speak, but Brandenburg held up his hand. "Ms. Garrett, why do you think this DVD has any bearing on this new case against your client?"

"It's evidence that John Finley was engaged in some activity important enough to keep him from coming to the aid of an innocent woman who was facing the death penalty."

"Yes, I can accept that, but do you have any evidence that the reason for his lack of action had anything to do with this new charge?"

With Oswald and Swanson as witnesses, Mary would have had a fighting chance to show a connection, but the fingerprint evidence was meaningless without evidence that proved that Finley had been on a ship smuggling hashish.

"I've attempted to gather that evidence, but the CIA and other government intelligence agencies have refused to honor our requests for information about the *China Sea* and Mr. Finley's involvement with the ship."

"I can't do anything about that, Ms. Garrett. I have no jurisdiction over the federal government."

"I've issued subpoenas to Homeland Security for information about Agent Belson and the *China Sea*.

They've refused to comply. You can hold a hearing and compel them to produce this evidence.

"I've also requested the payroll records of Homeland Security and the CIA and the personnel records of the agencies, and they've asserted national security as a reason for refusing the request."

"Your Honor, if I may," Pike interrupted, "Assistant United States Attorney Avery Bishop is in court to address these issues."

An African American in a severe gray business suit, carrying a black attaché case, stood up in the back of the room. He was bald and sported a thin salt-and-pepper mustache. Wire-rimmed glasses perched on a small, broad nose magnified his brown eyes.

"May I approach, Your Honor?"

"Yes, yes. Come through the bar of the court, Mr. Bishop."

"Thank you, Your Honor." Bishop handed a thick stack of papers to the clerk and an identical stack to Mary Garrett. "I've just handed the clerk and Ms. Garrett a motion to quash the subpoenas Ms. Garrett prepared, along with a memorandum of law. The United States government is asserting the state-secrets privilege as a bar to any inquiries Ms. Garrett might make on behalf of her client concerning a ship allegedly named the *China Sea*, Mr. John Finley, Mr. Arn Belson, and any persons or objects allegedly connected to this ship in any way. Supporting our motion is a declaration from the director of National Intelligence."

"We don't deal with many state secrets in the Multnomah County Circuit Court," Judge Brandenburg said with a chuckle. "I'm afraid I'm not familiar with that privilege."

Bishop smiled back. "Not to worry, Your Honor. I'm here to enlighten you. The state-secrets privilege is a common-law evidentiary privilege that permits the government to bar the disclosure of information if there is a reasonable danger that disclosure will expose matters which, in the interests of national security, should not be exposed. I'm here to make a formal claim of privilege on behalf of Homeland Security, the National Security Agency, the Defense Intelligence Agency, and the Central Intelligence Agency—the organizations on which Ms. Garrett served subpoenas."

Mary Garrett stood. "Your Honor, it appears that Mr. Bishop is conceding the existence of an intelligence operation involving hashish and the *China Sea*."

"If I may?" Bishop asked the judge.

"Go ahead, Mr. Bishop."

"The privilege was first asserted in 1953 in *United States v. Reynolds*. In that case, the widows of three crew members of a B-29 Superfortress bomber that crashed in 1948 sought accident reports on the crash but were told that the release of these details would threaten national security by revealing the bomber's top-secret mission. The United States Supreme Court held that the executive branch could bar evidence from the court if it deemed that its release would impair national security."

"If I recall correctly, Your Honor," Mary said, "in 1996, the accident reports were declassified and released and were found to contain no secret information. They did, however, contain information about the poor condition of the aircraft that would have compromised the Air Force's case. It seems to me that the privilege is being invoked here to cover up the involvement of the United States government in drug smuggling, and that is not a legitimate use of the privilege."

"Your Honor," Pike said, "the defendant has not established that any drugs were on the ship."

"We would be able to prove that there was hashish on board if I were able to subpoena the records concerning this matter," Mary said.

"Your Honor," Bishop answered, "the assertion of the privilege bars any discussion of this matter in this court. It is privileged and simply may not be discussed."

"And rightly so," Judge Brandenburg said as he skimmed the memo. "You can't let foreign powers and terrorists get the records you seek, Ms. Garrett. I'm not letting you go on a fishing expedition when it might compromise national security."

"Judge Brandenburg," Mary said, "I don't believe that the state-secrets privilege applies to criminal cases. It's a rule of civil procedure."

"The type of case makes no difference, Your Honor," Bishop argued. "The purpose of the rule is to keep our nation's enemies from learning secrets that could undermine the security of the United States of America."

"This is a death-penalty case, Your Honor," Mary said. "My client may die without the evidence we seek."

"Death-penalty cases are governed by the same rules of evidence that are used in shoplifting cases, Ms. Garrett. Mr. Pike's motions will be allowed, and I will not permit you to introduce any evidence or testimony about the *China Sea*."

Part Five

Death Row

2012

Chapter Forty-two

It was after two in the morning when Dana finished the record in *Woodruff*. She thought that the State's case in the second trial was thin, but the defense couldn't counter the evidence connecting the bullets that killed John Finley to the gun that was seized in the gang- and drug-related murder that Sarah Woodruff had investigated. Monte Pike had introduced logs from the evidence room that proved that Woodruff was the officer who took the gun to and from the courtroom. Then he put on testimony about throw-down weapons, guns stolen from crime scenes or arrested criminals that rogue police officers threw down at the scene of a shooting when they discovered that a person they shot was unarmed. Pike argued that Woodruff had taken the gun to hold as a throw-down if she ever got into that type of situation and had used it to murder Finley.

Mary Garrett had tried to have Sarah testify about the statements John Finley had made to her on the evening he was murdered, but the judge agreed with Monte Pike that the statements were hearsay and excluded them. Then Garrett had tried to raise a reasonable doubt by introducing the passports and ID found in the duffel bag, but Pike had argued that whatever Finley was involved in was irrelevant because the murder weapon was linked to only one person involved in the case, the defendant. Without the evidence about the *China Sea* incident and Finley's statements to Sarah Woodruff, the defense had very little to argue.

The jury had been out one day before finding Woodruff guilty of aggravated murder. It had taken them another two days to produce the findings that had forced the judge to impose a death sentence.

Dana had emptied her coffee pot sometime around one thirty, and what remained in her mug was lukewarm. She popped it in the microwave and grabbed a legal pad on which she'd been making notes. When the coffee had been nuked, she sipped from the mug and began making a to-do list on a new page. At the top of the list she wrote, "plane and hotel reservations."

Portland, Oregon, is one of America's most beautiful cities, but Dana Cutler wasn't thinking about the high green hills that towered over it, the distant snow-capped mountains you could see from, or the river that wound through it when her plane began its descent. Portland evoked dark memories for Dana. The only other time she'd been in the City of Roses, she was running for her life, she almost died, and she'd left with the blood of two men on her hands.

Dana picked up a rental car at the airport and

was downtown twenty minutes later. After checking into her hotel, she showered, then put on a white silk blouse and a severe navy blue business suit. Dana rarely wore anything but jeans and T-shirts, and she always felt a little odd in a suit, the way she imagined a Wall Street investment banker might feel if she slipped into black leather.

Dana walked the four blocks from her hotel to Mary Garrett's law office. Before leaving D.C., Dana had made an appointment with Garrett, and she arrived with a few minutes to spare. After a brief wait, the receptionist ushered her into the defense attorney's office.

Dana had done her homework, so the attorney's unusual appearance didn't surprise her. She soon found herself seated in a director's chair with a seat and back of black leather and arms and legs of polished metal tubing. The seat sagged a little, decreasing the height of the chair's occupant. Garrett sat behind a wide glass desk on a high-backed chair of black leather that Dana guessed could be elevated by pushing a button, so the diminutive attorney could always look down at her clients.

"When you made your appointment, you told my secretary that you were calling from Washington," Mary said. "You should know that I'm not a member of the Washington bar, and I can't practice there."

"I must not have made myself clear," Dana answered with her best smile. "I was calling from Washington, D. C., not Washington State, and I'm not here to consult with you on a legal matter."

Mary's brow knit. "Then why are you here?"

Dana handed Mary one of the business cards she'd had printed the day after her meeting with Patrick Gorman.

"I'm a reporter for *Exposed*, a D.C. newspaper, and I'm here on a story."

"Isn't *Exposed* a supermarket tabloid?"

"Primarily, but we're publishing more hard news now."

"That's right. Your paper broke the Farrington case."

"And won a Pulitzer Prize for our coverage. We're not all about alien abductions and Bigfoot sightings anymore." Dana leaned forward and tried to project sincerity. "Ms. Garrett, Patrick Gorman, my editor, is fascinated by Sarah Woodruff's case. Being charged two times with murdering the same person is highly unusual, and the unusual is what sells our paper."

"The case sounds odder than it really is," Mary said. "The DA rushed to judgment the first time and charged Sarah without evidence that John Finley was actually dead."

"I'd say the case still has some pretty amazing elements," Dana said. "We have a dead man with no past who may be a spy involved in a covert operation. Then there's the mystery ship, the vanishing night watchman, and the disappearing hashish."

"There's no denying that this is not a run-of-the-mill case," Mary conceded, "but before we go any further, I'd like to know what *Exposed* plans to do with this story. I appreciate your interest and the fact that you've flown to Portland, but Ms. Woodruff is my client, and her interests are my paramount concern. I can't discuss her case without her permission."

"Ms. Garrett, our coverage of your client's case can only work in her favor. I did plenty of research before I came here, so I know a lot about what happened. There will be an outcry once the public learns that an innocent woman is on death row because the government is withholding evidence that could clear her. The publicity should help your efforts to get cert granted."

"I don't think the justices are influenced by the opinion of your readers."

"Public opinion is a powerful force. Even justices of the Supreme Court are aware of it. One never knows what influences a judge's decision in a close case. Then there's the possibility of the story convincing a whistle-blower to come forward. Someone knows what John Finley was up to. Time has passed."

Dana hoped Garrett would decide that talking to her probably couldn't hurt her client's chances and might help.

"Ask me your questions," Mary said, "and I'll answer those I can without breaching attorney-client confidentiality. But I want your promise that you'll let me screen anything you plan to print to make sure there's nothing in the story that can compromise Sarah's case."

"I'll have to clear it with my editor, but I'm sure Mr. Gorman will go along with it."

"So, what do you want to know?"

"Why don't you fill me in on the two cases? As I said, I've read a lot about them, but I'd love to get your take."

Garrett gave Dana a quick recap of the events

that led to Sarah Woodruff's first arrest and the dismissal of her first indictment, followed by a short version of the second case.

"At Sarah's second trial, I tried to prove that Finley was involved in dangerous undercover work, but the intelligence agencies used the state-secrets privilege to stymie my inquiries. Then the judge kept out statements Finley made to Sarah on hearsay grounds."

"It looks like Ms. Woodruff's freedom rests on showing Finley's connection to a CIA smuggling operation," Dana said.

"Or drug dealers. Finley told Sarah that he thought that the crew member who murdered everyone on the *China Sea* made an arrangement with a Mexican cartel for the hashish. There were also rumors that Finley's kidnappers were after two hundred fifty thousand dollars that Finley supposedly was given to finance the smuggling operation."

"This is the first I've heard of money being involved."

"It was a rumor that was circulated on the street by drug dealers and users."

"How strong was the evidence that Finley was the survivor of the shootout on the *China Sea*?"

"That's a fact. The night watchman who called 911 told Tom Oswald, the investigating officer from Shelby PD, that he'd seen a man stagger off the ship and drive away. The guard thought the man might be wounded. He also saw another car that may have been following the wounded man.

"During Finley's autopsy, the medical examiner found a bullet wound in Finley's side that was older than the wounds caused by the bullets that killed him. Then there was the duffel bag found next to Finley's body, the one with the phony passports and ID. There were bloodstains on the bag. Some were old and some were new. If Finley was wounded on the night of the murders on the *China Sea* and shot again on the evening he died, it would explain the two different groups of bloodstains.

"Another thing. Shortly after Finley disappeared that first time, the bodies of two men with ties to a Mexican drug cartel were found just off a logging road. I think these were the men who kidnapped Finley, but I didn't have a shred of evidence connecting the men to our case, so the judge wouldn't admit any evidence about the dead men.

"Then there's the clincher. After Sarah was indicted the second time, I learned that Oswald lifted a latent print from a hatch covering the hashish. Shortly before Sarah's first trial was supposed to start, a deputy DA ran one of the unknown prints from Sarah's condo and matched it to that print found on the hatch. After Finley was murdered, they took his prints and made the match.

"It's clear to me that Finley was wounded on the *China Sea*. Sarah's condo was the closest place he could think of to go, so that's where he headed. The Mexicans were watching the ship and tailed him to Sarah's place, kidnapped him, took him to the area with the logging road, and were killed when Finley was rescued. But after the judge's rulings and the assertion of the state-secrets privilege by the government, I had no way to prove any of it."

"Do you think the men who rescued Finley were with the CIA?" Dana asked.

"Probably. Someone paid for that ship. Finley's company, TA Enterprises, is a shell corporation. I'm certain it was created to purchase the *China Sea* and finance the hashish smuggling operation. But who put up the money? My bet is the CIA. The passports and phony ID point that way, too."

"You're talking about the stuff found in the duffel bag?"

Mary nodded. "While I was preparing for Sarah's first trial, she told me some names she'd heard Finley mention: Dennis Lang, Larry Kester, and Orrin Hadley. In the duffel bag that was found with Finley's body were several passports and sets of phony ID. Lang, Hadley, and Kester were the aliases Finley used. He could have gotten the ID and passports on the street, but an expert I hired to look at them told me they were a first-rate job. He couldn't swear that only a government agency could make something that authentic, but they looked like something the CIA would turn out.

"That's why I made the discovery requests. If I could have proved that Finley was involved with drug smuggling or terrorists or the CIA, I would have had a viable argument that someone other than Sarah killed him. But I dropped the inquiries when Sarah's first case was dismissed and, as I said, I was stonewalled when I made them again after the second indictment. The attack on the state-secrets privilege is a cornerstone of our argument in the Supreme Court."

"Is there anything else you can think of that I should know?" Dana asked.

Mary looked as though she was going to say something, but she paused.

"Yes?" Dana prodded.

"Well, there was another odd thing that happened during the second prosecution, but I don't think it had anything to do with Sarah's case directly. On the other hand, you might be able to use it to spice up your article.

"Max Dietz prosecuted Sarah the first time. He just rushed to judgment. Then he kept information from me that the law compelled him to turn over to the defense. He was reprimanded by the DA. Shortly after, he disappeared."

"Just vanished?"

Mary nodded. "This was a few weeks before the motions in Sarah's case. The last person to see him was his secretary. He asked her for some blank subpoenas and took them into his office. He left a little later and hasn't been heard from since."

"Any idea what happened?"

"He was very depressed by his demotion out of the Homicide Unit after the first trial, and the most prominent theory is that he committed suicide after he was reprimanded for hiding the exculpatory evidence from me. But that's just a theory. No body has been found."

"I do have a last request. Do you think it would be possible to talk to Sarah?"

"I'll ask her, but it's her decision."

"Great."

"Tell me where you're staying. As soon as Sarah tells me whether she'll meet with you, I'll let you know."

Dana told Mary the name of her hotel and her room number.

"Another thing, are Officers Oswald and Swanson still on the Shelby police force?"

Garrett shook her head. She looked sad. "They're both dead."

"What?"

"Shortly before the second trial, they answered a 911 call about a robbery in progress at a convenience store and were gunned down by the robbers."

"Was anyone arrested?"

"No. There were no witnesses, and the clerk was killed, too."

"An interesting coincidence, don't you think?"

"You mean because all of the witnesses to what happened on the *China Sea* are either dead or missing? I've thought about that, but there's nothing I've heard that leads me to believe that they were murdered because of what they saw on the ship."

"Thanks for taking the time to talk to me, Ms. Garrett, and for what it's worth, I'd say you did a good job but kept running into a brick wall."

"I don't know how good a job I did. Sarah's on death row. But you're right about that wall. Someone doesn't want what Finley was doing made public, and it's not going to be unless the United States Supreme Court rules that they have to."

Chapter Forty-three

When Daphne Haggard opened her front door, she was assaulted by the scent of herbs and spices. Her husband was sweet, considerate, and great in bed, but she always told her friends that Brett had seduced her with his mastery of their kitchen. Daphne liked to think that she was considerate and good in the sack, but it was no secret that she couldn't cook worth a damn. Brett's passion was food and his flexible hours as an academic let him practice his hobby frequently. Daphne never knew what culinary delight awaited her on her return home. The divine aromas drew Daphne into the kitchen. Brett had his back to her, and she wrapped her arms around him and gave him a peck on the cheek.

"Out, woman," he growled. "Can't you see I'm working?"

"What am I smelling?" she moaned.

"I've conjured up a golden oldie," Brett said. "Chicken Marbella. You're smelling oregano, prunes, garlic. It's been marinating in the fridge all night."

"It looks heavenly, and I haven't eaten since breakfast."

Brett looked over his shoulder. "What happened to lunch?"

"A traffic fatality on Wentworth Road just as I was headed to Elsie's Café. I'm starving."

"Hang in for another twenty minutes. It'll be worth it," Brett assured her.

Daphne was about to answer him when the cell phone she used for police business rang. She tugged it out of her jacket pocket and walked into the living room, grateful for anything that would distract her from her growling stomach.

"Detective Haggard," she answered.

"Amal Shastri here, calling from the Orthosure offices in Omaha."

A friend of Daphne's at Princeton had been an upper-class Indian, and Shastri's clipped British accent made her think of him.

"Thank you for returning my call, Dr. Shastri," Daphne said.

"I was at a conference in New York City," the president of Orthosure said. "I have just returned today, or I would have gotten back to you sooner. I was intrigued. Your message states that you are a homicide detective?"

"Yes, sir," she said. "I'm with the Inverness Police Department in Wisconsin, and I was hoping you could help me solve a mystery."

"That sounds exciting. How can I do that?"

"Inverness is a college town in the northern part of the state. The area surrounding the campus is heavily forested. A few weeks ago, a student came across the remains of a human thigh."

"My goodness."

"She was pretty shaken up."

"I would imagine."

"We were set to search for other body parts when bad weather moved in. I didn't have much hope once the storm passed, but we got lucky and found the other thigh. The medical examiner X-rayed it. The victim's leg had been broken at some point and there was an orthopedic appliance—a stainless steel rod—that had been inserted to stabilize the fracture. When we examined the rod, we found Orthosure's maker's mark and a serial number. If I give you the number, could you identify the patient?"

"I couldn't, but the surgeon who inserted the rod should be able to."

"How can we find him?"

"Our records will tell me what hospital ordered the appliance. Part of the serial number tells us the year in which it was shipped. The hospital can give you the names of the orthopedic surgeons who operated in the given year. You'd have to interview them, but there should be a sticker from the rod with the serial number attached to the surgeon's notes. It would be in the patient's file."

"That's great."

"What is the serial number?" Shastri asked.

"05-8L9765G."

"OK, well that narrows it down. The 05 means 2005, so you have your year. I'll have my secretary call you with the name of the hospital."

Daphne thanked Shastri for his help and hung up. Then she smiled. Shastri was right, solving mys-

teries was exciting. It beat the hell out of rousting
drunks and dealing with domestic disputes. And
they had a grade A, first-class mystery on their hands
in little Inverness. It also looked like she would be a
step closer to figuring out the victim's identity any
day now. *Take that, Jessica Fletcher,* Daphne thought.
Ace detective Daphne Haggard is hot on the trail in The
Case of Severed Thigh.

Chapter Forty-four

Officer Earl Moffit had been a character witness for Sarah Woodruff during the penalty phase of her trial, and Mary Garrett had recommended him as a person to talk to for background. When Dana walked into the Starbucks on Pioneer Square, she spotted a man in jeans and a jacket with a Seattle Mariners logo, nursing a caffe latte at a corner table. The man looked to be in his early thirties. He had blue eyes, shaggy black hair, and a rangy, athletic build and matched Mary Garrett's description. The latte was the only thing that made Dana hesitate. On the East Coast, cops fueled their engines with harsh black coffee, and Dana had a hard time accepting the fact that cops in this land of Starbucks sipped these frothy drinks.

"Officer Moffit?" Dana asked.

When the man nodded, Dana took the seat opposite him.

"Thanks for meeting with me," she said.

"Mary vouched for you. She's one of the few defense attorneys whose word I'll trust."

"I know what you mean," Dana said. "I was a cop in D.C."

"Mary told me you're a reporter. Why'd you leave the force?"

That was the question she dreaded. "On-the-job injury," Dana said, giving Moffit the bland answer that usually satisfied anyone who asked why she wasn't a cop anymore.

"You were Sarah's partner?" Dana continued, hoping to head off further inquiry about her reasons for leaving the police force.

Moffit nodded. "For three years."

"You must have gotten along well."

"We did. Sarah was aiming at detective, but she was good on the street. She handled tense situations well and could be tough when she had to be."

"Can you give me an example?"

"Sure," Moffit said. Then he laughed. "We get this domestic violence call and pull up to this bungalow that hasn't seen a paint job since the Flood, with a yard that's like a zoo for weeds. We hear the screams as soon as we get out of the car. I knock and announce that we're cops, but the screaming doesn't stop, so we try the door. It's unlocked.

"When we get inside, this woman who looks like she weighs three hundred pounds is cursing a blue streak in Spanish—none of which I understand—at this guy with blood streaming from his nose and a gash under his eye. The guy is covered with tattoos and wearing a wife-beater undershirt.

"Now the guy isn't that big, but he looks like he pumps iron, and he's really irate. Right away I figure him for the abuser, and I wedge myself between the two of them with my back to the woman. I'm pushing the guy away when I hear movement behind me.

The guy gets a horrified expression on his face and starts screaming in Spanish. Sarah translated it for me when we were done with the call. The guy was screaming, 'Look out.' Then I hear a crack like a board breaking and the guy drives right through me. I grab him, and we're rolling on the floor, so I can't see what's happening.

"So this was the day I learned to forget about stereotypes. The woman was the abuser. She beat up her husband regularly. But when I went for him, she got protective and went for me with a carving knife. The crack was her wrist breaking where Sarah hit it with the handle of her gun. And the next crack was the woman's knee giving way. Sarah's real good at self-defense. In addition to the woman, I've seen her take down men who outweighed her by a lot."

"She sounds like someone you'd want watching your back," Dana said.

"Definitely."

"She also sounds like someone who would be capable of murder."

Moffit took a sip of his drink and mulled over Dana's comment. When he answered, he looked very serious.

"Sarah could do that, but I don't think she did."

"Tell me a little about her personality."

"Sarah's very tough, driven, and she likes a challenge. She skydives, she climbs mountains."

"She's a risk taker?"

"Yeah, but she's not crazy. She got me up Mount Hood the first year we worked together, and she took all of the safety precautions."

"Did she take risks on the street?"

"No. I would have asked for another partner if I thought she was a cowboy. But she liked the action. I can handle it OK, but I wouldn't be sorry if I never ran into another bad situation. I think she preferred tense situations."

"So she was a good cop?" Dana asked.

Moffit took another long drink of coffee. "Yeah, overall. She cut corners on occasion, but I always felt comfortable riding with her."

"Did she ever do anything illegal?"

"You're asking me if she was dirty?" Moffit sounded offended.

"I'm just asking."

"No, she was straight. I never saw her do anything crooked."

"Did Sarah ever talk about John Finley?"

Moffit nodded. "When he first moved to Portland."

"What did she say?"

"She told me about meeting him after she climbed that mountain in South America and how he showed up."

"Mary tried to get evidence that would prove John Finley was a government agent. Did she ever say anything about that?"

"Not to me."

"I think I've exhausted my questions. Do you want to tell me anything else?"

"Only that I don't think she did it. Everything I know points toward spooks. Finley sounds like he was into mysteries we average folks don't deal with."

Chapter Forty-five

The Willamette Valley Correctional Facility for Women had been selected by the Oregon Department of Corrections to house female death-row prisoners. Sarah Woodruff had the dubious honor of being the institution's first and only death row resident. A chain-link fence topped by barbed wire surrounded the low-slung, pastel yellow buildings. A service road circled the prison, and the land on the other side of the road had been ground down and stripped away. Anyone escaping would be visible to the guards until they made it to the evergreens that grew half a mile beyond the fence. In the distance were low green hills and a vast blue sky.

Dana was expected. After she signed in and passed through the metal detector, a guard led her down the prison corridors to the noncontact visiting room, where she waited for the institution's most famous inmate. Fifteen minutes later, a thick metal door opened on the other side of the bulletproof glass, and Sarah Woodruff shuffled in dressed in a baggy jumpsuit and wearing manacles. Her complexion was pasty, a result of the starchy institutional food and lack of sunlight, but the former policewoman held her head high despite her depressing situation. Dana was pleased to see that the prisoner had maintained her dignity.

Woodruff eyed Dana warily while the guard took off her chains. When the guard left, she sat in an orange molded plastic chair and picked up the receiver that was affixed to the wall.

"Thank you for seeing me," Dana said into an identical receiver.

"You're a reporter, right?"

Dana nodded.

"And you're here to do a story about my case?"

"Yes. We think we can stir up support for your cause by letting our readers know how the government kept you from getting a fair trial."

"You might make some money off the papers you sell, too," Sarah said.

"There's that, too. Even reporters have to eat."

"I hope exploiting me helps fatten you up, Miss Cutler."

Dana found it interesting that Sarah had made no effort to mask her cynicism, even though Mary Garrett must have told her that Dana was there to help. It was a good sign that Woodruff was not trying to manipulate her. She looked straight through the glass and locked her eyes on Woodruff's.

"Selling papers does put food on my plate. That doesn't mean I don't think you were fucked over. I'm in this for the money *and* because I think you got a raw deal."

"Mary said you were a detective with the D.C. police. What did you work?"

"Vice and Narcotics. Now I'm an investigative reporter. You use a lot of the same skills. The big difference is that I can't use a rubber hose to get people to talk to me."

Sarah didn't smile at the joke. "I wanted to be a detective," she said. "That dream ended the minute I was arrested."

Dana leaned forward. "We want to help you get your life back on track, and the first step is a new trial. There are so many unanswered questions in your case. Especially those involving the intelligence agencies. Hopefully, Ms. Garrett will get answers to them if the Supreme Court sends your case back on the national-security issue."

"That's where I was really screwed," Woodruff said, her anger barely contained. "The government shut us down. They raised that state-secrets bullshit, and I never had a chance."

"Why do you think the government worked so hard to keep the truth from coming out?"

Sarah laughed bitterly. "That's easy. Can you imagine the uproar if the public found out its government was dealing drugs? Someone somewhere is scared to death of what would happen if the truth about the *China Sea* came out. I'm certain that John was killed by the CIA because he could prove hashish was smuggled in on the *China Sea*."

"Before I ask you about the facts of your case, I'd like to talk a little about your childhood and how you ended up on the police force."

"Why do you need to know that?"

"I'm writing an article that I'm hoping will help you get a new trial, so I've got to make our readers see you as a real person."

"I'd rather not talk about my past. Can't you get all that from Mary? She had me write an autobiography for the sentencing phase of my trial."

"I need to hear it from you—how *you* see your life, not how an expert witness dissected it. All our readers know about you now is that you're a convicted killer."

"Nothing I tell you is going to endear me to them. My early life wasn't pretty. I was lucky to escape from it in one piece."

"There was testimony about abuse during the sentencing hearing."

"Yeah, well, those were some of my earliest memories of dear old Dad, may he rot in hell."

"How long did it go on?"

"Until he died, which fortunately was when I was nine. He was a trucker. There was a big pileup on an icy road in Montana. I hear he burned to death. I hope it's true."

Woodruff paused and caught her breath. Dana waited before asking about Sarah's mother.

"Living with that bastard took its toll. He beat her when he was home. She was a dishrag. She never protected me, even when I told her what was going on. She screamed at me, accused me of lying. She was drunk most of the time, and she'd drink enough to pass out when he was home so she could claim she didn't know what was happening. I got out of there as soon as I could."

Dana consulted her notes. "You ran away several times."

"They'd bring me back, and I'd plot my next exit. When I turned sixteen, I took off for good. I'd heard Oregon was a good place to go, and that's how I ended up here. I lied about my age. That was easy. I always looked older than I was. Got a job waitressing and soon found out that waiting tables was not what I wanted to do all my life. So I got a GED, worked my way through community college, scholarship to Portland State, and on to the police academy."

"Do you ever talk to your mom?" Dana asked.

"She died. I found out about that by chance. After I left, I never called, and to the best of my knowledge, she never tried to contact me."

"What made you choose law enforcement as a career?"

"It gave me a chance to arrest scumbags like my father," Sarah answered without hesitation.

Dana couldn't help admiring Woodruff's strength. She was impressed by Sarah's ability to hold herself together through the isolation and despair she must be experiencing on death row, and she was starting to like the woman. But before she got carried away, Dana reminded herself that with the right circumstances, even women of good character could kill.

Dana spent twenty more minutes on background before asking Sarah her first question about the incident that had put her on death row.

"I've read the transcript of your first trial, and I've got a pretty good grasp of what happened the first time you were accused of killing John Finley.

I'd like you to tell me what happened the night he was really killed."

"Yeah, well, that was interesting. It was a repeat performance. I was sleeping, and a noise woke me. I got my gun and went downstairs, and there was John, looking guilty as hell. I wanted to kill him. I really did, because of everything he'd put me through."

"Did you?" Dana asked.

"No, I did not," Woodruff answered without flinching. "John was alive when he left my house."

"Did he tell you why he broke in?"

"Yes. He told me everything."

"Why?"

Woodruff smiled. "When I came downstairs, I was furious. I fired a shot into the floor. He could see how mad I was, and he was desperate to talk me out of shooting him, so he spewed out his story to distract me and to convince me that he had no choice when he let me go to trial."

"Why did he return to your house? He had to know you wouldn't be very happy to see him."

"He was on the run, and he needed the passports and phony ID in his duffel bag."

"The one that was found with his body?"

Woodruff nodded. "He'd stashed it at my house the night he was kidnapped. I didn't know the damn thing was there until he told me."

"What was his version of what happened on the *China Sea*?"

"John was the ship's captain. He was using a false name, and the crew knew him as Orrin Hadley.

John told me that the *China Sea* rendezvoused with a freighter that sailed from Karachi, Pakistan, with a load of hashish. The Pakistanis transferred the load to the *China Sea* midocean. The hashish was supposed to be off-loaded at the dock in Shelby where the ship had been moored.

"The evening he was kidnapped, a crew member named Steve Talbot killed all of the other crew members and tried to kill John. John got lucky and killed Talbot in a gunfight. He assumed that Talbot was after the hashish and figured out that he couldn't be acting alone because there was too much of it for one man to get off the ship. He knew he had to get away before Talbot's accomplices arrived. He took the duffel bag with him when he escaped."

"Why did he stash it in your house in the first place?"

"John was wounded in the gunfight on the ship, and he had to get help. He drove to my condo because I was the only person he felt he could turn to. He was hoping I would help him and keep my mouth shut, for old times' sake."

"You said that John was on the run the evening he was really murdered," Woodruff said.

Sarah nodded.

"Who was he running from?"

"I never found out."

"What happened when he got to your condo on the evening he was kidnapped? I'm talking about the first time."

"He'd lived with me and still had a key. He hid the duffel bag as soon as he got inside. Then he started for the stairs. He was going to my bedroom to wake me so I could help him with his wound. He was halfway to the stairs when two men broke in and attacked him. That's when I came down and was knocked unconscious.

"John told me he was locked in the trunk of a car and driven to the place where the men planned to kill him. He was pulled out of the trunk and forced onto his knees. John was certain he was going to die. Then the man who was behind him collapsed and knocked John to the ground. As he was falling, he saw the other man's head explode. Moments later, several men appeared and removed his restraints. They were CIA operatives. John told me that the smuggling operation was run by the CIA."

"How did the CIA know where the kidnappers had taken Finley?"

"The Agency had the *China Sea* under surveillance as soon as it docked, but the men who were watching didn't realize what had happened on the ship. When they heard shots and saw John drive off, they followed John to my house. Then they heard more shots and saw the kidnappers leave with John. They followed and rescued him. John was driven to a safe house where his wounds were treated. When he recovered, he helped set up the sale of the hashish."

"Did John tell you who his kidnappers were working for?" Dana asked.

"He thought that Steve Talbot was dealing with a Mexican drug cartel and probably didn't realize that the CIA was behind the smuggling operation.

The people that tried to kill John were part of this cartel."

"Why did John wait so long to come forward?"

"Everything that happened on the *China Sea* was hushed up so the people who were going to buy the hashish from John wouldn't know about the killings on the ship and the cartel's attempt to steal the goods. John was undercover during my arrest and most of my trial. He told me he would have come forward, but he couldn't risk blowing his cover. He said he insisted on clearing me as soon as the deal was complete."

"Your neighbor told the police that she heard a loud argument the night Finley died. Did you argue?" Dana asked.

Woodruff nodded. "At one point, we were yelling at each other."

"You told everyone that you fired one shot into the floor before you realized that John was the person who'd broken in."

"That's right."

"Your neighbor thought she heard two shots."

"She was mistaken. One bullet was dug out of the floor in the entryway. I didn't fire again."

"How do you explain the coincidence of the murder weapon being a gun that was connected to one of your cases?"

Woodruff looked directly at Dana. "Remember who you're dealing with. The people who want this hushed up control the most powerful intelligence agency in the world. If they wanted me to be the fall guy for John's murder, how difficult do you think it would be for them to steal a gun from the police property room?"

"I see your point. Did Mary tell you about the men who were found on the logging trail?"

"Yes. Mary showed me autopsy and crime-scene photographs. I only saw the man in the leather jacket briefly before I was knocked unconscious, and my memory of the fight is hazy, but one of the men could be the man who was fighting with John."

"There were rumors that the drug dealers were after a quarter-million dollars that Finley was using to finance the smuggling operation. Did John talk about that?"

Woodruff's brow furrowed. Then she shook her head. "Mary mentioned it to me, but John never did. If he had that much money, he wouldn't want anyone to know about it, would he? I guess it could have been in the duffel bag. I never saw inside it. And he was pretty shaken when he was telling me what happened. I'd caught him breaking in, and I'd fired a shot into the floor. He had to be worried that I was going to kill him, because he could see how angry I was. John blurted out everything he told me. It wasn't orderly, the way I just said it. He was just saying things as quickly as he could think of them to convince me to let him go."

"Do you think he made up what he told you because he was desperate? Could the CIA story have been an invention?"

"If it was, who killed him?"

"What if the smuggling operation was John's idea or the idea of someone he worked with who had no connection to American intelligence?"

"You're forgetting the men from Homeland Security who made the *China Sea* and the hashish disappear."

"They may have pretended to be from Homeland Security so no one would question them when they took the hashish away. We could just be dealing with two different gangs of dope dealers."

"Dana, I don't know who killed John. I can only guess. The only thing I know for certain is that it wasn't me."

"*Exposed* is going to put as much pressure as we can on the Supreme Court so it will send your case back for a new trial and give you a chance to prove that."

"If they don't, I want to die as soon as possible."

"Don't give up hope."

The determination that had suffused Sarah's features faded away, and she looked tired.

"I don't have any hope, Dana. All I have are days that stretch on and on and are always the same. Do you have any idea what it's like to sit in a small cell all day with nothing to keep you occupied but your thoughts? I had a life. I've stood on mountaintops that pierced the clouds. I've skydived through space, floating like an eagle. Now I see the sky once a day for a half hour. Now all I have is the strong possibility that I will die for something I did not do."

During the return trip to Portland, Dana couldn't stop thinking about Sarah Woodruff. Everything about her was impressive: her self-possession in the face of so much adversity, the way she'd survived her childhood and made something of herself when it would have been so easy to give up, and the way she'd confronted Dana when most people would have tried to curry favor. Dana knew the danger in drawing conclusions about guilt or innocence. She had not been in Sarah's condo on the night Finley was murdered, but she couldn't help but feel that had she been, she would have seen Finley leave the condo alive.

Whether Sarah was guilty or innocent, Dana found it hard to believe that a jury would convict if it was in possession of all of the facts. There would have to be a reasonable doubt in the mind of a fair juror who learned about the *China Sea* and the drug dealers who were found murdered in the forest. She hoped that *Exposed* could raise a big enough stink to sway public opinion, and she prayed that her investigation would help take Sarah Woodruff off death row.

Chapter Forty-six

Dana could not believe that Monte Pike was the chief criminal deputy in the district attorney's office of a major metropolitan city. He looked more like a junior-high student than a law-school graduate; none of his clothes matched, and his hair was going in all sorts of directions, like the panicky participants in the running of the bulls. If Pike told her that he was blind and had dressed without help, Dana would have accepted the explanation. Dana also knew that the way Pike looked was deceiving. Mary Garrett had told her about the attorney's Harvard degree and his reputation as a brilliant, fair, but hard-nosed adversary.

"Thanks for seeing me, Mr. Pike."

"Hey, it's not often I get to meet a celebrity. Nice work on Farrington. It takes guts to go up against the president."

"I didn't have much choice."

"Still, most people would have crawled in a hole and shoveled dirt over themselves in your situation. So, what can I do for you?"

"As I told your secretary, I do some reporting for *Exposed* now, and the *Woodruff* case is my current assignment."

Pike smiled. "I'm not surprised. It's got conspiracies and CIA assassins, not to mention Mexican drug lords and ghost ships. And, like your paper's other favorite subjects—the Abominable Snowman, ETs, and the Loch Ness monster—Woodruff's defense is a complete work of fiction."

"You're saying that the *China Sea*, those five dead men, and the hashish never existed?"

Pike laughed. "The ship and the dead men are probably real. As to the hashish . . ." Pike shrugged. "We'll never know for sure. No, it's the defense that's a work of fiction. Sarah Woodruff shot John Finley to death and dumped him in the park. Ninjas and Mexican hit men had nothing to do with it. That's all part of Mary Garrett's cleverly constructed smoke screen."

"You sound like you're pretty sure of yourself."

"And you're probably thinking that I'm one of these cocksure prosecutors who decides who the bad guy is, then picks and chooses the evidence, discarding anything that doesn't fit his theory, but I'm not. Mary and I had this talk the first time she told me what Oswald had seen. I took a tough stand with her, but I double-checked every bit of evidence in the case as soon as she left my office.

"I take my position very seriously. I never, ever want to convict an innocent person. I just don't think that Sarah Woodruff fits into that category. And if you want to know why, read my closing statement at her trial. I never try to win by being the more theatrical attorney. I teach, Miss Cutler. My trials are seminars about a particular incident, in which I explain to the jury why they can convict with a clear conscience. Believe me, if you uncover evidence that changes my mind about Woodruff's guilt, I'll be in the judge's chambers that day asking for a stay of execution."

Dana had seen many people make self-serving statements, but she could see that Pike was sincere.

"I did read your closing argument. In fact, I read the transcript of Miss Woodruff's trial before I flew here. But I came to a different conclusion about the evidence you excluded. I think the jury was the proper body to decide its relevance. This whole business with the *China Sea* smells like a rogue operation, and people who conduct that kind of business would not hesitate to kill John Finley if they thought he was a threat."

"I guess we have to agree to disagree. Besides, I didn't invoke the state-secrets privilege, even if I agreed with its use. The feds did that."

Dana saw she wasn't going to get any more out of Pike, so she changed the subject.

"I understand that Max Dietz, the prosecutor who brought Miss Woodruff to trial the first time, has vanished."

Pike stopped smiling. "He has."

"Is there any new information about what happened to him?"

"His car was recovered from the airport, but it didn't yield any clues that told us what happened to him. Some people think he hopped a plane for parts unknown because he was depressed, but I don't buy that. None of his bank accounts were touched, and there's been no action on his credit cards, so what is he living on?"

"What about the quarter of a million dollars Finley was supposed to have had?"

"Yeah, I've heard that rumor. The problem is that no one has ever seen that money. I doubt that it ever existed. And if it did exist, the kidnappers or the people who rescued Finley have it, not Max Dietz."

"Where was Dietz last seen?"

"In his office. He asked his secretary for a handful of subpoenas. She brought them to him. A little later, he left. His secretary said that he seemed excited."

"Do you know why he wanted the subpoenas?"

"No."

"Were there any clues to Dietz's disappearance in his house or office?"

"None we figured out."

"What happened to his belongings?"

"They're stored in a warehouse where we keep evidence in open cases."

"Any chance I could see them?"

"Why, do you think they have anything to do with Woodruff?"

"I'm just curious."

"You know he was off the case by then."

"That's what I understood."

"So it's not likely his disappearance has anything to do with your story."

"I guess not." Dana stood up. "Thanks for seeing me."

"My pleasure. And I wasn't kidding. If you come up with anything that clears Woodruff, let me know. Sending someone to death row is an awesome responsibility. I'd have a hard time living with myself if I were responsible for an innocent person's execution."

As soon as Dana walked out of the Multnomah County Courthouse, she checked the to-do list she'd written on the back page of her notebook. She had talked to everyone she wanted to question, and only one task remained.

Dana was scheduled to take a red-eye out of Portland International, but she had several hours before she had to be at the airport. Dana packed and checked out. Then she talked to the concierge. He told her that it would take forty-five minutes to drive to Shelby. She set her GPS for the address of the warehouse and headed out Highway 30 toward Astoria. The highway ran along the Columbia River and gave Dana a continuous view of the green and tan bluffs of Washington State on the far bank.

During the drive, Dana reviewed everything she'd learned during her stay in Oregon. By the time she pulled into the warehouse parking lot, she had concluded that the only new information she'd picked up concerned Max Dietz's disappearance and the deaths of Jerry Swanson and Tom Oswald. The disappearance and the deaths were suspicious, but no facts connected them to the *China Sea*. More important, nothing she'd learned showed a connection between Justice Price and the *China Sea*.

The sun was starting to set, and Dana shivered when she got out of her car. No ship was moored at the pier, but Dana walked to the water's edge anyway and tried to imagine what the scene was like on the night of the murders.

The discomfort caused by the wind made Dana cut short her reverie, and she walked back toward the warehouse. It looked deserted, but she circled it anyway. On the side opposite the spot where she had parked her car, she found a door with a heavy padlock.

Dana decided that there was nothing more she could accomplish, so she headed back to her car. As she turned the corner, she discovered a black SUV parked sideways in the lot and a large man leaning against her rental. After her escape from the basement where she'd been held captive, Dana never went anywhere without a weapon. The Beretta that nestled in a holster in the small of her back brought her great comfort. She slipped it out before stopping far enough from the man so she could shoot him if he became a threat.

"It gets cold out here," the man said. Dana thought she heard a trace of a Scandinavian accent.

"Why are you leaning on my car?" she asked.

The man smiled. "I heard you were tough."

"Look, jerkoff, I don't have time for your routine. You may think you're cool, but I just find you annoying. If you know anything about me, you know that I have no problem killing if I feel threatened. So tell me what this is all about, or fuck off."

The man straightened up. All traces of amusement disappeared from his features, and his stare was as cold and cruel as Dana's.

"Tell Patrick Gorman that there is no story here."

Dana didn't respond.

"Your boyfriend, Jake Teeny, is in Sierra Leone. That's a dangerous place."

Dana cocked the gun. "Watch your mouth."

"That was simply an observation. And here's another one. It would be difficult for *Exposed* to print a story about the *China Sea* if its building was vaporized."

"Who are you?"

The man smiled. Then he turned without answering Dana's question and got into the SUV. Dana let him. As soon as he was out of sight, she leaned against her car. The mention of Jake Teeny had shaken her. Dana had lost all fear of death while she was a captive. That had enabled her to do anything, regardless of the risk. Falling in love had changed her. She still had no fear where her personal safety was concerned, but the idea that Jake might be hurt because of something she did filled her with dread and made her vulnerable, something she hated.

Dana started the car and drove onto the highway. It was ironic. The man had threatened her so she would kill the story about the *China Sea*, but his threats had made her realize that someone still thought that the incident could turn into a very big story. The question Dana had to answer was how much she was willing to risk to uncover it.

"Pat, it's Dana."

"Where are you?" Gorman asked.

"I'm on my way to the airport in Portland to catch my flight back to D.C."

"Do you by any chance have the scoop of the century packed in with your sexy lingerie?" the editor asked.

"I'm not carrying either of those items, you pervert."

"Do you have *anything* for me?"

"What I'm working on is too big to discuss without proof, and I wasn't able to get any hard evidence."

"We don' need no steenking evidence to print our stories," Gorman said in an atrocious Mexican accent.

Dana laughed.

"If you don't have a story for me, why are you calling?"

"You've got contacts with deep knowledge about the intelligence community, right?"

"Why do you ask?" Gorman said with all traces of humor gone.

"I was threatened by someone while I was conducting my investigation, and I want to know how seriously I should take the threat."

"What's the intelligence agency?"

"I'm guessing CIA, but it may be Homeland Security."

"Let me make a call. I'll get back to you."

"Thanks, Pat. If this wasn't important, I wouldn't ask."

"I know, Dana. That's the reason I'm willing to burn a favor for you."

Part Six

The Evil Twin

2012

Chapter Forty-seven

Ginny assumed that her workload would lessen now that she was part of the team preparing Audrey Stewart for her congressional hearing, but she soon learned that this was a false assumption. She staggered through her front door at ten o'clock to the sound of an urgent conversation coming from her living room. One of the speakers was a woman, and the voice sounded familiar. While Ginny was propping her attaché case against the wall in the entryway, the name "Millard Price" drifted toward her from the other room. She strained to hear the conversation as she took off her coat. She could detect the urgency in Brad's voice, but not what he was saying. Then she heard the woman say, "You've got to tell Justice Moss that this is way too dangerous for you to stay involved."

"What's too dangerous?" Ginny asked as she walked into the living room and saw Dana Cutler with Brad.

They looked like startled deer caught in the headlights of a Mack truck.

"What's up?" Ginny asked suspiciously when neither Brad nor Dana answered her question.

"I didn't hear you come in," Brad said.

"Maybe that's a good thing," Ginny answered. "What are you two discussing?"

"Business, honey," Brad answered, "and it's confidential."

"Not if you're doing something dangerous. I live here, too. And if it concerns Millard Price, I may be able to help. He was a partner at Rankin Lusk before he went on the Court."

"Please forget anything you may have heard," Brad begged her.

Ginny stared daggers at her fiancé. "This has something to do with the attack on Justice Moss, doesn't it?"

"Why would you think that?" Brad asked with a nervous laugh.

"Because, *dear*, I am not stupid. I distinctly heard your coconspirator tell you that you should tell your boss that whatever you are doing is dangerous, and the attack on Justice Moss is the only dangerous thing that's happened at the Court since you started working there."

"We are working on something that involves the Court, and it's something Brad can't discuss," Dana said. "And I just learned something that made it clear that amateurs should not be involved."

"Is this something serious enough to require police involvement?" Ginny asked.

Dana nodded. Ginny looked frightened. "You follow her advice, Brad."

Brad looked like he wanted to say something, but he couldn't bring himself to do it.

"I mean it," Ginny said. "You were almost killed in

the garage. I love you, and I can't stand the thought that your life might be at risk."

Brad's shoulders sagged and he sighed. "All right. You win. I'll tell Justice Moss that she should talk to Keith Evans."

"You're doing the right thing," Dana assured Brad.

Ginny looked relieved, and Dana looked at her watch.

"It's late," Dana said. "I should be going." She stood up. "It was good seeing you again, Ginny. When Jake gets back, we should get together."

"I'd like that. Maybe we could meet for lunch before that."

"You're on. I'll call you."

Brad followed Dana into the entryway and locked the door behind her.

"Are you going to tell me what you're involved in?" Ginny asked when they were alone.

"I really can't. It does involve Court business, and I promised I wouldn't tell anyone but Dana."

"So you can tell her, but you can't tell the woman you're going to spend your life with?"

"It's not like that. Dana is being paid to investigate a . . . a problem. This was a business conversation between a client and her employer."

"You're paying her?"

"I can't answer that, and please drop this, OK? How would you feel if I asked you to reveal confidential communications between you and a client or demanded that you tell me what you and a partner discussed in a business meeting?"

Ginny could see that Brad was upset, and she

knew he was right. She took his hands in hers and looked into his eyes.

"I'm worried because I love you so much, and I'd die if anything happened to you."

Brad took her in his arms. If he had to choose between a billion dollars and hugging Ginny, he knew where his heart would lead him.

In his dream, Brad was on the deck of the *China Sea*, and the ship had been converted into a strip club. Brad was sitting at a table covered with a white tablecloth and lit by a candle, watching naked, busty women with large derrieres cavort on a raised stage. Millard Price was sitting next to him, and he was wearing a sombrero and a serape. A near-naked woman perched on Price's lap. The judge was drunk, and he laughed as he stuffed hundred-dollar bills into her G-string. Then the woman turned toward Brad and thrust her breasts in his face.

"Do you want a private dance?" she asked, seconds before Brad shot up in bed and stared into the darkness.

"What's wrong?" Ginny mumbled.

"Nothing," he said, but the tension in his voice told her otherwise. "I've got to make a call."

"It's three in the morning," Ginny said, fully awake now.

"I know."

Brad grabbed his cell phone and left the bedroom. Ginny was pissed off by the secrecy. She debated staying in bed but decided that she needed to know what Brad was involved in, so she crept to the bedroom door and opened it a crack.

"I know it's late, Dana, but this can't wait," Brad whispered in the mistaken belief that Ginny could not hear him. "The shell corporation that was used to purchase the *China Sea* was named TA Enterprises. Remember Mary Garrett told you that Sarah Woodruff asked John Finley what TA meant and he joked that it meant tits and ass? Well, that's not it. You read Price's bio, right? He went to Dartmouth with Masterson, and they were the stars of the championship football team. Do you remember their nickname? They were the Two Amigos! TA.

"When the incident on the *China Sea* took place, Dennis Masterson was the head of the CIA, and Millard Price was a senior partner at Rankin Lusk and one of Masterson's closest friends. Smuggling hashish was an illegal operation that the CIA wouldn't be able to get the Congress to sanction, so Masterson hired Finley, an independent contractor, to be the front man, and he also went outside the Agency and asked his best friend, Millard Price, to set up the shell company that was used to buy the ship and fund the operation. The company was called TA Enterprises because one 'amigo' asked the other 'amigo' to set it up. Proving that won't be easy, but it does give us something to look into."

Dana said something.

"OK, it gives Keith Evans something to look into, but if he can show Price set up the company, he'll have a connection between Price and the *China Sea*, and we'll know for certain why Price wants to kill the cert petition in *Woodruff*."

Ginny listened until it was clear that the phone call was over. She crept back into bed and pulled the covers over her head. Now she knew why Brad and Dana were being secretive. They suspected that a sitting Supreme Court justice was involved in drug smuggling. It wasn't much of a stretch for Ginny to conclude that Brad and Dana also suspected that Millard Price had something to do with the attack on Justice Moss.

Ginny decided that something must have happened recently that made Dana believe that Brad should back off. People who would try to kill a Supreme Court justice would think nothing of killing a lowly clerk, so Dana's advice was sound. But Brad seemed convinced that they could show Price was involved with the murder attempt if they could prove he set up this TA Enterprises company. Ginny had an idea how that could be accomplished, and she didn't think there would be any risk to her or Brad.

Chapter Forty-eight

At seven thirty the next morning, Ginny booted up her computer and typed "Sarah Woodruff" into Google. She was worried that her search would be traced back to her, so she entered a password she'd seen one of the junior partners use. It didn't take her long to find the case that was before the Supreme Court and newspaper articles about Woodruff's two trials for killing the same man.

When she was finished, Ginny could see why digging into the case was very dangerous. Once the *China Sea* disappeared, Masterson must have thought he was home free. Then Max Dietz charged Woodruff with murder, and Mary Garrett started poking her nose into the *China Sea* affair. Masterson must have taken another deep breath when the first case was dismissed and no one had any reason to look into what happened in Shelby anymore. But the specter of the *China Sea* rose again when John Finley turned up dead for real and the only way Mary Garrett could defend her client was by proving that Finley was involved with CIA assassins and drug dealers.

Masterson must have thought he was safe when the trial judge blocked Garrett after the government asserted the state-secrets privilege, but Sarah Woodruff was sentenced to death, the Oregon Supreme Court ruled that the defendant's right to exculpatory evidence in a death case doesn't trump the state-secrets privilege, and the issue in the case became one of national importance. If cert wasn't granted, the case would die. If cert was granted, the case would get national scrutiny. While Masterson was with the CIA, he had a million ways to keep the lid on it, but he was on his own now, and he had to get rid of Justice Moss because she stood in the way of the Court denying cert.

As soon as Ginny felt she knew enough about the facts of the case, she ran an internal search in the firm's files for TA Enterprises. She was disappointed when the computer could not make a match, but she wasn't surprised. Anyone clever enough to run a major drug-smuggling operation under the nose of the federal government was going to cover his tracks.

If Price had created the papers used to incorporate the company and they weren't stored on a hard drive, there was another place they might be stored. During her first week on the job, Ginny had needed a file from a closed case that had been handled for a major client in 1970, before the firm had computers. When she couldn't find the file online, she had asked the secretary for the partner who'd assigned her the project where she could find it. The secretary had taken a distinctive key from a drawer in her desk and sent Ginny to the subbasement where the paper files were stored.

Ginny's secretary wasn't in yet, but her desk wasn't locked. Ginny found the key and took the elevator to the subbasement. When the doors opened onto the reception area of Rankin Lusk, they revealed a world of sparkling glass, shiny chrome, and polished wood. The subbasement was the dark side of the force. When Ginny got out of the elevator, she walked into an unpainted concrete corridor dimly lit by low-wattage bulbs. The air was clammy, and the odor of decay hung in the stagnant air. Both sides of the corridor were divided into storage bays. The file cabinets in the bays were vague shadows protected by chicken wire attached to a wood frame. The strands of a cobweb brushed across her face and she started before wiping it away. A flashlight would have come in handy, and she cursed her lack of forethought.

Each bay had a number. From her previous visit, Ginny knew that the first four digits referred to the year. She found a bin labeled with the year in which the smuggling operation had occurred. Gray metal filing cabinets filled the space. Each drawer in each cabinet had a label with letters in alphabetical order, so she opened the drawer labeled "Ta–Tm." She had to move aside to let the ceiling light shine on the files. To her delight there was a file for TA Enterprises. Ginny opened it. The file contained papers of incorporation in the Cayman Islands for the company, and correspondence. The letter on top had Millard Price's name on it. Ginny took out her cell phone and snapped pictures of each page in the file. She was almost through when she heard the elevator doors open. Ginny replaced the file and closed the drawer. Then she snapped her phone shut and hid it in her pocket. When she turned around, Greg McKenzie was standing in the doorway, his massive body blocking the light from the corridor.

"What are you doing?" McKenzie demanded.

Ginny had prepared a fallback position in case someone discovered her in the basement. Her heart was tripping, but she smiled and held up a thick file from an insurance case with a claimant whose last name began with a "T."

"I'm checking to see if there were any prior insurance claims by this guy. We think he might be a flake. What are you doing here?"

McKenzie stared at her for a few seconds before answering.

"Mr. Masterson sent me. He wants to see you."

"I'll be right up."

"He wants you now."

Ginny debated telling McKenzie to back off, but she was all alone and he scared her. McKenzie stood aside to let her out of the bay. Then he followed her to the elevator. The associate made no effort to give Ginny space. One massive shoulder was only inches from hers and she could smell the cloying scent of his aftershave.

On the ride up, Ginny wondered how Masterson knew she would be in the subbasement. Did he suspect she was looking into TA Enterprises? She wondered if her computer inquiries had raised a red flag somewhere. But how would anyone know that she was making them? She'd used the partner's password. But she'd used her own computer. Was the CIA or NSA tracking anyone who looked into TA Enterprises? Was there technology that could trace her search back to her computer?

When Ginny returned to the surface, the sight of people on the other side of the elevator doors made her feel safe, at least for the moment. McKenzie herded her toward Masterson's office.

"Tell Mr. Masterson that I've got Ginny Striker," McKenzie snapped at Masterson's secretary. Ginny assumed that a secretary for a senior partner would normally be shown a lot of deference by someone who wanted to be made a partner, but McKenzie showed the woman none, and the secretary was clearly intimidated. She buzzed her boss. A moment later, she told McKenzie to go in and told Ginny to wait. Ten minutes later, McKenzie came out and glared at Ginny.

"He wants you," he said. Then he turned his back on her and walked off.

Masterson smiled when Ginny walked into his office, but he didn't offer her a seat. He was sitting at his desk, the sleeves of his white silk shirt rolled back to reveal corded forearms. The knot of his tie was pulled down and his shirt collar was open.

"How are you getting along at the firm?"

"Fine. It's very interesting work, especially my assignment with Miss Stewart's nomination hearing."

"And you're fitting in, feeling comfortable?"

"Definitely."

Masterson leaned back in his chair. "I imagine a

day at the firm is a lot less exciting than what you were used to in Oregon."

"Quite honestly, Mr. Masterson, not having to dodge reporters is a big relief."

"I can empathize with you from my days at the CIA. Everywhere I went, there were cameras flashing and microphones shoved in my face. Knowing what we know, I wonder how you and I would have voted if we were back in colonial times and considering what to do with the First Amendment."

Ginny forced a laugh. Maybe it was a coincidence that she'd been sent for while she was looking for the TA Enterprises file.

Masterson picked up a thick folder and held it out to Ginny. "There are articles in here that Audrey has written on national-security issues and memos from her days in the CIA. I want you to make a digest of them with a synopsis of her position on torture and the limits of interrogation. She's going to be grilled on that for sure, and we need to be able to cite her actual opinions word for word."

"I'll get right on it."

"Good. I'd like it by the day after tomorrow."

"No problem," Ginny assured him, though she knew that creating the digest and finishing her other assignments by the deadline meant working late into the night.

"Is your fiancé enjoying his work at the Court?"

Ginny felt a chill pass through her. "Very much."

"And he likes working for Justice Moss?"

"Yes."

"That was something." Masterson shook his

head. "If a Supreme Court justice isn't safe in the sanctuary of the Court, none of us are."

Ginny nodded, afraid to speak.

"I understand you were in the subbasement."

"Yes," Ginny answered.

"That place has always unnerved me. It's like a medieval dungeon, don't you think? A woman was attacked down there a few years ago. A janitor tried to rape her."

Ginny's stomach rolled.

"Retrieving files from that graveyard is the job of a secretary or legal assistant. Who sent you down there? I'll make certain it doesn't happen again."

"Actually, no one sent me. I was just looking for a file in an insurance case."

"You won't need to go to the subbasement to complete this assignment," Masterson said. "It was nice talking to you."

Ginny felt sick as she walked to her office. What had McKenzie told Masterson? Had the associate seen Ginny taking pictures of the TA Enterprises file? Had Masterson assigned her the task of digesting Stewart's articles and memos because it would make her work into the night? There would be few other people in the office after six. She would be vulnerable. How could she protect herself? There was only one person she could think of to call. As soon as she was in her office, Ginny shut her door and phoned Dana Cutler.

Chapter Forty-nine

Dana had neglected her other cases while she was in Oregon, and she played catch-up starting the morning after her visit to Brad Miller's apartment. She was finishing a report in an industrial-espionage case when she heard the ringtone of the cell phone with the number few people knew.

"Yeah?" Dana said.

"It's Pat; I've got an assignment for you. We're going to do a feature on Indian legends like shape-shifters and Indian vampires."

"Do Indians believe in vampires?"

"Don't be a bigot. Surely you don't think that the only cultural group that can have vampire legends are lily-white Eastern Europeans? You're not an Aryan supremacist, are you?"

"Definitely not where vampires are concerned. Go on."

"Anyway, a good place to start is the National Museum of the American Indian. Have you been there?"

"Not yet. Jake did a photo shoot inside, but I was out of town conducting surveillance."

"Well, here's your chance to level the cultural playing field with your boyfriend. Somebody in that place should know a few legends you can use. Why don't you drop over as soon as you can so you can get a jump on the story."

The National Museum of the American Indian, part of the Smithsonian Institution, was located at Fourth Street and Independence Avenue. The museum was one of the more interesting architectural structures on the Mall. The adobe brown, curvilinear building was designed to resemble natural stone formations and was a stark contrast to the buildings that surrounded it.

The height of the tourist season had passed, and the crowds at the museum were sparse this early in the day. When Dana entered, she found herself in a large open space where she could look up unimpeded to a dome ceiling five stories above her. A ramp wound upward to the exhibits on each floor. From the top of the ramp, an observer could look down on the visitors as they entered. It was an excellent place to check to see if someone you were meeting had a tail.

Gorman had not given Dana a description of the person she was going to meet or a name, but she assumed he'd given her contact her description. After wandering aimlessly around the entryway for a few minutes, Dana concluded that no one was going to approach her there, so she started up the ramp and began wandering through the exhibits. She was alone in one of the galleries studying an exhibit of Pacific Northwest Indian artifacts when a man walked in front of the display case. He was wearing a Washington Nationals baseball cap, a shiny Nationals jacket, jeans, and running shoes. His complexion was pale, and his brown eyes were focused on a collection of Tlingit cedar-bark baskets.

"Do you think the Tlingit Indians believed in vampires?" he asked.

"Beats me," Dana answered, "but I'm a reporter working on a story for *Exposed* about Indian legends, so read the paper next week and you'll know the answer to your question."

"If you go to the end of this exhibit and look left, you'll see a stairwell. Why don't you go up to the landing on the top floor and check for vampires. I'll join you when I'm satisfied you haven't been followed."

Dana entered the stairwell and walked to the highest landing. A few minutes later, Gorman's contact joined her.

"What do you want to know?" he asked. Dana appreciated the lack of chitchat. She also noticed that he hadn't told her his name, and she assumed he'd only give her a false one if she asked.

"I was working on a story and I was threatened. I'm guessing the person who threatened me was sent by Dennis Masterson. How worried should I be?"

The man chuckled. "That one is easy. Having Masterson mad at you is like being on the receiving end of DEFCON 1. When Masterson was head of the CIA, he could send a drone with a nuclear warhead into your bathroom while you were on the potty."

"But he's not head of the CIA now, so how dangerous is he?"

"Very. He can't send the drone anymore, but someone like that has assets that will do whatever for a price, and Masterson has the money to pay the price."

"OK, you've succeeded in scaring me," Dana said.

"Then I've done you a favor. Do not fuck with this guy."

"One more question. The person who made the threat was about six two; solid build like a linebacker, blond, and I thought I heard a Scandinavian accent."

"The Swede. I think his name is Thomas Bergstrom, but I wouldn't bet on it. He uses a lot of aliases. When Masterson was with the CIA, Bergstrom was the person he used for the dirtiest assignments. I would take any threat he makes very seriously."

"Would it do me any good to go to the authorities?"

The man laughed. "Masterson *is* the authorities, even if he's not in government anymore. My advice, do what you were told to do or be prepared to sit up with a shotgun every night for the rest of your life. Oh, and don't start your car, ever."

"You've made your point."

"Good, because the person who set up this meet likes you and wants you to live to a ripe old age. That story you were working on is not worth your life."

"One more thing. I know where I can find Masterson, but where can I find Bergstrom?"

The man's face lost all trace of humor. "Are you wearing earplugs? Did you fail to hear everything I just told you? The last thing you want to do is find this guy, because it could be the last thing you do."

"I appreciate your concern, but I still want to know."

"Yeah, well, that's something you can do on your own. It's a crime to help someone commit suicide."

The man shook his head before stalking off. He looked sad, like a patient teacher who had tried his best but had finally given up on a spectacularly dull student. Dana knew that she'd screwed up. Pat had called in a chit for her and she'd blown it. She was deciding whether she should go after the contact and apologize when her cell phone rang.

"Dana," Ginny Striker said, "I may be in trouble and I need your help."

Chapter Fifty

Ginny's office was three doors down from the fire stairs in a row of broom-closet-size spaces that were reserved for new associates. By seven thirty, an eerie silence had replaced the hum of activity that filled the floor during working hours. The only sound Ginny heard was made by a vacuum cleaner on the far side of the building. There were usually a few of her fellow wage slaves toiling away in the evening, but the last person to leave had said good-bye at seven fifteen.

Ginny concentrated on a memo Stewart had written justifying waterboarding and other interrogation techniques that sounded vaguely similar to stuff she read about when she was studying the Spanish Inquisition. She had to admit that the assignment was interesting, even if Stewart's positions were appalling. She shuddered when she thought that the woman who'd written these tracts might soon be sitting on the Supreme Court, and she felt a twinge of conscience about the part she was playing, no matter how small, in seeing that she got there.

The hum from the vacuum cleaner grew louder,

and Ginny stood up to shut her door. When she looked down the aisle she saw a tall, broad-shouldered man wearing a baseball cap and the uniform of the cleaning crew slowly maneuver the machine in and out of a group of cubicles used by the secretarial staff. Most of the cleaning crew was Hispanic, and the man's blond hair and Nordic features surprised Ginny. She stared for a moment, then shut her door.

Ginny made some notes on a legal pad. She paused to think about a way to spin the conclusion of Stewart's memo so the nominee wouldn't sound like a cross between Hannibal Lecter and Torquemada and was suddenly aware that the vacuum cleaner sounded like it was right outside her door.

When The Swede arrived at the fire exit, he left the vacuum cleaner running to cover the sound of his approach and pulled his Glock out of his coveralls. Masterson had called him that afternoon and told him that one of the firm's associates had seen Ginny Striker using a cell phone to take pictures of the contents of a file in the drawer marked "Ta–Tm." He believed it was the TA Enterprises file. Masterson wanted the cell phone, he wanted the names of anyone who had seen the pictures, and he wanted Striker neutralized.

"Drop the gun," Dana Cutler commanded from the entrance of the secretarial cubicle in which she'd been hiding since six that evening.

Most people would freeze in this situation, but

Bergstrom reacted instinctively and sprayed shots in Dana's direction as he powered backward through the fire door. Dana threw herself to the floor and barely avoided the bullets that flew by her. She was starting to look up when she heard the steel door slam shut. For a moment, she toyed with the idea of following Bergstrom. Then Ginny's door opened and Striker stepped into the hall to see what had made the dull cracks she'd heard over the whine of the vacuum cleaner.

"Get back," Dana shouted, even though she was pretty certain they were safe. Ginny backed into her office and closed the door, and Dana scouted the area around Ginny's office before knocking.

"What happened?" Ginny asked.

"The cleaner was getting ready to kill you. I had the drop on him, but he surprised me and got away."

"Were those shots I heard?"

Dana nodded.

Ginny stepped back and sank onto a chair. Her breathing was shallow.

"Don't worry. You're safe," Dana assured her.

"For now. And what about Brad?"

"I have someone watching your apartment. I'll have Brad ask Justice Moss to authorize police protection until we're certain you're both safe."

"And when will that be?" Ginny asked.

Dana wished she knew.

"Did you get an early parole, or did Spartacus lead a second slave revolt?" Brad joked when Ginny and Dana arrived at the apartment at eight thirty.

But his smile disappeared rapidly when he saw the frightened look on Ginny's face and Dana's grim countenance.

"What happened?" he asked.

"A man tried to kill Ginny, and we think Dennis Masterson sent him."

"Did you call the police?" Brad asked as he crossed to his fiancée.

"No," Dana answered. "This is something we should talk to Keith about."

"Why did someone try to kill you?" Brad asked.

"Let me sit down," Ginny answered. "I have something to show you."

She sat on the couch, and Brad sat next to her. Ginny opened her cell phone and showed him the photos she'd taken of the TA Enterprises file.

Brad gawked. "Where did you get this?"

"The firm keeps old, closed files in the subbasement of our building."

"More important, why did you go looking for this file?"

Ginny colored. "When you called Dana in the middle of the night, I eavesdropped on your conversation. You talked about being stymied without proof that Millard Price was connected to TA Enterprises, and it dawned on me that there might be a file in the office."

"And Masterson found out you'd been rooting around in the files?"

"He must have if he sent someone after her," Dana said.

"At least you know that Price set up the company," Ginny said.

"That information is not worth your life," Brad said.

"If you give these pictures to Justice Moss or the FBI, Masterson won't have a reason to go after me anymore," Ginny said.

"I'm not so certain. A prosecutor would need you to lay a foundation for the admission of the pictures at a trial. You're the only one who knows where you found them, and I'll bet that file has ceased to exist."

"I know one thing for certain," Dana said. "From this point on, you two are through with anything to do with the *Woodruff* case and Millard Price. There is no upside to your continued involvement, and as we learned tonight, there could be a very big downside."

"Justice Moss is in Texas giving a speech," Brad said. "She'll be back in two days. When she returns, I'll brief her about the pictures and what Dana learned in Oregon. Then I'll tell her to turn the information over to the FBI. What are you going to do, Dana?"

"I'm not sure," she said, but Dana knew damn well what she was going to do. The man who tried to kill Ginny tonight had threatened her and the man she loved. She was not going to sit around and wait for Bergstrom or Masterson to make the next move. She was going to track down Bergstrom and make certain the people she cared about were safe.

Chapter Fifty-one

A shell company with offices in Dubai rented Dennis Masterson's penthouse under the name Ivan Karpinsky. Masterson used the penthouse for sexual encounters with women other than his wife and for clandestine meetings. When Masterson responded to his doorbell, he found Millard Price standing on his welcome mat wearing a heavy black overcoat with the collar turned up and a fedora with the brim pulled low. The hat served the dual purpose of a disguise and protection from the heavy rain that was inundating the metropolitan area.

"You look like a private eye, Millie," Masterson joked, using the nickname Price had acquired at Dartmouth, where the effeminate moniker was the exact opposite of his violent play on the football field.

"There's nothing funny about this situation, Dennis," Price said as he brushed by his bemused friend.

"Let me fix you a drink," Masterson said while Price was tossing his hat, scarf, and overcoat onto a chair.

"Scotch. The good stuff. You owe me."

"Calm down," Masterson said as he stepped behind his wet bar. "The file is gone." He didn't tell his friend about the attempt to make the person who'd photographed it vanish, too. Price was squeamish, and the less he knew, the better off everyone was. "What I'd like to know is why there was a file in the first place."

"It was an oversight. And you were never very clear about why I was incorporating the damn company. If I'd known . . ."

Masterson handed his friend a glass three-quarters full of twenty-five-year-old single-malt liquor.

"I told you it was covert. If it was even remotely legit, I wouldn't have needed you to incorporate the company. In any event, there's no harm done."

Price gulped down a quarter of the scotch. "She's Miller's girlfriend, Dennis. Why is Miller's girlfriend looking into the company that purchased the *China Sea*? Felicia's got to be behind this."

"Moss is unquestionably the problem," Masterson said quietly.

"You *cannot* go after her again," Price said emphatically. "I can't believe you tried to kill her."

"You'll be singing a different tune if cert is granted and every investigative reporter in the country starts looking into the *China Sea*."

"She's a justice of the United States Supreme Court."

"Unfortunately."

"Promise me there will be no more violence."

"I won't lie to you, Millie. We go back too far. I am not going to let that case destroy my life, or

yours. Did you know that Dana Cutler has been
nosing around in Oregon?"

"The investigator who helped bring down Farrington?"

Masterson nodded. "Our mole in the Court
bugged Moss's chambers, and I've had someone on
Miller since Moss told him to look into the case.
He met with Cutler, and a few days later she flew to
Oregon."

"Did she find anything?"

"She must have figured out your connection with
the case if Ginny Striker was looking for the TA
Enterprises file."

"What are you going to do now?" Price asked.

"I'm going to devote my efforts to putting Audrey
on the Court so we can bury that damn case forever
and never again have to think about that fucking
ship."

Following Dennis Masterson was the only way
Dana could think of to find The Swede or Thomas
Bergstrom or whoever the fuck he really was, so she
staked out his law offices. Masterson was driven to
and from work in black chauffeured town cars outfit-
ted with tinted windows. A major problem was presented by the fact that Rankin Lusk contracted with
a company that had a fleet of identical cars. Anyone
at Rankin Lusk who wanted to use the service got
into the town car in the parking garage in the basement of the building. Since Dana did not have X-ray
vision, she would have no way of knowing which car

Masterson was using, but she solved this problem by bribing one of the garage attendants, who called her with the information minutes before one of the town cars pulled out of the underground garage.

The heavy rain played havoc with visibility and helped disguise the fact that Dana was tailing the limo. When the car stopped in front of a high-rise apartment building, Dana parked across the street and watched the driver escort Masterson to the front door while shielding him from the downpour with a large black umbrella. Dana knew where Masterson lived and she knew this apartment house wasn't it. Since she had no plan, she decided to stay in her parking space and see if anyone interesting turned up. She wasn't disappointed.

Forty minutes after Masterson was dropped off, Millard Price arrived in another town car. Dana didn't make him at first, but the justice took off his hat to shake off the rain when he got under the overhang that protected the front door.

Price came out an hour later and got into his waiting car. Dana didn't see any reason to follow him so she stayed put. She was glad she did. Thirty minutes after Price left, Thomas Bergstrom entered the building. Half an hour later, he, too, drove away. Dana followed The Swede across the state line into Virginia. If she expected Masterson's strongman to live someplace exotic like a houseboat or gated mansion, she was disappointed. Bergstrom lived in an upper-middle-class housing development in a house designed to look like it should have been in a New England village. Dana concentrated her binoculars on the front window and saw Bergstrom embrace an attractive brunette, who had gotten off her living room couch when the garage door opened. Dana panned across the front of the house and saw a tricycle and a soccer ball on the front porch.

Thomas Bergstrom seemed to live a modern-day version of *The Adventures of Ozzie and Harriet*, only Ozzie never threatened Dana's friends. If Ozzie had done that, there would have been a good chance that Ricky and David would have grown up without a dad.

Chapter Fifty-two

When Brad arrived at his office the next morning, Harriet Lezak was already toiling away at her computer. She stopped working when Brad walked in.

"Can we talk?" Harriet asked. She sounded worried.

"Sure, about what?"

Harriet shut the door. "I've been going back and forth with myself all week, and I've decided that I have to tell somebody."

Brad had no idea what Harriet was talking about.

"You know I went out for a run the evening Justice Moss was attacked?"

Brad nodded.

"I came back just before the assault. I was probably taking a shower when it happened. But I didn't know a thing about it because it was in the garage. As soon as I was dressed, I went to see Kyle Peterson, one of Justice Price's clerks. Do you know him?"

"We've met. He's on loan from Rankin Lusk, where Ginny works."

"Price circulated an opinion, and Justice Moss wanted my take on it. I came across a problem with one of the footnotes. Kyle worked on the draft, so I went to see if he was still in. The door to his office was closed, but I was absorbed with the legal issue and I was distracted, so I opened it without knocking. Kyle was seated at his desk and he was bent over, stuffing something into his attaché case. He was shocked to see me. Not surprised—shocked. He stared at me for a second. Then he pushed the attaché under his desk."

"What did Kyle put in the attaché?"

"I can't be one hundred percent certain. That's why I didn't talk to anyone immediately. But it's been eating at me. I mean, what if I kept my mouth shut and something else happened?"

"What was it, Harriet?"

Lezak looked at Brad. She was usually opinionated and very sure of herself, and he was not used to her being uncertain.

"I think it was a black ski mask."

"A ski mask?" Brad repeated dully.

"You can see why I waited. It made no impression on me at the time, because I didn't know about the attack. A few days after the attack, I heard that the person who tried to kill Justice Moss wore a black ski mask."

Brad remembered that Millard Price had brought Peterson to the Court after one of his clerks had an accident. Was the "accident" planned so Price could insert an assassin into his staff?

"How certain are you about this?" Brad asked.

"I just saw it for a second."

"Why are you talking to me? Why haven't you gone to the police or the FBI?"

"You have experience with stuff like this, and you saw the attacker. Before I tell anyone, I want to know if you think he could have been Kyle. If I accuse him and I'm wrong, his career could be ruined."

Brad closed his eyes and tried to remember the fight in the garage. Did Kyle resemble the killer?

"Kyle has an athletic build and so did the assailant," Brad said, "but I only saw the man for a few moments. At the beginning, I was above him on the ramp. Then I was on the floor looking up. Then he had me from behind. Then I was on the floor again. None of those positions make it easy to gauge the assailant's height. And everything happened so quickly."

"Damn. I was hoping you'd be sure."

"I can't be."

"What should I do?"

"I think you should tell what you told me to my friends from the FBI."

Justice Moss was in Texas giving a speech, so Brad met Maggie and Keith in her chambers. Keith could tell Brad was nervous.

"What's up?" Keith asked as soon as Brad shut the door.

"I share an office with Harriet Lezak, another law clerk. She just told me something she saw shortly after Justice Moss was attacked. It might give you the break you need to solve the case."

"If that's true, why do you look so uncomfortable?" Keith asked.

Brad hesitated. "There are some things that have happened that I can't tell you about right now."

Keith looked confused. "Do you know something that makes you question what this witness is going to tell us?"

"No, it's nothing like that. I just can't talk about it for reasons I can't explain, but I'm hoping that will change soon. In the meantime, listen to what Harriet has to say. She may be able to tell you who attacked Justice Moss. If her information pans out, I may be able to tell you why she was attacked."

As soon as they finished questioning Harriet, Keith Evans and Maggie Sparks walked over to the office Kyle Peterson shared with Wilhelmina Horst. When Maggie knocked on the doorjamb, Horst looked up from the case she was reading.

"Can I help you?" she asked.

"Is this Kyle Peterson's office?" Maggie asked.

"Yes."

"Is he around?"

"No, he hasn't come in yet."

Keith looked at his watch. "Does he usually come in after ten, Ms. . . . ?"

Horst looked back and forth between the agents. "Who are you?" she asked suspiciously.

Maggie flashed her identification. "Maggie Sparks and Keith Evans. We're special agents with the FBI," she said with what she hoped was a disarming smile. "And you are?"

"Willie Horst. I clerk for Justice Price, too."

"So, Ms. Horst, is Mr. Peterson usually here by ten?"

"Yeah. He's usually in before I get here."

Sparks frowned. "Do you have his cell or home phone and his address?"

"What's this about?" Willie asked.

"We needed to ask him some routine questions about the attack on Justice Moss," Keith answered.

"Well, I can't just give out that information, even if you are with the FBI. You need to talk to the Clerk's office or someone on our police force."

"You're right," Maggie said. "By the way, were you in the building when Justice Moss was attacked?"

"I already talked about this to one of our police officers. They'll have a report."

"I'm sure they do. But while we're here . . ."

"I was working out in the gym."

"Do you know where Mr. Peterson was?"

"No."

"Did anyone see you while you were working out?"

"Do you mean, do I have an alibi witness? No. And I've already told all this to the police."

"We appreciate that, Ms. Horst," Maggie said. "We'll follow your suggestion and get Mr. Peterson's address from the Clerk. And we'd appreciate it if you didn't call him to say we're on our way."

An hour after securing a search warrant, Keith Evans and Maggie Sparks parked outside Kyle Peterson's apartment building and waited for backup. The attorney lived in a new condominium complex a few miles over the state line in Bethesda, Maryland. A Starbucks, a sushi restaurant, and other establishments catering to young professionals stood on either side of the entrance. When the backup arrived, Sparks went inside and flashed her ID at the security guard. After getting a master key, Evans, Sparks, and four more armed agents rode the elevator to the eighth floor.

"Mr. Peterson," Evans called out after pressing the doorbell twice. When there was still no response, Evans nodded at Sparks, who inserted the key and eased open the door.

Guns drawn, the agents stepped cautiously into a spacious living room with sliding glass doors that opened onto a narrow balcony and found themselves surrounded by chaos. Bookshelves had been overturned, their contents strewn across the floor. A glass coffee table had been turned on its side, and a lamp, its bulb still glowing, lay on a faux Persian rug. In the kitchen, cabinet doors had been flung open, and cookware and shards of glass covered the floor.

"This does not look good," Evans muttered.

"You think?" Sparks whispered back.

The agents spread out and edged toward a narrow hall. At the end was a closed door. Evans took a deep breath and pushed it inward. The bedroom was a wreck. Closets and drawers were open and clothes littered the room.

"Fuck," Evans said as he holstered his gun. The curse had been elicited by the nude body sprawled across the black silk sheets on Kyle Peterson's bed. Duct tape sealed his mouth, and Peterson's hands had been cuffed behind him, causing his back to arch. The law clerk's body was disfigured by burn marks and razor cuts.

"Keith!"

Evans turned and saw an agent pointing at something in Peterson's closet. He and Sparks walked over and looked down at a stack of racist propaganda: newsletters from white-supremacist groups mixed with neo-Nazi literature and anti-Semitic tracts.

"Pardon the pun," Evans said, "but it looks like our boy was a closet racist."

"What's that?" Maggie asked as she pointed toward a black mound stuffed into a corner of the closet.

Keith prodded it with his toe, and a black turtleneck flopped over, exposing a black ski mask and black slacks.

"It looks like Lezak did see Peterson stuff a ski mask into his attaché," Maggie said. "Do you think his buddies decided they couldn't trust him when he muffed the hit on Moss?"

"That's one theory," Evans answered.

"What's another?" Sparks asked.

"I don't really have one, but Brad seems to. It's useless to press him. I know he'll tell us what he knows when he's ready. Right now, let's ask Justice Price about his law clerk."

"Ridiculous!" Millard Price said. "Kyle wasn't a racist."

"There's a lot of evidence to the contrary in his apartment."

"Then someone planted it. Do some police work. Check into his history. I've known him for years, and I've never seen him do anything or heard him utter a word that would make me believe he is— was—a bigot."

Price shook his head. He appeared to be genuinely shaken by the news that his clerk had been murdered.

"We will follow up, Justice Price, but we have a witness who saw Mr. Peterson stuffing a ski mask into his attaché case right after Justice Moss was attacked, and we found the ski mask and clothing that matches the clothes the assailant wore in Mr. Peterson's apartment."

"I just can't believe it."

"It would explain how the killer disappeared," Maggie Sparks said. "All Peterson had to do was strip off his clothes in an area that wasn't covered by a surveillance camera, return to his office, and leave the Court as he would normally."

"Have you reviewed the tapes to see if that's what happened?" Price asked.

"We have someone on it right now."

"I'm betting you won't find any incriminating evidence on the tapes. This is a setup."

"So you never saw anything that would lead you to believe that Kyle Peterson would do something like this?" Maggie asked.

"That's what I've been telling you."

"I understand your reaction," Keith said. "When you work with someone every day, and you think you know him, and something like this happens, it can be very disconcerting. We get the same reaction from the neighbors of serial killers."

"It's inconceivable to me that Kyle was a racist, let alone a killer," Price insisted.

"I hope there's another explanation," Keith said. "We certainly won't stop investigating. Thank you for taking the time to talk to us."

"Of course."

"If you do think of something, please call," Maggie said as she handed the judge her card.

As soon as the door closed behind the agents, Price closed his eyes and leaned his head against the back of his chair. Dennis was behind this. He was sure of it. That poor young man. Kyle was a decent, hard-working sort. He didn't deserve this.

Price leaned forward and put his head in his hands. Was Kyle murdered by the person who tried to kill Felicia Moss? Price was overwhelmed with guilt because he was responsible for getting Masterson's assassin a job at the Court. Dennis had told him he needed someone to keep an eye on the case. He'd never said anything about the law clerk being a trained killer. If he'd only refused, Price thought. There probably weren't enough votes to grant cert in *Woodruff.* And what if the case did get a hearing? Was it worth killing people to keep the *China Sea* operation hidden?

Price ran a hand down the side of his face. He didn't know what to do. Maybe the killing was over. Maybe this insanity would stop if the FBI decided that Kyle was the person who tried to kill Felicia. If Audrey Stewart became a member of the Court, the *Woodruff* case would die, and everything would be OK. That was a hope he had to hang onto.

Chapter Fifty-three

When her phone rang, Daphne Haggard was getting ready to leave the police station to join Brett for dinner at Inverness's only Thai restaurant before attending a student production of *Frost/Nixon*. She checked her watch and debated whether to take the call. Her sense of duty trumped her hunger pangs.

"Is this Detective Daphne Haggard?"

"Speaking."

"I'm Jim Haynes, an orthopedic surgeon in Madison. I understand you're looking for the name of one of my patients."

"Does this concern an orthopedic appliance made by Orthosure?"

"Yes."

"Thank you for calling," Daphne said excitedly. "I am *very* interested in identifying your patient."

"What's this all about?" the surgeon asked.

Daphne told him how the appliance was discovered.

"God, that's terrible," Haynes said.

"It is, and I'm hoping you can give me the information we need to identify the victim."

"I can definitely do that."

Dr. Haynes gave Daphne a name and said that the patient would be twenty-eight now. They talked a few minutes more before Daphne thanked the doctor and ended the conversation. It was too late to do anything tonight, but Daphne finally had a name.

Chapter Fifty-four

Even though Kyle Peterson was dead, Brad was relieved to find a police officer sitting outside Justice Moss's chambers. If Kyle was part of a white-supremacist group, there was nothing to prevent them from making another attempt on his boss's life. But Brad was not convinced that Kyle was a racist. He could have been set up by the real killer, or he could have been the assassin, but his motive for trying to take out Justice Moss might have been tied to the *Woodruff* case.

"How was Texas?" Brad asked.

"I always get a kick out of talking to law students before the real world has corrupted them."

Brad laughed. "I never knew you were such a cynic."

"Life's knocked me back and forth between cynicism and optimism. I prefer the latter. Then I hear about Kyle Peterson, and I want to give up on people altogether. Do you think he was the person who tried to kill us?"

Brad hesitated.

"You have some doubts?" Moss asked.

"I think it's possible. Kyle was tall and lanky. His build is vaguely similar to the man I fought with.

And they did find the clothes in his closet. What do you think?"

"I thought the man who attacked me was thinner than Peterson. I even entertained the thought that the killer might have been a woman."

Brad frowned. "I never thought of that."

Justice Moss shook her head. "I was looking at that gun. Then I was trying to pick it up. I only concentrated on the person who attacked me when I was trying to get off a shot, but he was up the ramp by then, some distance away. I just don't know."

"I guess we'll have to wait until the investigation is complete."

"I heard Peterson died very violently," Justice Moss said.

"That's what Keith—Agent Evans—told me. It sounded pretty gruesome."

"Does the FBI have any idea who killed him?"

"Their working hypothesis is that Kyle had a falling-out with the other people in the assassination plot."

"If Kyle was part of a white-supremacist group, it looks like I was wrong to suspect Millard of being involved with the attack. But what if Peterson isn't the assassin? What if the clothing was planted in his apartment by the real killer?"

"Harriet saw him putting the ski mask in his attaché."

"I forgot about that." Justice Moss sighed. "Before Peterson was killed, I was certain of Millard's involvement in the attempt on my life. It made sense. What goes on in conference is secret. Not even you clerks know. That means that one of the justices had to have told the people who wanted me dead that I was responsible for deferring the vote on *Woodruff.* But my theory means nothing if the attempt on my life was for reasons having nothing to do with that case."

"That's true, but finding those racist tracts was pretty convenient. It offers a clear-cut explanation for an attack on an African American and closes the door on any further investigation into a link between the attack and *Woodruff v. Oregon.*"

"You think Peterson was set up to derail our investigation?" Moss asked.

"He could still be the person who attacked you, but he might not be some kind of Aryan Nation, White Brotherhood assassin."

"Why the doubts?"

"We've discovered a link between Justice Price and the *China Sea.*"

Brad told his boss about Dana's investigation in Oregon and the discovery of the TA Enterprises file in the subbasement. Then he showed Justice Moss the pictures Ginny had taken with her cell phone.

"It looks like Justice Price was upset about the possibility of *Woodruff* being granted cert because he's afraid that his part in the drug-smuggling operation will become public knowledge," Brad said.

"After seeing the pictures of the TA Enterprises file, I'm almost positive that Justice Price was involved with the *China Sea* in some capacity," Moss said.

"Proving his involvement or anything else that happened that night may be impossible, Judge. The ship is gone, along with the dead men and whatever was in the hold. Oswald and Swanson are dead, and God knows where the night watchman is or if he's alive. They're the only people who could give eye-witness testimony about the murders, and Oswald is the only person who had an opinion about the hash-ish. There's still Oswald's report about the hashish and the dead men, but that's also worthless as evidence without Oswald.

"And as far as the file in the subbasement is concerned, I'd be shocked if Dennis Masterson hasn't taken care of it. Our photos prove that Justice Price created the TA Enterprises shell corporation but there's nothing in the pictures that proves why he did it or ties the file to the *China Sea*.

"Finally, John Finley is dead, and his statements to Sarah Woodruff are hearsay. And, not to put too fine a point on it, a person facing execution is not the best witness if you are trying to prove someone else committed the crime."

"This is very disturbing," Felicia Moss said when he was done.

"Dana has gone as far with this as she can, and I think it's too dangerous for me to continue working on the matter. Dennis Masterson knows Ginny was poking around in the TA Enterprises file. The day she took the pictures, a man tried to kill her."

"Oh, my God," Moss said.

Brad told Justice Moss about the incident at the law firm. She looked grim as she listened.

"I should never have involved you," Moss said when Brad was done. "I don't know what I was thinking, especially when I thought Millard might have been behind the attack."

"It's time to confide in Keith Evans, Judge," Brad said. "We can trust him to be discreet. We're not detectives. Let Keith do his job. Dana's right. It's time for the amateurs to step down and let the professionals take over."

"I agree. You have no idea how grateful I am for your help, Brad, but in light of what you've told me, I definitcly want you to cease any involvement in the matter."

"I will after I do one more thing. I don't think you should have any contact with the FBI. When we started this, you told me how much trouble you could get in if anyone found out that you were going outside the record to investigate a case that was in front of the Court. Let me brief Keith. I'll tell him that everything was my idea."

"How will you explain knowing about my motion to defer voting on the *Woodruff* cert petition and Millard's actions in the conference?"

Brad's brow furrowed. Then he brightened. "Wilhelmina Horst and Kyle Peterson both talked to me about the way Justice Price acted when he came back from the conference. I'll just say that Kyle told me. No one will be able to find out what he really did."

"All right, but as soon as you've briefed Agent Evans, you will shed your secret identity as an ace detective and revert to being a mild-mannered law clerk. That's an order. And until this is over, I'm giving you and Ms. Striker police protection."

Brad didn't make a single complaint about the order, and he was grateful that Ginny was going to be protected. He was anxious to back away from their investigation of international drug dealing and intrigue and go back to his peaceful humdrum existence.

Chapter Fifty-five

All during dinner and the play, Daphne's brain was swamped with ideas for discovering the identity of the person who had dismembered her victim. The body parts had been found in the forest surrounding the campus. That didn't mean that the victim had to be a student at Inverness, but she was young, so Daphne decided that the college registrar's office was not a bad place to start.

As soon as she got to work the next morning, Daphne placed the call and asked if the victim had been a student at the school. After some hemming and hawing about the confidentiality of student records and a few transfers to people further up the food chain, she learned that no one by that name had been a student at Inverness University. Daphne was disappointed until she remembered that the law school had a separate registrar's office. She slapped her palm against her forehead. "Of course, dummy," she murmured. "A twenty-eight-year-old would be in graduate school."

Rather than put up with the obstruction she knew she'd encounter from the registrar, Daphne decided to pay a visit to the dean of the law school.

Daphne had met Tom Ostgard on a number of occasions since moving to Inverness, and her Ivy League degree had given her the credibility she'd needed to convince him to let her co-teach a course in the law school's clinical program.

There had been heavy flurries that morning, and the stillness that accompanies the fall of fresh snow still cloaked Inverness. The children were in school and a lot of the townsfolk had chosen to stay indoors. The college students paid no attention to the cold and wandered across campus with red noses and cherry-colored cheeks.

The Robert M. La Follette School of Law was housed in a redbrick building that stood on the eastern edge of the campus, away from the undergraduate schools. It had been named for "Fighting Bob" La Follette, who was Wisconsin's twentieth governor and had served the state in the House of Representatives and Senate in the early part of the twentieth century. The dean's office was on the third floor, and Daphne climbed the stairs for the exercise, dodging students too engrossed in legal arguments to pay attention to where they were going.

Tom Ostgard, a nationally respected scholar in the area of property law, was a reed-thin man in his early sixties. He had a fringe of gray hair surrounding his shiny dome and wore wire-rimmed glasses that magnified his brown eyes.

"You're not here to arrest me, are you?" joked Ostgard, who was fascinated by Daphne's connection to a world of mayhem and disorder that he had never encountered.

Daphne smiled. "Have you been up to something I should know about?"

"Sadly, no. My life is still that of the dull academic. Seriously, though, what's up? You're going to teach next semester, aren't you?"

"I wouldn't miss it for the world. The students are great, and I love being back in academia."

"Then what can I do for you?"

"You know about the body parts we found in the woods?"

Ostgard sobered.

"We've made an identification, and I need to know if the victim was a law student. When I tried to get information out of the registrar's office at the college, it took me forever, so I thought I'd go to the top and see if you can cut through the red tape."

"Of course. Give me the name."

Ostgard grabbed a pen, but he set it down as soon as Daphne identified the victim.

"I'm afraid you've made a mistake," Ostgard said.

"I don't think so. My information is pretty solid."

"Then check it again. Harriet Lezak is not only alive, but she's a clerk at the United States Supreme Court."

Daphne's face showed her confusion. "That's a very prestigious position. No offense, Tom, but I thought the justices took their clerks from schools like Harvard and Yale. Has La Follette Law ever placed anyone else on the Court?"

The dean looked torn.

"What's the problem?" Daphne asked.

"I know something about the appointment that I swore to keep secret," Ostgard said.

"This is a murder investigation, Tom."

"I know. That's the only reason I'm considering telling you, but I need your assurance that you'll keep what I say confidential unless it's absolutely necessary to reveal it."

"I need to hear what you know before I can make that type of promise."

Ostgard hesitated. Then he sighed. "I'm going to have to trust you to use discretion, because revealing what I say could have a major impact on the law school's future."

"Go ahead."

"La Follette School of Law has never had a graduate selected to clerk at the Court. Even our best graduates would consider the application process a waste of time. Those positions are usually reserved for law-review students at elite law schools. Actually, it's not that often that a student is given a clerkship right out of law school. Most of the Supreme Court clerks serve a clerkship with a federal appellate judge first."

"So what happened this time?"

"A few months before the term ended last year, I received a visit from a man named Oscar Hagglund. Mr. Hagglund said he was representing Justice Millard Price and that everything he was going to say was in confidence. Hagglund said that Justice Price was trying an experiment. He wanted me to send him the résumés of the law-review students in the graduating class so he could select one of them to be his clerk. The purpose of the experiment was to see if there was a difference between the work performed by graduates of schools like Yale, Harvard, NYU, Stanford, and Columbia and a top graduate at a school like La Follette. Of course, I was thrilled that Justice Price had selected our school, and I sent the résumés to the address Mr. Hagglund gave me."

"Was the address different from the address of the Court?" Daphne asked.

Ostgard nodded. "It was a post office box. Hagglund explained that Justice Price was using this address to keep his project secret."

"What did Hagglund look like?"

"He was a big man. He looked very fit." Ostgard closed his eyes for a moment. "Blond hair, blue eyes, very Scandinavian. I detected an accent—Swedish, Danish, I'm not certain, but my ancestors came from those parts, and he sounded a little like my grandfather."

"What happened after you sent the résumés?"

"A week later, Hagglund called and told me the justice's choice."

"Did the choice surprise you?" Daphne asked.

"Yes and no. Harriet was third in the class, but she had no other distinctions besides her excellent grades. If I remember correctly, she worked her way through college and did well at a small liberal-arts school. I don't remember the school, but it was in Iowa. Then she worked as an accountant for a few years before applying to law school, so she was a little older than most of the students. Harriet received some financial aid, but she worked for her tuition here until she received a scholarship when she made law review. She had no extracurricular

achievements except the review, which is understandable if you're working your way through. Still,
her résumé was rather sparse.

"Ned Randall, who graduated first, was editor of
the law review. He'd been in Iraq with the Marines
before applying to law school. His undergraduate
record was not exceptional, but he'd been a star athlete. And Marla Jones, who graduated second in the
class, is an African American who is very active polit-
ically and had a very varied résumé. Of course, given
Price's politics, that may have worked against her."

"Can you get me Miss Lezak's records? I'd like to
ask her parents if they've talked with her recently."

"Harriet is an orphan. An aunt raised her, but I
think she passed away, too. That's why she had to
work her way through."

"Did she have any close friends, a boyfriend?"

"I don't know anything about her social life."

"When is the last time you saw Miss Lezak?"

"At graduation, but I didn't speak to her very
much. I did have a very nice chat with her when I
relayed Justice Price's offer of the clerkship."

"How did she react?" Daphne asked.

"She was stunned, literally speechless. I told her
she would have to go to Washington and interview
with Justice Price. She was very excited. She'd never
been out of the Midwest. She was concerned about
one thing. She'd accepted an offer from a very good
firm in Chicago, but I assured her that any firm
would gladly defer her job for a year if she was clerking at the Court. I even offered to call the firm. I'm
a personal friend of one of the senior partners."

"I'll call Washington to find out if Miss Lezak is working at the Court," Daphne said, "but I'd like to get as much background as I can before I do that. Do you think there's anyone at the law-review office who knew her—another student or a professor?"

"Let me call the law-review office," Ostgard said.

Ten minutes later, a tall, attractive blonde dressed in jeans and a forest green cable-stitch sweater was ushered in by the dean's secretary.

"Ah, Gayle. Thanks for coming. Have a seat," Ostgard said. "Detective Haggard, this is Gayle Blake, one of our shining stars."

The young woman's smile vanished when she heard that Daphne was with the police. Ostgard laughed.

"Not to worry," he assured Blake. "You're not in any trouble. Detective Haggard needs to ask you some questions about Harriet Lezak."

"She graduated," Blake said.

"I know that," Daphne said. "And you don't have to worry about getting her in hot water. This conversation will stay here. I don't plan on writing a report about it. What I'm interested in is background. For instance, how well did you know her?"

"Not well, and I can't think of anyone who did. Harriet worked very hard, and she always completed her assignments on time, but she didn't socialize."

"No beers after putting the review to bed?"

"She wasn't a hermit. She joined the staff when we went out for a group dinner or, like you said, a beer. But she was quiet, kept to herself. I know she spoke up on occasion. She had political views. But I honestly can't remember anything she said, not one conversation. Oh, she did run a lot. It was her way of blowing off steam. She'd run for miles on the trails behind the campus."

"So there was nothing wrong with her legs?"

Blake's brow furrowed. "You know, she did mention a biking accident once. We were talking about working out. I do a lot of cardio in the gym. She said she used to ride a bicycle, but she broke her leg a few years back and decided that running was safer."

"What about boyfriends or just friends?" Daphne asked.

"I never saw her with a boy where it looked romantic. She had a study group: some of the other third-years on the review. Oh, and I did see her walking around campus with a woman on a few occasions toward the end of the term. They looked friendly. Actually, now that I think about it, Harriet and this woman looked very similar, like sisters. So maybe she was a relative."

Chapter Fifty-six

Brad waved to Keith Evans as soon as he spotted the FBI agent. Brad had asked Keith to meet him in a neighborhood Greek restaurant a few blocks off Dupont Circle because he didn't want anyone at the Court to know about the meeting.

"Thanks for coming," Brad said as soon as Keith was seated across from him.

"I'll do anything for a free meal," Keith joked.

"On my salary?" Brad said. "And you'll be buying *me* dinner when you hear what I have to tell you."

The waiter appeared and Keith ordered Chicken Vasilikos with a side of Dolmathes. Brad asked for Spanakopita and a Greek Salad.

"I want to be up-front with you," Brad said as soon as the waiter left. "I can't prove what I'm going to tell you with evidence that would be admissible in court. I'm also going to ask you to promise to keep a few things I tell you to yourself and out of any report you write and to stop asking questions about any area I tell you I can't go into."

"OK."

"You know how a state criminal case gets a hearing in my court, right?"

"I think so. When someone is convicted, they file appeals and keep filing them until they are turned down at the highest state level, usually the state supreme court. If they think there's a federal issue, they file a petition for a writ of certiorari asking the U.S. Supreme Court to take up the case. How did I do?"

"A-plus. We've got a case out of Oregon that raises a very tricky federal issue. The defendant is on death row. She was convicted of murdering her boyfriend. While the case was in the state trial court, the defendant's attorney tried to get evidence that would establish an alternative theory of the crime, that drug dealers and the CIA had reasons to kill the boyfriend. As part of her strategy, she issued subpoenas for the records of the CIA and other intelligence agencies. The feds blocked the attempts by invoking the state-secrets privilege. That's the issue in the Court. Can the state-secrets privilege be invoked to prevent a defendant in a death-penalty case from securing exculpatory evidence? Are you with me so far?"

"Yes, Professor Miller."

Brad leaned across the table. "I think Justice Moss was attacked because she interfered with an attempt by Justice Millard Price to deny the petition for cert."

A look of incredulity spread across Keith's face, and he put down his fork.

"Let me get this straight. You're accusing a Supreme Court justice of hiring a hit man to kill another justice?"

"I think there's a good possibility Justice Price had some involvement in the assassination attempt. And I think Dennis Masterson is behind the plot."

Evans's mouth dropped open. Then he laughed. "You are fucking kidding me! Masterson is one of the most powerful men in this town."

"And he was the head of the CIA when the events in Oregon took place. Let me tell you everything we've found out."

Keith listened intently as Brad laid out what he, Dana, and Ginny had learned about the *China Sea* incident and TA Enterprises.

"You've been a busy beaver," the agent said when Brad finished.

"You've got to admit that I had a good reason for asking Dana to look into the *Woodruff* case."

Keith was about to respond when his cell phone rang. He checked the caller.

"I have to take this," he said. Keith got up and walked into the narrow hall that led to the restrooms.

"What's up?" Keith asked Tyrone Bagley, his supervisor.

"Daphne Haggard, a homicide detective in Inverness, Wisconsin, called for the agent in charge of the investigation into the assassination attempt on Justice Moss. She was driving to the airport in Milwaukee to catch a flight to D.C. I'm going to give you her flight number and time of arrival. I want you to meet her at the airport in the morning."

Keith fished out a pen and wrote down the information.

"What's this about?"

"A receptionist took the message. She was going to wait to give it to you but she decided it might be important so she brought it to me."

"And?" Keith asked.

"The message says that Haggard believes there is a good possibility that one of the clerks at the United States Supreme Court is an impostor."

Chapter Fifty-seven

Justice Moss called Brad minutes after his alarm went off to tell him that she wanted him in her chambers as soon as he got in. The judge hadn't told him why she wanted to meet, but Brad remembered that the justices were in conference later in the morning to decide the fate of petitions for writs of certiorari. He wondered if *Woodruff* was among the petitions that would be discussed.

When Brad arrived at the Court, Harriet was already at her desk.

"I'm off to see the Wizard," Brad said, in case someone needed him.

Harriet grunted but didn't look up from her monitor.

Until the attempt on her life, Felicia Moss had been one of the more spirited justices, and the energy with which she attacked her job had made Brad forget her age. This morning, she was slumped in her chair looking every bit like a woman in her seventies.

"We're discussing the petitions for cert this morning," the judge said as soon as Brad shut the door. "I've asked Millard to meet with me before the conference starts."

"Why are you doing that?" Brad asked, worried that he knew what his boss was going to answer.

"I'm going to confront him. I want you to be here because you know everything our investigation uncovered."

"You're making a mistake, Judge. I don't think it's wise to meet with Justice Price. What if we're right and he was involved in the plot to kill you?"

"Do you remember when Millard visited me the morning after the attack?"

Brad nodded.

"He was very upset, and I don't think he was faking. Millard is involved in some way in the *Woodruff* matter; the papers your fiancée discovered prove he created the Cayman Island company, and I'm convinced his opposition to Woodruff's cert petition has nothing to do with its merits. But I can't believe he would be part of a plan to murder me."

"I met with Keith last night and brought him up to speed. He knows everything I know. Let's bring him into the meeting."

"Millard won't talk freely with an FBI agent in the room."

"What makes you think he'll talk with me here?"

"I plan on having you step out as soon as you tell Millard what you know."

"You're going to be alone with him? He's a big man, Judge. He could kill you."

"I don't think he'll try to hurt me, but we'll soon know how good a judge I am of human nature."

* * *

Air traffic control had instructed the pilot of the plane carrying Daphne Haggard to let the detective off before any other passenger. Keith's credentials had gotten him through security, and he was waiting at the end of the gangway when the bleary-eyed redhead walked into the boarding area pulling her carry-on behind her.

"Detective Haggard, I'm Keith Evans, a special agent with the FBI. How was your flight?"

"As good as a red-eye can be."

"Do you have any more baggage?"

"No, this is it."

"Do you want some coffee or something to eat?"

"I don't think you'll want to waste time eating when you hear what I have to say. To tell the truth, I was afraid I wouldn't be taken seriously."

Keith smiled. "I'm the agent in charge of the investigation into the attempted murder of Justice Moss, and I can assure you that an easy way to get my attention is for a homicide detective to leave a message stating that she thinks a Supreme Court clerk is an impostor. So, what makes you think one of the clerks isn't who they're supposed to be?"

On the way to the parking garage, Daphne filled in Evans on the discovery of the missing thigh and how the victim was identified.

"What did you do after you talked to the dean and the student?" Keith asked.

"I called the Supreme Court. They told me that Harriet Lezak is clerking for Justice Moss. The problem is that pieces of Lezak are also in the Inverness city morgue."

"Have you tried a DNA match?"

"I'm on that. We sent a tissue sample to NamUs right away so they could run it through their database, but that takes three months or more, unless it's a priority case."

"This case will jump to the top of the list as soon as I get a chance to call Texas. What about using Lezak's tissue or saliva for the test?"

"I'm trying to run down something to use for a comparison. So far I haven't had any luck. Lezak is an orphan, so there's no family to contact. She did have her own apartment just off campus, but it was cleaned when she moved out, and it's been rented for months."

"Do any of her friends have something of hers with DNA on it?"

"Everyone says she was also a loner with no real friends. One student saw her walking around campus with a woman whose description fits the woman Gayle Blake saw her with. He also thought there was a strong resemblance. But I have no leads on the identity of the woman."

"Do you think the woman who was seen with Lezak is the person who took her place?"

"That's what I'm guessing, but it's just a guess at this point."

"Did you bring Lezak's school file? I'd like to see it."

"It's in my bag," Daphne said.

"What about a picture?" he asked. "Do you have a photograph? I've talked to Lezak. I'll know right away if the person in the photo is the woman who's clerking for Justice Moss."

"There's one in her file. I'll get it out when we're in the car."

"This is terrific police work," Keith told Haggard. "Exceptional, but personally I hope you've made a terrible mistake."

"That makes two of us," Haggard said, "but I don't think I have."

Millard Price was smiling when he entered Justice Moss's chambers. Brad decided that the justice hadn't guessed why the judge wanted to talk to him, or he was a very good actor.

"What's up?" Price asked.

"Sit down, Millard. Brad and I have something to tell you."

Price looked back and forth between the justice and her clerk. Both looked somber. Price stopped smiling and took a seat across from his fellow justice.

"What's going on, Felicia?"

"I know why you've been so upset about Sarah Woodruff's petition for cert," Moss told him.

"*Woodruff?* What makes you think I'm upset about that case?"

"If you're not worried that we'll grant cert, you should be," the judge said. "Once the case becomes a topic of discussion in the national media, someone is going to dig up the goods on TA Enterprises, the hashish-smuggling operation, and the five dead men on the *China Sea*."

"I'm really not sure what you're getting at. From

what I've read in the record, there's no proof that there was hashish on the ship or any dead bodies."

"There is proof that you were involved in establishing the shell corporation that bought the ship."

The judge turned to Brad. "Show Justice Price the pictures of the file."

Price looked angry when he finished studying the blowups Brad had made from the photos on Ginny's phone.

"Where did you get these?" he asked. "These documents are in a client's file in my old firm. They're confidential. Anyone who took these is guilty of theft."

Moss focused her gaze on her judicial brother. "And you're guilty of a conflict of interest, Millard. Did you help buy that ship for the CIA? If you did, why didn't you recuse yourself?"

"What I did or did not do in my capacity as an attorney for a client of Rankin Lusk is privileged information."

Justice Moss leaned toward Price. When she spoke, there was steel in her voice and a hint of the menace she must have radiated during her days on the street.

"Brad is going to tell you everything we know about the *China Sea* so you can decide how you wish to proceed. If you don't recuse yourself from the case, I will repeat in conference everything Brad will tell you, and I'll let the justices decide how to deal with you."

Brad's voice shook as he told Justice Price—without naming Dana or Ginny—what had been uncovered about Woodruff's case. Price maintained a blank expression during the narrative. If they'd been expecting Price to break down and confess, Justice Moss and her clerk were disappointed.

"I haven't heard anything but guesswork and hearsay," Price said when Brad was finished. "You'd never get any of that admitted in court."

"Our conferences are not courts of law, Millard," Felicia said quietly. "The hearsay rule doesn't apply. But common sense does, and I believe that our brethren will be as upset with you as I am when they know what happened on that ship and the attempts that you and your school friend made to cover it up—attempts that may have included an attempt on my life.

"Tell me, Millard, what will you do if a member of the House of Representatives begins impeachment proceedings? How will you and Dennis Masterson cover up what you did when the government and the press put this sordid episode under a microscope."

The smug look disappeared from Price's face, and Brad could tell that he finally understood his position.

"Thank you for your help, Brad. Why don't you leave me and Justice Price so we can continue this discussion?"

Brad was torn. He wanted nothing more to do with the *China Sea*, but he didn't want to leave his boss with a man who might try to kill her. Moss saw his indecision. She smiled.

"I'll be fine, Brad. Please go. And tell Carrie I don't want to be interrupted."

Brad stepped out and gave Carrie the message. He rounded the corner and was about to step into his office when his cell phone vibrated. He looked down to check the caller ID and almost ran into Harriet Lezak.

"Sorry," Brad said.

"No problem."

Harriet headed down the hall.

"Hey, Keith," Brad said.

"Don't react. Just say yes or no. Is Harriet Lezak with you?"

"No. She just left our office. Why?"

"She's an impostor. The real Harriet Lezak has been dead for months."

"Jesus!"

"I'm pulling into the Court garage. I'll be upstairs in a few minutes."

As Brad disconnected, he remembered that Justice Moss and Justice Price were alone and Harriet had been heading in the direction of the judge's chambers. He sprinted back. Carrie had been sitting at her desk moments ago, but he didn't see her. Then he saw a foot jutting out past her desk. He walked around it and found the judge's secretary sprawled on the floor. He knelt quickly and felt for a pulse. As soon as he found one, Brad rushed to the door of Justice Moss's chambers and yanked it open. Harriet was standing in the middle of the room, pointing a gun at Price and Moss. She turned her head toward Brad, and Justice Price launched himself across the room with the determination he'd shown decades earlier on the gridiron. Harriet turned back and fired. Price staggered but he was close enough to wrap Lezak in a bear hug. His momentum sent them crashing to the floor. When they hit, Harriet's right arm was pinned to her side and the gun was pointed down her leg. Price held her so tightly that she couldn't turn the barrel toward him.

Brad scanned the room for a weapon and grabbed a heavy ceremonial gavel that had been given to Justice Moss by the NAACP. Price and Lezak were thrashing around on the floor. The justice was bleeding badly and he was weakening. Lezak got some space between their bodies and started to sit up. Brad smashed the gavel on her skull. Blood poured from her scalp. She turned her head toward Brad and he whipped the gavel into her face with so much force that the head of it flew off.

Lezak slumped back, but she still held the gun. Brad stamped on her wrist and her hand opened. As he kicked the gun away, Lezak grabbed his ankle and whipped it up. Brad toppled over. Lezak heaved Price off her. Brad got to his knees. Lezak turned to face him. The handle of the gavel was jagged where the head had snapped off. Brad didn't hesitate. He plunged the jagged edge into Lezak's neck. Blood spurted out and her hands flew to the wound just as the door flew open and Keith Evans ran in, followed by two members of the Supreme Court police force and a redheaded woman Brad had never seen before.

Chapter Fifty-eight

Two days later, Justice Moss and Brad Miller sat quietly in the judge's chambers while Keith Evans brought them up to speed on the investigation.

"Justice Price passed away last night," he said.

"Oh my," Felicia said. A tear drifted down her cheek. "He saved my life, you know. When Harriet pulled the gun, he begged her to spare me. Then he took the bullet that was meant for me."

"Lezak would probably have killed him anyway," Keith said. "When we swept your chambers, we found a listening device. She could hear everything you said in here, which means she heard you and Brad lay out the investigation. She couldn't let Price talk, and you were a witness *and* you were going to vote to grant Woodruff's cert petition."

"Has Harriet—or whatever her real name is— has she said anything?" Brad asked.

"She's still not able to speak."

"How did she become a clerk?" Brad asked. With everything that had gone on, he'd never had a chance to find out how Keith knew "Lezak" was an impostor.

Keith told them everything Daphne Haggard had discovered in Inverness.

"Without Price, we can't prove everything," Keith said, "but here's what I think happened. Masterson would have kept track of Woodruff's case. When the Oregon Supreme Court denied her appeal, he must have told Price that they needed a mole on the Court to keep track of the way some of the more liberal judges were leaning and to try and influence them. I'm guessing that Masterson made a study of the students at the top of second-tier law schools until he found one who looked like one of his operatives. Daphne Haggard told me how excited Dean Ostgard was at the possibility of placing a La Follette grad in a Supreme Court clerkship. It wasn't much of an effort to get him to keep Price's experiment secret, and the real Harriet Lezak was thrilled by the opportunity to get the most prestigious law job in the country.

"A few months before the offer was made, the impostor befriended Lezak. She may have posed as a fellow runner and killed Harriet in the forest during a run. Then she chopped up the body to hide it and stall identification as long as possible in case someone stumbled across the body parts."

Keith addressed Justice Moss. "Once Price hired Lezak, he maneuvered you into taking her on as your clerk. Her first chance to influence your decision in *Woodruff* came when you assigned her to write a memo about the legal issues raised by the case. Brad has reviewed the phony Lezak's legal work. He said it was pretty high quality. She's probably a lawyer or had legal training. She used her memo to convince you to vote against granting cert, but you had reservations about the case. That made you a potential target. I'm guessing that Masterson told her to take you out when Price told him that you were responsible for convincing the justices to defer the vote on *Woodruff* in the conference."

"Do you have a case against Masterson?" Justice Moss asked.

"I'll be honest with you, Judge. If we can't get the phony Lezak to talk, we have nothing."

"Agent Evans," the judge said, "I will do everything in my power to see that the events on the *China Sea* receive as much publicity as they possibly can. Once the other justices learn what's happened, I'm guessing that cert will be granted. There are going to be congressional inquiries, investigative reports. Dennis Masterson will not get away scot-free."

"I wish I shared your enthusiasm," Keith said. "Masterson is a powerful man, and the CIA has a vested interest in keeping its dirty secrets hidden from the public eye."

"You're right, of course. But the Agency has got to draw the line somewhere, and I hope it's at the murder of a United States Supreme Court justice."

"One can always hope," Evans said, but he didn't sound like he expected the Agency to act honorably. He looked at his watch. "I've got to run. I'm driving Haggard to the airport, and I'm cutting it close."

As soon as Detective Haggard buckled her seat belt, Evans handed her a copy of the *Washington Post*.

The headline read "Small-Town Ivy League Detective Solves Supreme Court Murder Case."

"I thought you might like to show that to your husband and your boss," he said.

Daphne blushed. "I'm afraid I've been given more credit than I deserve."

"Not true. And I'm not the only one who thinks that was one great piece of detective work. In fact, I've been authorized to ask you if you have any interest in joining the Bureau. The people who make the big decisions have spoken to your boss in Chicago, and he had great things to say about you. Personally, I think you'd make one hell of an agent."

Daphne's breath caught in her chest. Joining the FBI was like making the majors if you played baseball. She'd thought about it a lot when she was in Chicago, but she hadn't dreamed about it at all since she'd moved to Inverness.

"I appreciate the offer, but I'm going to have to talk it over with my husband. He has a good job teaching, and he'll have to be part of any decision I make."

"You'll be back in D.C. to testify, so take your time. The offer is serious."

Daphne thought about the offer to join the Bureau while she checked in and went through security. And the offer wasn't the only thing distracting her. Daphne had become a celebrity during her time in D.C. As soon as the press learned about her academic background and her brilliant detective work, she had been the subject of stories like the one Keith

Evans had shown her. She'd also fielded a number of book and movie offers, as well as invitations to appear on TV and radio shows.

Daphne had called Brett every night before she went to bed to tell him what had happened during her day. She treasured their talks because they introduced a note of normalcy into her insanely hectic D.C. routine. As soon as she was in the boarding area, Daphne called Brett.

"Where are you?" he asked.

"I'm waiting for my plane. It's going to board in twenty minutes."

"I missed you."

"Ditto."

"So, tell me, are the rumors true? Are they really thinking of having Charlize Theron play you in the movie?"

"Not you, too," Daphne moaned.

"Hey, I need to know who I should fantasize about when we're making love."

"You are such an asshole."

Brett laughed. Then he got quiet. "Are you going to be able to settle down and go back to writing traffic tickets?" he asked.

"Detectives don't hand out traffic tickets," Daphne answered, but she knew the question was serious. It was another version of "How you gonna keep 'em down on the farm after they've seen Paree?"

"I was invited to apply to join the FBI," Daphne said after a pause. "It was a serious offer. The implication was that the application was just a matter of form."

"What did you tell them?" Brett asked.

"That I had to think about it and that I wouldn't do anything without talking to you."

"So, how are you leaning?"

Daphne could hear the tension in Brett's voice.

"The agent who tendered the offer started out as a small-town cop in Nebraska. I asked him about the adjustment, and he was pretty honest. He told me he got his offer the same way I was getting mine, after he found a serial killer who had stymied the Bureau. He told me that agents move around a lot and they're not home much. The work is exciting but it's high pressure, and it doesn't leave much time for friends and relationships. His marriage was a casualty of the move."

"When I couldn't get a teaching job, you stood by me," Brett said. "And when I got the offer from Inverness, you gave up a future on the Chicago force so I could be happy. If you really want to make this move, I'll support your decision. I can always find a teaching job. What I don't want is to have you wondering about what could have been and regretting that you didn't make the best of your big opportunity."

Daphne smiled. "You have always been my big opportunity, Brett. I did move to Inverness for you, and I'll admit there were times when I wondered whether I'd made too big a sacrifice. Then I'd see how happy you are when you come back from class, and I'd know I'd made the right choice. I like Inverness. We're known and respected there. Chicago or D.C. would be a rat race. My career might take off, but would our marriage survive the separation and constant moves that would be inevitable if I worked in the Bureau? I'm not willing to risk your happiness and what we have. So, yes, I'm ready, willing, and able to hand out traffic tickets and kiss my brilliant future in the Bureau good-bye."

"I love you."

"I love you, too."

"So, you never answered my question about Charlize Theron . . ."

Daphne laughed. "Call me Charlize when we're in bed, and I'm going to Taser you."

Brett laughed. "Hurry home, kiddo, and we'll see what happens."

Chapter Fifty-nine

Dana called Brad half an hour after Keith Evans left. She was upbeat, which was unusual for her.

"I just got some good news," Dana told Brad. "Jake called and he's coming home this week."

"That's great. Let's get together."

"Will do. So, what's going on with the case?"

"Lezak still can't talk. If she doesn't, Keith thinks Masterson may walk. The judge is determined to push for a congressional investigation. That might not lead to an indictment, but it will make the *China Sea* incident public."

"That's the main reason I'm calling. I promised Pat Gorman a scoop, and I'd like to deliver, but I need the judge's permission to go public. Can you see if I can get it? I'll keep the judge's involvement quiet. Tell her if she wants to shine a big spotlight on Dennis Masterson, a story in *Exposed* will do that in spades. *Exposed*'s motto is 'All the innuendo Pat sees fit to print.'"

Dana and Brad talked a little longer before they hung up. She was looking forward to exposing Dennis Masterson, but she was frustrated by her inability to develop a plan that would put Masterson and Bergstrom in prison. She was also stressed out because she was balancing her investigations for her clients with the tail she'd put on Bergstrom.

When she needed to, Dana employed retired policemen or moonlighting cops to help her. She was doing that now so she could watch Bergstrom, who spent most of his time at home or at a gym where he pumped iron and practiced mixed martial arts. Dana's financial resources were limited, and the strain of twenty-hour days was starting to show. She knew she couldn't keep up the tail much longer or her business and her health would fail, so she had decided to end her surveillance of The Swede. If nothing happened that night, the Congress and the press could deal with the problem.

That evening, Bergstrom broke his routine and left his house at ten. He headed toward a rural area of Virginia where farms outnumbered housing developments. Bergstrom turned off the highway onto a narrow country road, and Dana took a chance by turning off her headlights. She followed Bergstrom into a small village and saw him turn into the deserted parking lot of a closed general store. Dana pulled into a side street a block from the store. She had brought several weapons with her, and she checked them before taking a video camera with a long-range directional mike out of her backseat.

Dana approached the general store through a narrow alley. When she arrived at the end of the alley, she could see Bergstrom sitting in his car. Ten minutes later, headlight beams illuminated the street. Bergstrom got out of his car when a non-descript Buick pulled into the lot a space away from his car. Dana activated the video camera and the mike when Dennis Masterson got out of the passenger side of the car. She began to listen.

"Why the meeting?" Bergstrom asked.

"They operated on the woman I placed on the Court. The word I get is that she'll be able to talk soon."

"Has she given the cops any information so far?"

"No, but she's been out of it since she was injured."

"Is this someone you've worked with before?"

Masterson nodded.

"Then she knows the drill."

"She killed a Supreme Court justice. No one will show her mercy. People are unpredictable when they're facing death and are given a way of avoiding it."

"Maybe so, but what do you want me to do about it?"

"You can get to her, silence her."

Bergstrom laughed. "Are you nuts? She'll have an army guarding her."

"You're the only one I can count on to do this."

"Then you're in trouble. I don't do suicide missions."

"You don't understand. She can put us in prison."

"Correction, Dennis. She can put you in prison. She doesn't know me."

Masterson stared hard at Bergstrom. "We sink or swim together, Tom."

Bergstrom sighed. "I thought you would say something like that."

What happened next happened so fast that Dana wasn't certain of what she'd seen until she viewed the DVD. Bergstrom hit Masterson in the throat with the rigid fingers of his left hand, stunning him. At the same time, he whipped out a gun with his right hand and fired through the passenger window, killing Masterson's driver. After shooting the driver a second time, Bergstrom fired a third shot between Masterson's eyes. When he was certain both men were dead, The Swede dropped the weapon next to Masterson's car, took off his gloves, and drove away.

For a moment, Dana toyed with the idea of following Bergstrom and taking him out. But the plan was far too dangerous, considering what she'd just seen. Dana backed into the shadows in the alley and checked the DVD. She'd turn it over to Keith Evans and let him get the credit for catching the man who'd killed one of the most powerful men in the country.

Chapter Sixty

Brad Miller walked into the chambers of Justice Moss and found her slumped in her chair, looking exhausted. He wasn't surprised. A normal term of the Court was demanding. Any case the justices decided affected not only the litigants but thousands of people who were not participants in the case. Just think *Roe v. Wade* or *Miranda v. Arizona*. When you added murder to the equation, it was easy to see why the justice's nerves were frayed.

Two weeks had passed since the fight in the judge's chambers that had resulted in Millard Price's death. That incident had to share top billing with the murder of ex-CIA director Dennis Masterson. When *Exposed* broke its story about the involvement of the Two Amigos in the *China Sea* affair, no other news story had a chance of stealing a headline.

"You wanted to see me?" Brad said.

"Sit."

Brad took the chair Justice Moss indicated.

"I just got back from the cert conference. The vote to grant cert in Sarah Woodruff's case was unanimous. From the way everyone was talking, there's an excellent chance that we're going to send Sarah Woodruff's case back for a new trial."

"That's terrific!"

"It's not official yet that we're granting cert, so keep this between us, but I thought you and Dana Cutler had a right to know."

"Thank you."

"You're owed a lot more than a heads-up about the outcome of a case, Brad. Sarah Woodruff and I owe our lives to you."

Brad didn't know what to say, so he said nothing. The judge closed her eyes and pressed her fingers to her eyelids. When she opened her eyes, she sighed.

"I've always known that I was getting old, but I haven't *felt* old until this term. I don't know how much longer I can take the pace."

"You're not thinking of quitting, are you?" Brad asked, tamping down the alarm he felt at the possibility that the Court could be deprived of a great legal mind.

"There's a strong possibility that I won't be back next term."

"Don't quit. You say that Dana and I saved Sarah Woodruff, but that's not entirely correct. If you hadn't stood up for her, she would be facing execution. You're a hero to me and a lot of other people. And I don't mean just because of *Woodruff*."

Moss smiled. "That's touching, Brad, and I'm not going to make any rash decisions, but I don't think I could take another term like this."

Brad laughed. "If that's what you're worried

about, you're going to be on this court for a long time. I can't imagine that there will ever be another term of the United States Supreme Court like this one."

Brad, Ginny, Dana, and Jake were in a festive mood when they met for dinner at Michelangelo's, an Italian restaurant a few blocks from the offices of *Exposed* where Patrick Gorman ran a tab. The bill was being picked up by Gorman to show his appreciation for everyone's help in breaking a political scandal as big as the Farrington affair. He was already talking about a second Pulitzer, but what made him really giddy was the new advertising revenue from large corporations that used to use his newspaper to collect parakeet droppings.

"I have an important announcement," Brad said as soon as they'd made their wine selection. "Now this is hush-hush until tomorrow. Justice Moss just told me this in confidence an hour ago. So I need your blood oath that you'll keep it between us." Brad looked directly at Dana. "No spilling the beans to Mr. Gorman. Swear?"

Dana forced herself to look solemn and crossed her heart.

"So, give," Ginny said.

"They're granting cert in *Woodruff*, and her read is that the case will probably go back for a new trial."

Everyone applauded.

"The judge thinks there's a majority who want to rule that a defendant's need for exculpatory evidence trumps concerns of national security in a case where the defendant is facing the death penalty. Of course, a lot can happen between now and when the case is decided."

"I wonder if the DA will try Sarah again," Ginny said.

"It'll be a tough case to win with all the doubt that the evidence about the *China Sea* will cast over the State's case," Dana said.

"And there will be all sorts of adverse publicity about the CIA smuggling drugs and Masterson trying to kill Supreme Court justices to hush up what happened," Jake said. "If I was the defense attorney, I'd argue that people who would kill a judge on our high court would think nothing of killing that guy Finley."

"An argument I'm sure Mary Garrett is crafting as we speak," Dana said.

Ginny cleared her throat. "Mr. Miller isn't the only person with breaking news. I know a thing or two also."

"Give," Jake said.

"Tomorrow, Audrey Stewart is going to take her name out of consideration for a spot on the Court for . . ."

Instead of finishing her sentence, Ginny gestured to her friends.

"Health reasons," they said in unison, before breaking into laughter.

"How did you guess?" Ginny asked with a cynical smile.

"I can't believe President Gaylord nominated

Stewart in the first place," Brad said. "There were so many other worthwhile candidates."

"Yeah, but none of them had Dennis Masterson backing them," Ginny said. "There were rumors around the office about a late-night visit by Masterson to the White House. I'm guessing a lot of dirty secrets died with our senior partner."

"Secrets powerful enough to force the president to nominate Audrey Stewart to the Supreme Court?" Jake asked.

Dana cast her lover a look of pure scorn. "Grow up, Mr. Teeny. The guy was the head of the CIA. He probably knew what kind of underwear you buy."

"Mine are pretty dull, but yours . . ."

Dana slapped Jake playfully, and everyone laughed just as the waiter arrived with the wine Dana had ordered. Dana didn't know that much about wine. She'd just ordered the most expensive bottle on the wine list because her friends deserved it and Patrick Gorman could afford it.

Dana raised her glass. "To Sarah Woodruff," she said when everyone's glass was full.

"And Felicia Moss," Brad added.

"Amen," everyone said.

Part Seven

Subpoenas

2012

Chapter Sixty-one

A month and a half after the shootout at the Court, the *China Sea* was off the front page and Dana Cutler's life was back to normal. One of the jobs that Dana's work on the *Woodruff* investigation had disrupted involved the defense of an investment banker who had been indicted in a white-collar fraud case. Dana had spent the day in the defense attorney's office briefing him on her investigation and advising him on the witnesses and documents that had to be subpoenaed for trial. The meeting had broken up late, and Dana was so tired that she'd worried about having an accident driving home. A sound bite on the news about the hunt for Thomas Bergstrom woke her up.

An hour after Dana had given Keith Evans the video of Bergstrom murdering Dennis Masterson and his driver, the FBI had raided Bergstrom's house. They were too late. Bergstrom's wife and children were there, but Bergstrom had disappeared into the ether. So far, the radio announcer said, the international manhunt had not turned up a single clue to The Swede's whereabouts.

Bergstrom's disappearance was one of the few setbacks in the investigation into the violence at the Supreme Court and the mystery surrounding the *China Sea*. Cheryl Fortier—the woman who had impersonated Harriet Lezak—was talking as fast as she could in hopes of staying off death row. In addition to clearing up the roles of Millard Price and Dennis Masterson in the sordid affair, Fortier had told the FBI that Dave Fletcher, the night watchman, had been killed soon after Oswald and Swanson left the dock, and his body had been dumped at sea.

Jake was sound asleep when Dana tiptoed into their bedroom. She dropped her clothes where she took them off and went into the bathroom to wash up. Dana had stopped thinking about Bergstrom and the *China Sea* by the time she arrived home. While she flossed, her thoughts turned to her boring day and the stacks of subpoenas with numbers and names and addresses she had helped write. Suddenly mental tumblers clicked into place in the recesses of her brain, and she grew cold.

As soon as she finished in the bathroom, Dana fixed herself a cup of strong coffee. Then she went to her home office and worked out the logical inferences of her brainstorm. Dana booted up her computer and checked her notes from her visit to Portland. The name she wanted was buried in them. Dana checked the time. Washington, D.C., was three hours ahead of Oregon, so there was a chance she could catch the person she needed to talk to before she went to sleep. Dana dialed information and breathed a sigh of relief when the operator told her that LuAnn Cody's number was listed.

"Ms. Cody, my name is Dana Cutler, and I'm calling from Washington, D.C.," Dana said as soon as they were connected.

"D.C.?"

Dana could hear the confusion in her voice.

"I'm a reporter, and my editor wanted me to fact-check a story we're going to run in the paper that involves the Multnomah County District Attorney's office."

"I don't understand. What kind of story? I'm a secretary. Shouldn't you be talking to one of the attorneys?"

"No. I had a very nice meeting with Monte Pike when I was in Portland a while back. Your name was mentioned, and I wrote it in my notes, but I've misplaced them. So I wrote the paragraph from memory, and then I wasn't certain I got it right. That's why I'm calling, to make certain that we print what really happened."

"I still don't know why you need to talk to me."

"Right, I'm sorry. I should have explained. Mr. Pike mentioned that you were Max Dietz's secretary. This detail has to do with the day he disappeared. We want to be accurate when we print something. Like your name. I have it down as L-U-capital A-N-N, no space. Is that right?"

"Yes. But what did you want to know about Mr. Dietz? I mean, I'm not sure I should be discussing him with a reporter without asking one of the attorneys."

"Well, I'll ask you the question. If you don't feel comfortable, I can give you my number, and you can call back after you talk to someone. Is that fair?"

"I guess. What do you want to know?"

"OK, I wrote that the last time anyone saw Mr. Dietz, he asked for some subpoenas, you typed them for him, he took them and left the office, and he wasn't seen again."

"No, that's not what happened," Cody said. "I didn't type them. Mr. Dietz just asked me for several subpoenas, and I gave him blanks, and he took them into his office."

"Wouldn't you have typed them normally?"

"Yes, but he didn't ask me to that time."

"Thanks. I'll change that." Dana paused as if she were making a note. "You don't happen to know why he wanted the subpoenas, do you?"

"No, he never said."

"Well, thanks a lot. Sorry to take up your time, but I wanted the story to be accurate."

"Has anybody figured that out, what happened to Mr. Dietz?" Cody asked.

"Not that I know. But I'll let you know if I learn the truth about his disappearance."

Dana hung up and stared into space. She worked everything through twice more to make certain she wasn't fooling herself. Of course, she could be wrong, and her flight to Oregon could be a waste of time. Even if she was right, it was highly unlikely that she would be able to find the proof she needed. But she had to try, so she called the airlines and bought a round-trip ticket to Portland.

Chapter Sixty-two

It was raining in Portland when Dana's plane touched down, but it always rained in Portland, so she didn't read the foul weather as an omen. Dana drove her rental car to the hotel where she'd stayed on her last visit to the City of Roses. After she checked in, she headed for Mary Garrett's office. While she walked, she debated the morality of what she was about to do, a debate that had begun to rage as soon as she'd hung up the phone after speaking with LuAnn Cody. If she went through with her plan, she might learn the truth, but a murderer might go free. If she used deceit to get what she wanted, justice might be served, but she would have to betray a trust.

Mary Garrett rarely greeted visitors at the door to her office because their height disparity became apparent as soon as they met, but she made an exception for Dana Cutler.

"Come on in," Garrett said when her secretary showed Dana in. "I can't thank you enough for the work you did for Sarah."

Dana's features didn't betray the guilt she felt. "I just wrote the stories. You wrote the petition for cert."

"I have no doubt that your exposé had a lot to do with cert being granted."

"Since the justices never reveal their reasons for granting cert, we'll never know how much influence *Exposed* had on their decision. What matters is that there is a good chance you'll get Woodruff's case reversed."

Garrett motioned Dana into a client chair and took one next to her.

"You were mysterious on the phone about why you're visiting," Garrett said. "What's up?"

"I have a strange request, Mary."

"Let's hear it."

"I want you to hire me as an investigator in Sarah's case. It won't cost you anything. I'll charge you one dollar."

Garrett cocked her head to one side. "Why do you want to be my investigator?"

"To protect your client. I may have figured out something about her case, but I won't know if I'm right until I examine the contents of Max Dietz's office. When I was here last, Monte Pike told me it's in the evidence room because Mr. Dietz's case is still open. I could have gone to Pike with my suspicions, but I'm more interested in seeing if I'm right than helping either side in this case."

Garrett wasn't smiling now. "You have me thoroughly confused," she said.

"Good. If I'm right, the less you know about what I'm thinking, the better off you and Woodruff are."

"I don't like this."

"I don't expect you to. Think of it this way: If Monte Pike is with me when I examine the evidence, he can use anything incriminating I discover against your client. But the attorney-client privilege will shield me from his questions if I'm Sarah Woodruff's agent. So, will you get me into the evidence room?"

Chapter Sixty-three

Monte Pike was puzzled by Mary Garrett's discovery request. Why would she want to inspect the evidence gathered by the police in Max Dietz's case? Garrett's secretary had left the DA's office as soon as she delivered the motion for discovery, so Pike didn't get a chance to question her. He assumed she wouldn't know why her boss had filed the motion anyway and wouldn't tell him anything if she did. That left a mystery for Pike to solve, but he loved puzzles. Unfortunately, he had no clue to the solution of this one, and the only conclusion he drew was that Garrett suspected a connection between Max's disappearance and Sarah Woodruff's case. Pike had no idea what that connection might be when he called Garrett and told her that the evidence would be in a conference room in the DA's office whenever she wanted to examine it. He had asked what she was looking for, but Garrett had given him a polite version of "That's for me to know and you to find out," so he was no wiser when Garrett broke their connection.

The next day, another mystery presented itself when Dana Cutler followed Mary Garrett into the conference room. Pike flashed a bemused smile.

"What a pleasant and unexpected surprise. But I'm afraid reporters aren't allowed to look at evidence in an ongoing case, no matter how famous they may be."

"Cutler's my investigator, Monte," Garrett said.

Pike looked perplexed and could see that Garrett was pleased by his obvious confusion.

"I guess I could ask if Ms. Cutler is licensed in Oregon," Pike said, "but you'd find some way around that."

Mary started to say something, but Pike held up his hand.

"I'm fine with Ms. Cutler helping the defense as long as she promises that she won't report about anything she sees that is not public record."

Mary turned toward Dana.

"I'm fine with that," Dana said.

"OK, then." Pike pointed to one of the DA's investigators who was sitting in a corner of the conference room. "Bob Hunsacker is here to keep an eye on you."

"Hey, Bob," said Garrett, who knew the investigator.

"Ms. Garrett," he answered with a nod.

Pike took another hard look at Dana. Then he shook his head.

"Do either of you ladies want some coffee?" Pike asked.

"I know how bad your office coffee is, Monte,"

Mary said. "Just the offer is enough for a prosecutorial misconduct charge."

Pike laughed. "Have fun," he said before closing the door behind him.

Mary had tried to get Dana to tell her what she was looking for, but Dana insisted that the lawyer couldn't be hurt by what she didn't know. Dana suggested that Mary go through the evidence as if she *did* know why they were there. Dana could see that Garrett was annoyed, but she was relieved when Woodruff's attorney decided to play along.

Brown cardboard boxes were stacked on the conference table and the floor. There were Magic Marker notations indicating where the contents of each box had been found. Dana started with the boxes filled with evidence taken from Dietz's house so Hunsacker would not be able to figure out what she was doing. She knew that Pike would get a full briefing on what Hunsacker had seen as soon as she and Mary were gone.

One hour and fifteen minutes after Dana started, she opened the first box she actually wanted to examine. It held the contents of Dietz's office desk. She wasn't disappointed when she found nothing of interest. The real object of her search was a plastic trash bag that held everything that had been found on Dietz's desk. Dana's heart beat rapidly as she unwound the tie that secured the neck of the bag and emptied the contents onto the tabletop.

Dana was an excellent poker player, and she kept

any emotion from showing as she sifted through the contents of the bag. Halfway through the mess, her long shot came through in the form of a crumpled, half-filled-out subpoena. Out of the corner of her eye, she saw Hunsacker watching her closely, so she controlled her desire to read the subpoena and made it the fifth piece of paper she studied. It only took her a moment to see what Dietz had written and, in that moment, she knew she was right.

Instead of feeling elated, she felt sick.

Chapter Sixty-four

Sarah Woodruff had a huge smile on her face when she walked into the visiting room at the Willamette Valley Correctional Facility for Women.

"I don't know how to thank you," Sarah said. "The stories in *Exposed* created a political climate that almost forced the Court to take my appeal. Mary won't say it, but I know she thinks she's going to get them to send my case down for a new trial and force the government to reveal what they know about the *China Sea*. When I'm free, I insist on taking you to dinner at the best restaurant in Portland."

"You may not want to when you learn why I'm here."

Sarah stopped smiling. "What's up?" she asked, her voice suddenly chilly with suspicion.

Dana lowered her voice. "I know you killed John Finley."

Woodruff turned pale.

"You don't have to worry about me. I made certain Mary hired me as your investigator. Everything I know is covered by the attorney-client privilege, so

I can't be compelled to talk to Monte Pike or anyone else."

"If you think I killed John, why are you protecting me?"

"Finley put you through hell the first time. I don't know what went on when he died. I'm certain that you didn't kill him in the heat of passion, but this is not my fight."

"So why put your nose where it doesn't belong?" Woodruff asked angrily.

"Plain old curiosity. Once I figured everything out, I had to know if I was right."

"What do you think you know?" Woodruff asked.

"I went through the evidence that was taken from Max Dietz's office. I was looking for one item. Dietz asked his secretary for a stack of subpoena forms on the day he disappeared. He made a mistake on one of the forms and crumpled it up. But he didn't throw it away. It was a subpoena to a bank for any account belonging to you."

"So what?"

"The investigators who looked into Dietz's disappearance missed the significance of the subpoena, and I almost did, too. You grew up poor, Sarah. Your salary as a police officer is the most money you've ever made. How were you able to pay Mary Garrett's retainer and finance a gold plated defense?"

Woodruff didn't answer, but Dana saw her fists clench hard enough to turn her knuckles white.

"There have been rumors from the start of the case about a quarter of a million dollars that John Finley was given to pay the crew and other expenses, but no one ever found that money." Dana caught herself. "Correction, no one but you."

Dana waited for a response. When there was none, she continued.

"Here's what I think happened. Finley was wounded when he fled the ship. If he stopped to hide the money or the duffel bag, the kidnappers would have got him before he reached your condo. And he couldn't stop, because he was wounded and needed medical help. But he couldn't go to a hospital, and you were the only one he knew who could help him.

"You've told everyone that you didn't know that Finley had hidden his duffel bag in your house on the evening he fled the *China Sea*. I don't believe that. I think you found the bag when you were released from the hospital and took the money. Then you hid the duffel bag, but you didn't hide it in your house. If you had, the police would have found it when they searched your place.

"The first time you were arrested, you knew you didn't kill Finley and you were desperate to help Mary Garrett prove your innocence in any way she could, so you told her several names you claimed John Finley had mentioned. Those names were Orrin Hadley, Dennis Lang, and Larry Kester, the names in the false passports that were found in Finley's duffel bag when his body was discovered.

"You couldn't tell Garrett where you saw those names without admitting that you'd found the duffel bag and looked inside it. Once you admitted that, anyone looking for the money would know you'd stolen it. So you made up a story about overhearing Finley say the names.

"I think you believed that Finley had been killed by his kidnappers and that everyone connected with the money would believe the drug dealers or the CIA had the cash. But you couldn't leave the money in your house. You had to hide it. So you went around Portland making deposits of less than ten thousand dollars in many banks, so they wouldn't have to file reports with the government, which the banks must do for cash deposits in excess of ten thousand. That's the money you used to finance your legal defense.

"Then you learned that Finley didn't die, and you knew he'd show up eventually, looking for his money. And when he did, you killed him with the throw-down gun you stole from the evidence in the drug case. To cover yourself, you fired a shot from your service gun into the floor in the entryway so you could explain the shot your neighbor heard. How am I doing so far?"

Woodruff was staring at Dana with a look of pure hatred. Dana didn't blame her.

"Unfortunately for you, the police made a match between the throw-down and the drug case and found your signature on the log, which made you the last person to handle the gun after the drug case was over. And you had the misfortune of having a nosy neighbor who saw Finley go into your condo on the evening you killed him.

"Then it got worse. Max Dietz figured out that you'd taken the missing money and tried to black-mail you with a threat to serve the subpoenas on the banks unless you gave him the quarter million you took from Finley. I think you killed him and buried him somewhere to protect yourself."

"You don't expect me to respond, do you?" Woodruff asked.

"You're too smart for that."

"All of what you've said is theory, anyway. You don't have hard evidence to support any of it."

"Not now, but I have an idea how I could get some. I'm betting that there are still accounts with amounts of less than ten thousand dollars that were opened in several banks around the time you were first accused of killing John Finley. If I'm wrong, there will still be bank records showing the deposits and withdrawals. I'm betting, post 9/11, getting the skinny on those accounts would be a snap for Homeland Security, the FBI, or the CIA. What do you think?"

"Do you plan to tell your theory to anyone?" Woodruff asked.

"No. I told you, I made Mary hire me so I wouldn't have to get involved, but Monte Pike knows we were looking for something when Mary and I went through Dietz's stuff. He's supposed to be a genius. I guess we'll find out real soon just how smart he is."

Chapter Sixty-five

Someone knocked on Brad's office door. When he looked up, Ginny was standing in the doorway.

"This is a pleasant surprise," he said. "Why aren't you in the salt mine?"

Ginny sat down. Justice Moss had not hired another clerk yet, so Brad had the office to himself.

"Remember you told me that you didn't think I'd get in trouble at the firm because I took pictures of the TA Enterprises file?" Ginny asked.

"Sure. Masterson's dead, and that associate . . ."

"Greg McKenzie."

"Right, McKenzie. He's not going to open his mouth. If he wants to make partner, McKenzie will want everyone at Rankin Lusk to forget how tight he was with Masterson, so he's not going to talk about the TA Enterprises file. I think you can forget about the CIA, hashish, and ninja assassins and go back to worrying about your billable hours."

Ginny sighed. "I sort of miss the ninjas. They're a lot nicer to deal with than the partners."

She was quiet for a moment, and Brad could see that something was bothering her.

"I'm thinking of leaving Rankin Lusk," Ginny said.

"What brought this on?"

"When you said that McKenzie would try to distance himself from Dennis Masterson and keep his mouth shut about my part in exposing the TA Enterprises file, you made a fatal error in your analysis. You assumed that Rankin Lusk is a caring, moral entity, when in fact it is a collection of sociopaths who are interested in one thing and one thing only, the bottom line. Dennis Masterson was the firm's biggest rainmaker, and his death will cut into profits. Anyone who makes any attempt to expose a rainmaker is a villain in the eyes of the firm, even if it is clear that the rainmaker is a murdering swine. Anyway, I am being treated like a leper by almost everyone, and any support I've received has been whispered by people who look around nervously when they talk to me."

Brad looked the woman he loved in the eye. "Do you want to be associated with the type of people you've just described, regardless of the money?"

Ginny smiled ruefully. "No. I've pretty much decided to quit, but we're going to be hit pretty hard financially if I leave."

"We will be poor but honest, like characters in a Dickens novel."

"Oliver Twist didn't have student loans."

Brad smiled. "We'll be OK, kiddo. Between Justice Moss and Justice Kineer, we have enough heavyweights on our side to get work. And this time, look for something you really want to do. Don't just think about the money. This is your second job at a huge law firm, and they've both left you with a sour taste in your mouth."

"Your term on the Court is more than halfway through. Have you given any thought to what you'd like to do?"

"I guess I do have to start thinking about next year. The government doesn't pay that well, but the work is exciting. I'm thinking the Justice Department or a job in the Congress."

Ginny sighed. "Now that I've decided to leave Rankin Lusk behind, I feel like a great weight has been lifted from my shoulders. And you know what else?"

"No, what?"

"I do think we'll be OK."

Epilogue

Monte Pike sat in one of the conference rooms in the district attorney's office with his jacket off, his sleeves rolled up, and his feet propped on a corner of the long table that dominated the room. Pike had put the *Woodruff* case on the back burner while he waited to see what the Supreme Court did. He had plenty of other cases to keep him occupied, and the four months it had taken for the Court to reverse had helped him to come at the case with fresh eyes.

Pike was reading the unanimous opinion of the Court, which held that the state-secrets privilege could not be used to keep exculpatory evidence from a defendant facing the death penalty. Pike knew that Mary Garrett was going to come at him with artillery blazing this time around, and he would be lucky if he got a conviction. He took a sip of his latte as he stared at the boxes that covered the table. They were the same boxes filled with evidence relating to Max Dietz that Garrett and Dana Cutler had gone through months ago. Bob Hunsacker had no idea what the women had been looking for. Now Pike was going to go through the boxes to see if he could figure out what had piqued Cutler's and Garrett's interest.

Pike finished the opinion and laid it beside his drink. He stared down the table at the boxes as if willing them to give up their secret.

"Where are you, little fella?" Pike asked the evidence. "Better tell me now and save yourself a lot of pain, 'cause you can run, but you can't hide."

Acknowledgments

Supreme Justice was a lot of fun to write because it gave me an excuse to tour the United States Supreme Court as part of my research. I argued a case there in 1978, but I was in my early thirties and only in my fifth year of practice and way too nervous to ask for a tour. My thanks to the Honorable Diarmuid O'Scannlain for contacting Kathleen Arberg, the Court's public-relations officer, who arranged for the tour and was a gracious host. But my special thanks go to Bill Suter, the clerk of the Court, who took time from his busy day to act as my tour guide and answer my questions. He was a great help in making this book as realistic as possible, and he is not responsible for anything I got wrong. I am especially grateful for his recommendation that I purchase *The Supreme Court of the United States*, by Fred J. Maroon and Suzy Maroon (Lickle Publishing Inc., 1996), whose superb photographs and text helped me describe parts of the Court that Mr. Suter could not show me and areas I'd seen but had trouble remembering accurately.

My thanks to Professor Sue Deller Ross of Georgetown Law School for introducing me to former Supreme Court clerk Rebecca Tushnet, who answered my questions about a clerk's daily routine. Thanks also to my son-in-law Andy Rome for hooking me up with Richard Bartlett, another former clerk. I also made good use of Edward Lazarus's descriptions of the life of a Supreme Court law clerk in his book *Closed Chambers* (Crown, 1998).

I could not have written *Supreme Justice* without help from several experts: Brian Ostrom and Dr. Karen Gunson rode to the rescue once again by answering questions about medicine and science—areas in which I am woefully ignorant. Charles Gorder, Barry Sheldahl, and Fred Weinhouse helped me develop an issue that could, theoretically, come to the Court someday. Finally, the help of ship captain Sid Lewis was invaluable.

I don't know about other authors, but I need a good editor to take my first draft and make it into a book that can be published. Sally Kim did an excellent job cleaning up my mess. Thanks also to Maya Ziv, her assistant; Jonathan Burnham; Heather Drucker; the HarperCollins sales force and art department; and all the others at HarperCollins who have given me so much support over the years.

I can never thank Jean Naggar, Jennifer Weltz, and everyone at the Jean V. Naggar Literary Agency enough. I'm also grateful to my assistant, Robin Haggard, and Carolyn Lindsey for their research skills. Thanks also to Daphne Webb for her expertise in all things relating to Wisconsin.

And finally, I thank Doreen, my muse, who is always in my heart.